THE MIST RISES OVER NOTCHEY CREEK

A HARLEY HENRICKSON MYSTERY

LIZ ANDREWS

CHAPTER 1

The mist had fallen again. It was midnight and Dr. Patrick Middleton lay alone in silence. His was the silence of regret.

Whispers had woken him, whispers in restless dreams from the mouths of ghosts not yet buried. They whispered to him of the past, of his wife now dead for over thirty years, and of others, those he'd abandoned, abandoned yet never forgot.

For memories are not mere illusions. They are alive and well in the minds of haunted men.

His eyes tired from chasing shadows on the moonlit ceiling, he rose from his bed. He plucked his glasses from the side table and perched them instinctively on the bridge of his nose. Over the last forty years, those tired blue eyes had poured over countless texts, recording the lives of men long dead, their actions immortalized in the taps and rings of his typewriter.

And like the man who tempted fate, he tied his housecoat about his waist, and he ventured out into the autumn night, a lantern in his hand.

He had to see her.

On the hillside, his three-hundred-year-old mansion stood like a brick fortress, the kitchen lights aglow like the eyes of a watchman, awoken by an old man's guilt. A brood of dark clouds eclipsed the October moon, muting his green lawn to a sea of charcoal, dappled in hues of silver starlight. To the east, tucked in the quiet folds of the foothills, lay the small town where he'd spent the last thirty years of his life, only a few slivers of light peering from the curtained windows. What moonlight remained illuminated the surrounding apple orchards and pumpkin patches and hay fields as they rolled eastward toward the mountains, where the blue-gray peaks of the Smokies melded, stack by stack, toward the night sky.

The heavens were dark.

God and his angels always seemed to abandon him on his darkest of nights.

And from those mountains, cresting from a vein of the Tennessee River, Notchey Creek wound its way like a snake toward Patrick, the mist hanging heavily over its dark waters, gathering a pale blanket of fog on the creek bank.

He could hear her now. She was calling to him.

And like one lured by a siren's song, he idled down the hill toward the creek, with his lantern held out before him like a shield. Trees huddled around him, and he dared not look into the surrounding forest, aware that his mind could create far more terrifying things than that of the hand of creation. The lantern's low flicker cast shadows at his feet, shadows that were morphing and mutating into various creatures, becoming more embellished with each step taken. Though he'd travelled this path countless times, he found himself disoriented by the darkness, only scant ribbons of light permeating the dense tree branches above.

He took in a deep breath and released it into the chilly night air. He was gathering himself, gathering himself for what lay ahead. How could love and horror be so entwined, he asked himself. How could it seize his mind with one thought, one memory?

But he had to see her. Now was the time.

It was late October, a month after the Autumn Equinox, a time known as Samhain to the ancient Celts when herdsmen would gather in their cattle and farmers would harvest their fruits and vegetables, hopeful the sun's nourishing light would not abandon them during the dark winter months ahead. So too was it Hallowmas, a time when spirits were believed to enter the earthly realm through the between places, where water meets land, where mountain meets sky, where spirits rise from ancient waters to walk freely about the earth until dawn.

"Are you here?" he whispered, checking the creek's water, then its bank. "Please, tell me you're here."

But only the creek answered his calls, its ripples roaring with each step he took, the autumn wind howling through the tree branches above. If evil were to exist out here tonight, he thought, he would never know it, not until it was too late.

Before he could call a third time, he froze with the lantern suspended, the flame flickering over the creek before him. He stared into the dark waters, where the currents shimmered like golden ribbons beneath the harvest moon.

His breath caught in his throat.

Liquid strands of yellow hair were forming on the surface, encapsulating a face, ghostly and beautiful and pale.

"Oh, god," he cried, falling to his knees on the creek bank. "Oh, god, forgive me."

She had returned. Was she aware that her existence had been lost to time, to history, to memory? Lost to all but him?

But it hadn't been lost. Not forever. Not to everyone. For fate has an odd way of reminding one of things, an odd way of unearthing those forgotten ghosts from the past, those ghosts that lie patiently in one's heart, whispering their secrets, waiting for someone to reveal their untold stories to the world.

And as he lowered his hand into that freezing water, hoping to caress that golden hair, that pale and beautiful face, another figure appeared alongside it, a dark one, extinguishing those golden locks, shadowing that pale face. And like the mist settling over the dark creek, a heaviness descended on Patrick Middleton, deadlier than the weight of his conscience.

CHAPTER 2

Eighteen Hours Earlier

Flames rose above Harley Henrickson, dissipating into the gray morning sky. Since four that morning, she'd been in the fields, stacking the sugar maple boards in a latticework pattern, the structure climbing over six feet. Then, with the strike of a match, she'd set the entire thing ablaze, watching in awe as fire billowed from the massive shoulders, filling the fields with a blanket of smog.

Past the flames, the world at dawn was cold and damp. In the last two hours, the morning mist had left her long dark hair matted beneath her cap and her overalls sodden. The wet chill of a Smoky Mountain autumn stung her ears and fingertips, and she drew her hands toward the flames, warming them.

Though she'd completed this exercise every fall since childhood, she still found herself mesmerized by the rising flames. She drew in the aroma of damp earth and woodsmoke, watching the flames as they flickered and popped. Fire was a dangerous mystery, no doubt, capable of similar feats of magnificent creation and undiscriminating destruction. And as with every great force, it should be treated with due respect and caution.

"'Man is the only creature that dares to light a fire and live with it,'" she whispered, reciting the quote by Henry Jackson Van Dyke, Jr., "'because he alone has learned to put it out.'"

Harley drew a garden hose from the grass and released a steady stream of cold water over the flames, stymying the heat just enough to reduce the sugar maple boards to charcoal and not to soot. Later, she would filter her whiskey through the charcoal, lending the spirit's signature smoky taste. For some time she stood like that, watching the flames in meditation, and when the sugar maple had at last reduced to a smoking mound at her feet, she rested the garden hose in the grass and headed across the fields to the Henrickson whiskey distillery.

As she hiked, she took her time, slowing her gait to a saunter. As busy as her days were, this was her one true pleasure in life. A veil of mist hung over the Smokies, the blue-gray peaks floating like islands in a sea of fog, appearing more like a painting really, the mountains gliding in sweeps of watercolor, each layer a subtly different shade of blue from the next, changing with the light.

The view would remain like that until around ten o'clock when at last the sun would burn the mist from the valley, ushering it back to the heavens once more. Only then would the last of the fall color be visible, the burnt sienna, umber, and nuances of green and gold, covering the foothills like a patchwork quilt.

The Henrickson whiskey distillery rose over the hill, a red ten-thousand-square-foot barn lined with charred oak barrels, a weather-vane perched to its tin roof. Fallen leaves and tall strands of yellow Johnson grass clung to Harley's boots as she strolled down the hill in its direction. As she approached the white double doors, something cold and slimy began rooting against her backside. She glanced over her shoulder and into the eyes of an enormous, mud-caked pig, its tail bouncing like a corkscrew.

"Matilda, no!" she said as the pig rooted at her overalls, first moistening the pocket, then progressing to an all-out chew. She tried to protect the honey crisp apple tucked in her pocket, but Matilda bit through apple and overall in tandem. Moments later, she pulled a handful of mush from her pocket only to find Matilda licking it from her palm.

At times like this, Harley wondered where she'd gone wrong raising Matilda. In the early years, theirs had been a love story inspired by the likes of *Charlotte's Web*, with Harley as an ever-adoring Fern, saving the rejected runt, Matilda, from the litter that had cast her aside.

She'd nursed Matilda with a bottle, slept with her in her bed, and bathed her in the kitchen sink with Johnson's baby soap. Over time, that minuscule, pink piglet had morphed to the size of a pony, a veritable garbage disposal that ate anything animate or inanimate in her path. In short, Matilda was a pest.

"Matilda," Harley said, attempting a stern voice, "Matilda, look at me." To her surprise, the pig stopped chewing and gazed up at her with guileless innocence. "You have a trough," she said, pointing toward the barn. "And you have a trough full of food. Good food. People food. Whatever Uncle Tater doesn't eat, he gives to you. So why do you feel the need to eat everything you see?"

Matilda tilted her head to one side in momentary consideration and released a single snort. Then she rooted at Harley's left pocket, the one that held her leather notebook.

"Not my notebook! Not my notebook!"

The notebook held a series of cocktail recipes she hoped to launch at her family's liquor store, Smoky Mountain Spirits, that week. When she dipped her hand in her pocket, the notebook's pages were soiled and the leather cover slick with saliva.

As a last-ditch effort, Harley tried to fend off Matilda with her right hand, pulling at the distillery's door with her left. As she fiddled with her key in the lock, she whispered a quote from Agatha Christie. "'But surely for everything you love you have to pay some price.'"

"Mornin,' Harley!" Harley's great-aunt, Wilma True, who was also the distillery's secretary, buzzed into the barnyard on her lawn mower. Aunt Wilma and Uncle Buck's turkey farm was less than a mile from the distillery, and even if lawn mowers weren't suitable means of transportation in Notchey Creek, Wilma would've ridden hers regardless.

"That pig gettin' the best of you again?" she asked.

The lawnmower buzzed down like a dying bee, and the seat belched as Aunt Wilma hoisted her weight to the ground and readjusted her pink muumuu and matching shower cap. She'd done something else to her hair apparently, and Harley hoped it hadn't fallen out in the process.

"Matilda!" Wilma yelled across the barnyard. "Matilda, you old heifer. Get on over here!"

At the sound of Wilma's voice, Matilda trotted across the barnyard and waited patiently at Wilma's pink house shoes.

"Now you sit," Wilma said.

Matilda fell back on her haunches and gazed up at Wilma with quiet reverence. "You know she thinks she's a dog, don't you?"

Wilma pulled a Little Debbie from her pocketbook and dangled the cake in front of Matilda. "Little Debbies," she said, glancing up at Harley. "Old gal can't get enough of 'em."

Harley winced. Aunt Wilma and Uncle Buck had a reputation for peddling expired snack cakes in the neighborhood. Once they'd dispensed the Piggly Wiggly of its daily allotment of expired Little Debbies and Ding Dongs and HoHos, they stacked the boxes for another few months on their coffee table, ready for unwitting guests. Once, when she was in the third grade, she'd eaten an abominable pink Sno-ball and had to miss three days of school afterward.

Wilma removed the cake from its wrapper and popped the cake into Matilda's mouth. "Yeah," she said, watching as the pig chewed and snorted with approval. "You can't beat that Little Debbie. She's been my dietician for years."

Wilma smacked Matilda on her backside. "Now, you get on back to the barn, and I don't wanna hear hide nor hair out of you for the rest of the day."

Matilda trotted back to the barnyard, her hind legs squeezing together like the two ham hocks they were.

"Y'all spoil that pig too much," Wilma said, unlocking the

distillery's front door. "Heck, I bet she eats better than I do." She glanced around to her ample backside and grinned. "And that's sayin' a lot, ain't it?"

Once inside, Wilma headed for her desk and Harley straight for the sink. As she knelt over the running water, scrubbing her hands with soap, she caught a whiff of odor that made her lip curl. Matilda's attack had lingered. With no time to go home and change or shower, she would smell like pig and...apple sauce for the remainder of the day. She dried her hands on a towel and prepared herself for another day of the absurd.

In the adjoining office, Wilma sat at her small desk and placed her pink pleather pocketbook in the side drawer. She looked up, and upon examining her great-niece's appearance - the long dark pigtails, the thick-lensed glasses, the camouflage hat, the flannel shirt - she cocked a brow in disapproval. "Well, I see you got yourself all gussied up for work again. And what's up with them ugly butt glasses? I ain't seen you wear them since you was in high school."

"Lost one of my contacts."

"Now that is a shame."

Harley hung her barn coat by the door, waiting for Wilma's usual speech.

Wilma tucked a pencil behind her ear and began. "I mean it ain't like you're out here all the live-long day. What about them days you work at the store downtown? That's public, ain't it?"

Over the years, Aunt Wilma had assumed the responsibility of managing Harley's love life or lack thereof. At a young age, she'd lost both her mother and her grandmother, and with the recent passing of her grandfather, Jackson Henrickson, Aunt Wilma had felt the need more than ever to act as a surrogate parent.

While Harley recognized the sentiment as being from a place of caring, it did not keep that caring from being, at times, overbearing. Over the years, Wilma had threatened her with a series of blind dates, the latest being a one-legged chicken farmer Wilma and Uncle Buck had met at the VFW club.

"Your granddaddy would've liked for you to have somebody,"

Wilma said, taking a more conciliatory tone. "To love, I mean. And you ain't so bad homely like you was when you was a youngin."

Gee thanks, Harley thought.

But Wilma was right, she supposed, if only on a purely superficial level. She hadn't been the most attractive child, a fact that had been pointed out to her regularly by both children and adults alike. And in dealing with the loss of her mother and grandmother at a young age, she'd turned inward, relying on books rather than people for comfort and support.

As a result, she'd been a quiet and shy child, which, in turn, had been misinterpreted as being weird. Now, as an adult, she was no longer shy, per se, but she was definitely on the quiet side, always watchful of people and situations.

"And what about the rest of your life?" Wilma asked. "You can't spend the rest of it here in Notchey Creek. Now, I know Tater and I have needed you these long years, especially since your granddaddy passed, and we do appreciate you staying on to help us out. But we're good now, honey. We got enough money to hire some outside help. You can do something else with your life, something more meaningful with all them brains you got in your head."

When Harley's grandfather had become ill with cancer eight years prior, she'd given up a scholarship at Harvard and had used her entire life savings to save the ailing distillery and care for her grandfather. As she'd watched her peers leaving for college to pursue their dreams, she'd felt sad, of course, but knew she'd made the right decision.

With the loss of that opportunity, she'd gained another one: caring for the person who'd been a grandfather, a father, and a mother to her most of her life. From her perspective, it was the only decision possible. But someday, she told herself, she would go to college and pursue the education she'd sacrificed.

Wilma readjusted herself in the office chair and to Harley's relief, changed the subject. "You been at the whiskey since early this mornin'?"

"Busiest time of the year."

"Well, I'll get you a pot of coffee made up here directly."

"That'd be great, thanks. I'll just go upstairs and check on the whiskey."

On the way to the stairwell, Harley walked past her great-aunt's desk. The older woman had removed her pink shower cap, revealing an army of curlers bound to dyed red hair. Harley paused in the doorway, perplexed. As eccentric as Aunt Wilma was, she wasn't a forgetful person.

"Aunt Wilma," Harley said, motioning toward the top of her head. "I think you may have forgotten to take out your curlers this morning."

Powder compact in hand, Wilma glided on a coat of pink salmon lipstick and smacked her lips. "Oh no, honey, them's is supposed to be in there. You see, this here's gonna be a permanent." She angled her head, giving Harley an aerial view. "Them needs to stay in *all* day."

Harley started up the stairs, realizing that day, like all other days in Notchey Creek, wouldn't be normal. On the third floor, she half expected to find her grandfather kneeling beside a charred oak barrel as he once had, his eyes closed in quiet concentration as he sipped from a small whiskey tasting glass.

To her, he'd always appeared more like a monk lost in prayer than a whiskey distiller, but instead of a habit and tonsure, he'd worn a pair of denim overalls and a University of Tennessee Volunteers baseball cap. But the upper room was empty of his presence, with only her memories left to fill the space.

"Needs more time," her grandfather had always said, at last opening his eyes from the tasting glass to meet hers.

Harley removed that same tasting glass from the shelf, and after unplugging the cork from the barrel, filled the glass with whiskey and took a sip. She drew in the aroma of caramel, vanilla, and char, rolling the sweet smokiness over her tongue. And as was usually the case, it needed a little more time.

Whiskey was a patient spirit, not held to timetables or human impatience. "It'll be ready when it's ready," her grandfather had always said, "and it's best not to rush it." According to Jackson Henrickson, all of the best things in life took years to develop richness - friendships, marriages, and bottles of whiskey being just three of them. At the age of twenty-six, Harley believed that to be true as well.

Returning to the sink, she rinsed the whiskey taster before placing it on the shelf. As she dried her hands on a towel, she thought of her grandfather, the man who'd been not only her mother and father but also her very best friend. Oh, how she missed him.

"You all finished up outside?" Wilma called from the stairwell.

"Charcoal's down to a smolder," Harley said, coming back down the steps. "Should be ready for Uncle Tater to collect in another hour or so."

"If he's even up by then," Wilma said. "I swear that brother of mine. His bedroom was as quiet as Grant's tomb this mornin' when I passed by the house. He and Floyd must've tied on a big one at Bud's last night."

Bud's Pool Hall was a notorious beer joint and the favorite watering hole for Uncle Tater and the large cast of characters he called friends. Ever the social butterfly, or in this case, barfly, Tater never missed a chance to hold court. They always hoped they wouldn't find him in a jail cell in the Notchey Creek police station.

"Coffee's about ready," Wilma said, not glancing up from her nail filing. "And how about that new whiskey upstairs? Let me guess. It ain't ready yet?"

"Not ready. But almost."

Wilma blew nail dust from her emery board. "Figures. Waitin' on that old stuff is like waitin' at the Walmart pharmacy on a Saturday." She returned to her nail filing. "Well, anyway, them bottles is filled up and sealed, waitin' for you on the counter yonder."

Harley retrieved her barn coat from the hook, and as she guided her arms through the sleeves, Wilma said, "Oh, and Tina called earlier. Says you need to answer your friggin' cell phone. Says it's aggravatin' how you never pick up, and I've got to agree with her on that. Secondly, she said it's an emergency. Says she needs to talk to you ASAP." Wilma lowered her voice conspiratorially. "Of course, she always says it's an emergency, don't she? I swear that girl can stir up drama like a bear can stir up a honey bee's nest."

Tina Rizchek, Harley's childhood best friend, seemed to call her at all hours of the day or night with self-perceived emergencies. "I'll give her a call," Harley said over her shoulder, then hurried out the door before Wilma could catch her again.

Fallen leaves and blades of wet grass clung to Harley's boots as she trekked across the barnyard, passing Uncle Tater's two-story white farmhouse, a house that had sheltered their family since its inception a hundred years prior. Behind the farmhouse stood a little house of necessity, unused for decades, but kept erected for posterity's sake. Further down and nestled along the hill was a spring house, used during the nineteenth century to store the family's perishable goods. She could hear the creek babbling beside her, but she could not see it for the veil of mist blanketing the water and most of its bank. Finding her trusted seat, she sat down, flinching as her back rested against slats of cold wrought iron.

Cradling the coffee mug in both hands, she blew on the surface, her breaths indecipherable from the rising steam. As she took small sips, she enjoyed the nature occurring all around her, the twittering of birds, the scampering of squirrels. The undisturbed forest behind Uncle Tater's house was an ideal habitat for God's creatures, the quiet only scattered by the occasional passing of a car.

She drew her gaze up the trunk of a neighboring tree. Shrouded in morning dew, the intricate handiwork of the orb weaver was revealed, the craftsman long awake and at work, having consumed yesterday's web and started anew. Harley studied the spider, amazed that its bulbous black and yellow body contained six different kinds of precious silk, used to craft some of nature's most amazing artworks. And though often associated with ugliness and fear, few other creatures did greater for humankind than the spider.

Not everything has to be beautiful for us, she thought, *not if we can appreciate the function it provides to the world, not if we can appreciate beauty of a different quality.*

And in a season associated with death and decay, the orb weaver only seemed to teem with life.

Harley's cell phone vibrated in her pocket, and she drew the receiver to her ear. "Morning, Tina," she said. "Is everything okay?"

As usual, it wasn't, and Tina began their conversation as she often did, frantic and breathless. "Oh, my gosh, Harley, you won't believe it."

She probably wouldn't. Nonetheless, she said, "Okay, slow down. Now, tell me what's happened."

"I was drivin' into work this morning 'n at."

Tina, a native of Pittsburgh, had moved with her family to Notchey Creek in the fifth grade after her father had taken a job with the Tennessee Valley Authority. Despite spending the last sixteen years in East Tennessee, Tina had retained her Pittsburgh accent, which became more pronounced when she was stressed.

"And I decided to take a shortcut, you know, drivin' up past Briarwood Park 'n at. And that's when I seen him."

"Saw who?"

Tina groaned in duress. "Oh, I knew I shoulda went a different way."

"Saw who?"

"Steven Tyler. He was sittin' up in bed there lookin' at me."

"Who?"

"You know, from Aerosmith."

Silence on the line.

"Oh, for Pete's sake, Harley. Will you please get cable? Read an entertainment magazine every once in a while? Aerosmith is a legendary rock band. Their lead singer is Steven Tyler."

"And you're saying he was sitting in a bed on the side of the road in Notchey Creek looking at you?"

"No, silly, of course it wasn't him. It was one of those stupid scarecrows. But I'll tell you, Harley, they really did dress it up like him. Big black wavy wig, leopard print pajamas, pink feather boa."

Each year as part of the fall celebrations, the Notchey Creek Chamber of Commerce invited the local businesses to stage scarecrows in front of their respective properties. The rules, lax at best, carried only one stipulation, that said scarecrows had to represent the business in some way. Given Tina's description of the pajamas and the bed, Harley wagered a strong guess.

"Beds-to-Go?"

"Yeah, Beds-to-Go. Oh, gosh, I hate that place. Anyhow, that's not why I'm callin' you. You see when I saw Steven Tyler...I mean the scarecrow, it freaked me out so bad, I crashed my van in the creek."

Tina's Plymouth Grand Voyager was at least twenty years old. Once the Rizchek family minivan, they'd traveled to countless sleep-overs, track practices, and high school football games in the not-so-comfort of its back seat. No one knew exactly how many miles were on the van because the odometer had broken when they were in the seventh grade. After Tina graduated from culinary school and opened a bakery-cafe on Main Street, she painted the van bubblegum pink and fastened a giant model cupcake named "Rosie" to the luggage rack.

A groan oozed down the line. "I think the radiator's busted, and there's steam coming from her hood. And I don't know what I'm gonna do cause—"

"I'll come by there now, and we can call a tow truck. We can use my truck for your deliveries."

Another groan, this time of relief. "Oh, thank goodness...but that's only part of the reason I'm calling. You see, the other reason is that there's a man here...in the ditch."

Harley sat forward in her seat. "What?"

"Yeah, and I think...well, I'm pretty sure... he's dead."

CHAPTER 3

*I*t was just after seven a.m. when Harley's red 1958 Chevy truck rumbled down Main Street, having traversed the region's intricate web of country roads. As the truck entered downtown, it passed beneath Main Street's parallel rows of maples, the amber, gold, and red leaves forming a canopy over the wide, paved street. Leaves fluttered like confetti in the truck's headlights, while others danced beneath the tires, creating a flurry of movement and shadow.

Behind the maples stood Notchey Creek's half-mile stretch of three-story brick buildings, many built during the 1830s when the town was but a small coal and timber mining outpost.

Today, the buildings served the many Smoky Mountain tourists who flocked to Main Street on nights and weekends, the restaurants and shops decked out with awnings in a myriad of stripes and colors. Patio tables and park benches flanked the sidewalks, favorite spots for outdoor dining or resting one's feet after a long day of antique shopping or leaf gazing. Though Notchey Creek had its fair share of tourists, they tended to be older and more affluent, preferring the town's quieter atmosphere to that of its bustling neighbors, Gatlinburg and Pigeon Forge.

Main Street was quiet that morning. Just a few people walked past the dark storefronts, lacking their mid-afternoon tourist traffic. Harley slowed her truck to an idle in front of the town gazebo, where The Notchey Creek Historical Society had hung a banner advertising Pioneer Days, a fall harvest festival celebrating the town's agrarian past. Each year, the festival drew thousands of tourists and thousands of their much-needed dollars, all donated to the historical society. To make Main Street more festive, colorful wreaths, hay bails, and scarecrows adorned the streetlights, and terracotta pots full of chrysanthemums filled the spaces between.

Harley turned left onto Briarwood Avenue and headed north toward Briarwood Park, a stretch of tall pines and walking trails connecting the elite neighborhood of Briarwood with downtown. At this hour, the deserted road appeared ghostly and gray, enveloped in a veil of early morning mist. Ahead, in the truck's headlights, Harley spotted Tina's pink minivan peeking from the ditch and the giant model cupcake, Rosie, lying in the middle of the road, sans cherry. In the grass behind them, the Beds-to-Go scarecrow display had fared much better: Not a hair on Steven Tyler's wig was out of place and his queen-sized bed was perfectly made. Propped on a bed of fluffy pillows, he grinned at Harley, his corncob hands holding a sign that read: *Dream On.*

Tina, on the other hand, wasn't grinning. She shivered in a black wool sweater, an embroidered jack-o'-lantern smiling from her chest. Her orange sequined miniskirt did not detract from the purple and green tights encasing her short legs, nor her three-inch orange stilettos as they tapped against the pavement. Secured to her peroxide blonde locks were orange, black, and purple extensions that fell past her shoulders as she looked intently at each of her long fingernails, painted with scenes of a haunted house.

Regarding Tina's fashion sense, Harley had always thought of a quote by their beloved East Tennessee native, Dolly Parton: "It costs a lot of money to look this cheap."

And so it was with Tina. Harley supposed they were both misfits of sorts, but where Tina was loud, Harley was quiet; flashy where she was bland; and practical where she was more theoretical. Somehow they'd formed a friendship in the fifth grade, and the timing couldn't have been better for Harley. At the age of ten, she was a friendless orphan and was in desperate need of someone. Tina had been that person for her, and despite their apparent differences, Harley was eternally grateful.

Harley stopped the truck at a safe distance, and before she could turn off the engine, Tina scuttled over and tugged at the driver's side door.

"Oh, thank goodness, Harley. I didn't think you were ever gonna get here."

When Harley opened the door, Tina threw her arms around her, as much for comfort, it seemed, as for warmth. Tina released her and feverishly rubbed her hands together. "Gosh, it's cold out this morning."

Harley reached inside the truck and took one of her barn coats from the passenger seat before handing it to Tina. Tina made a face of disgust as she led her arms through the sleeves, but the need for warmth overcame that of vanity, and soon she was holding the coat close to her body.

"Where is he?" Harley asked, looking over Tina's shoulder. "The man you saw?"

Tina pointed behind them to the ditch. "He's over there. And he's still not moving."

Tina's stilettos scuttled behind Harley in single file as the two women made their way toward the ditch. A blanket of mist covered a large portion of the road's shoulder, making it difficult to see anything of substance beyond. It was then Tina latched onto Harley's elbow, pointing to something in the ditch below. Harley paused, her eyes focusing in the early morning light.

A flash of something.

Black.

A garbage bag, perhaps? But on closer inspection, the garbage bag turned out to be a black raincoat, slick with dew. Inside the coat lay a man, face up, his eyes closed, his pale face etched with dirt and bits of grass. He'd been a handsome man once, Harley surmised, but time and something else, something terrible had been unkind to him.

A road map of scars coursed down the contours of his face, making his age indecipherable. He could've been anywhere from fifty to seventy years of age, she guessed. A pale triangle of flesh peeked from his shirt collar, exposing a pair of dog tags linked by a silver chain. But the tags were turned away, obscuring any identifying information. She deflected her gaze to the wet grass and thought of her late mother, a regressive pain pressing against the back of her eyelids.

"Who do you think he is?" Tina asked.

Harley examined the mismatch of tattered clothes, the pants too short, the shirt sleeves too long. "I'm not sure," she said. "Maybe a vet who's fallen on hard times."

"What in the world's he doing here?"

Harley had a guess. A tragic one. Taking careful steps, she lowered herself into the ditch, Tina watching her from the road's shoulder.

"Harley, what are you doing?" she asked. "You're not going to touch him, are you?"

"Just a little."

Crouching to her knees, Harley pressed her fingers to the side of the man's neck, checking for a pulse.

Behind her, Tina screamed.

The man's eyes had popped open, and he was staring ahead, not at Harley, but at something beyond her, to a horror only he could see.

"Get out of there, Harley!" Tina yelled.

But Harley drew herself closer to the man, and when he did not lash out, she said in a gentle whisper, "Sir, we're here to help you."

At the sound of her voice, the man's eyes shot back in his head, the white sockets twisting back and forth. "I need to know."

"You need to know what?" Harley asked.

"I need to know what happened."

Taking the man's hand in hers, Harley waited for him to continue.

"That boy. I need to know what happened to that boy."

"Harley, please!" Tina yelled from the bank. "Get out of there!"

"What boy?" Harley whispered, drawing her face closer to his.

"Innocent. He was innocent."

Behind her, Tina's fingernails beat against her cell phone, the sound of numbers being pressed, dialing Jed's number. But that was the last she heard because the man was stumbling to his feet. He rose above her, his arms thrashing out in front of him for balance.

Harley shrunk back in the wet grass, shielding herself from any violence he might intend. But he was staggering then out of the ditch and headed in the direction of Briarwood Park, crawling toward the tree line, his eyes fixed on the woods.

"Jed's on his way," Tina said, her voice shaking.

But the man had already disappeared among the tall pines of Briarwood Park.

CHAPTER 4

"What do you mean he just disappeared?"

Sheriff Jed Turner towered over Harley and Tina, his muscled arms flexed against his hips. Since he'd arrived at the scene, his attention had been placed solely on Tina, treating Harley as he had since they were children, as invisible. Behind him, two deputies emerged from the woods where they'd been searching for the man in Briarwood Park.

"Nothing," one of the deputies called out to Jed.

"Let's head on back to the station," he told them. "Nothing of importance here."

At 6'5" and over two hundred pounds of muscle, Jed Tuner still held the stature and fitness of a professional football player. Harley wondered how often he replayed that fateful day on the field when a vicious tackle left his ligament torn to shreds, not only sidelining him for the season but also for the entirety of his professional career.

In the year since, he'd retired with millions to his small hometown of Notchey Creek, the only place where he was still considered a hero. After a brief and unsuccessful stint as a sports commentator for the University of Tennessee Volunteers, he'd run for county sheriff, which he'd won by a landslide. And in a county with meager crime rates and where football is king, it mattered very little to anyone that Jed lacked prior law enforcement experience. To the still-wealthy Jed, acting as sheriff was a mere hobby.

"Harley doesn't think it's nothing," Tina said. "The guy said somethin' weird to her before he took off, somethin' about a boy."

"What boy?" Jed asked, skeptical.

"I don't know. But it sounded like something bad might've happened to him."

"We've had no reports of anyone missing or otherwise, especially no boys. Sounds like some nonsense being spewed by a drunk."

"Harley thinks maybe he was a veteran," Tina said. "She says he might have information on file somewhere, so maybe we could contact his family."

With a wave of his right hand, Jed dismissed all of their claims. It was hard to believe that at one time when they were children, Jed and Harley had been unlikely friends. She thought back to that summer and wondered how the sensitive boy she had once known had morphed into the mountain of belligerence he was as an adult. She had a theory.

WHEN JED and Harley were in the fourth grade, the district's art teacher began offering free art classes in the summer, and being low on money and high on interest, Harley had signed up immediately. On that first afternoon, all of the students were stunned when Jed Turner, still wearing his little league football pads, walked into the classroom, a bag of art supplies tucked under his burgeoning muscles. He'd kept his head down as he moved past the teacher, then down the long line of desks, taking a seat in the last row.

And he'd remained like that all summer, with his head down, working in a comfortable silence, coloring, sketching, and painting. Art had seemed cathartic to the young football star, who was the most massive boy in their class, and who'd already exhibited a special talent on the football field. In that classroom he hadn't had to prove himself to anyone, it seemed, not to his coaches, and especially not to his overbearing father.

Weeks passed, summer grew on, and when it was time to pair off students for a final collaborative art project, their teacher had paired Jed and Harley together. "You two will work on a landscape portrait," the teacher had told them. "A summer field of wildflowers."

Of course, Jed would be disappointed by the pairing, Harley thought, and she dreaded what could only be an uncomfortable situation. But he merely took a seat beside her and spreading out a clean canvas, asked if he could please borrow one of her brushes. He had used the last of his allowance on watercolor paints bought in secret, he said, and not wanting to ask his father for more money, had not been able to afford any brushes.

"Sure, " Harley said and offered him the pick of whichever of her brushes he liked.

He did so with a smile, and after agreeing that he would work on the foreground and she would focus on the sky, the two worked side-by-side in a collaborative silence.

"But your sky isn't blue and white," Jed said with interest one afternoon, looking up from his field of wildflowers to Harley's skyline of beiges, blues, lavenders, and peaches.

"Because skies aren't necessarily blue and white, Jed," she said. "They're lots of different colors, depending on the time of day, the season, the weather. I guess you could say they're nuanced. Like people are."

"Nu what?"

"Nuanced. Varying shades of color, slightly different."

He gazed down at his cornflowers, purple dots in an equally monochromatic green field, then back to Harley's sky. He drew his paintbrush and dipped it in a series of pastels, accenting the purple flowers with a spectrum of colors. They popped.

He grinned. "Wow, look at that!" Almost reflexively, he rested his palm, as large as a catcher's mitt, it seemed, across Harley's delicate fingers. "Thanks, Harley," he said. "You have a good way of looking at things."

She returned his smile, and with no feelings of uneasiness, they returned to their work. Days passed, and Jed had taken to walking Harley to the Johnsons' house where Pearl Johnson had been babysitting her while her grandfather was at the distillery. And that was when everything changed.

Harley still remembered it as if it had happened only moments before, and she wondered if Jed ever thought of that afternoon as well. As they were walking along Briarwood Avenue, naming all of the different colors they could think of, laughing when Jed said "aborigine" for "aubergine," a pickup truck shrieked to a stop beside them and Jed's father, Roy Turner, a mechanic at Frank's Auto Body, sprung to the curb and grabbed Jed by the shirt.

"What do you think you're doin' boy, huh?" he yelled.

Jed, already as big as his father, seemed to shrink to a helpless animal under his grip. "But I didn't do anything, Daddy."

"Didn't do nothin'? Didn't do nothin'? Coach just called me. You know what he said? He said you've been skippin' practice. Said you've been goin' to some silly art class taught by a fruit. 'My son takin' a sissy art class?' I said. 'I don't believe it.' Well, is it true boy? Is it true?"

He ripped the bag of art supplies from underneath Jed's arm and held them up. "Well, I reckon it is."

He threw the supplies in the road and flung Jed to the ground, yelling, "Get in that truck! Get in that truck! You're goin' to practice by-god. You wanna wind up like me? Stuck in this one-horse town the rest of your life, fixin' cars for peanuts? You've got talent, boy. Real talent. Talent I never had. Ain't never gonna have. Now get in that truck."

His father stomped to the driver's side, jumped in the seat and slammed the door behind him. A crumpled Jed lay on the sidewalk, tears running down his burnished cheeks.

"Jed," Harley said, crouching down beside him and resting her hand on his shoulder. "Jed, are you okay? Oh, Jed, I'm so sorry."

But he would not make eye contact with her, and still sobbing, he jerked his body away. He continued to cry, his breaths coming in rasps, which at last settled to intermittent sniffles. Then, as if he were making a pact with himself, he wiped his eyes on his shirtsleeve and glared up at Harley with hatred. "Get away from me, Harley Henrickson, you stupid dork! You, sorry for me? How dare you even come near me. You're so ugly and stupid and weird. Don't you ever talk to me again!"

He hoisted his body up, and turning his back like an iron wall to Harley, he jumped in the truck and slammed the door. His father revved the engine, and the old pickup roared down the street, leaving the bag of art supplies in the roadway.

Crestfallen, Harley reached down and picked up the spilled paints, brushes, and unfinished canvas, still missing the remainder of Jed's flowers, and she tucked them under her arm. She returned to the home where she still lived with her mother and stowed them in the attic where they remained at present. Untouched and unfinished.

"Shoo!" Jed said, breaking Harley from her reverie. She snapped back to the gray morning, the fog-laden field, and to the woods of Briarwood Park, where the homeless man had disappeared moments before.

"You two are free to go," he said. He had already turned his back to them and was issuing out further orders to his deputies. When he finished, he marched to his police cruiser and lowered his girth into the driver's seat, his expression relaying that the disturbance had been a waste of his time, and he could have spent his morning on something more important.

"Jed's bein' such a jagoff," Tina said beside Harley. "I bet it's over what's-her-name. She broke up with him, you know. That model. Cheri or whatever."

Cheri, known to the locals as "Ole Cheery" because she was anything but cheerful, was the model Jed had been dating off-and-on again for the last few years. She flounced around town in her leather leggings and oversized sunglasses, illegally parking her Porsche on Main Street, and had she carried a leash, Jed would have been on the end of it. Since Jed's forced retirement from the NFL, their relationship had turned rocky, some speculating "Ole Cheery" was just a gold digger, and once Jed lost his fame, if not his fortune, Cheri would lose her attraction for him as well.

"I don't know why he's still cryin' over that one," Tina said. "I never thought she was so great. Needs a pierogi. Maybe that's why she's always in a bad mood. Cause she's always hungry."

"She's a symbol, Tina," Harley said, "a symbol of the life Jed had before his injury."

Tina shook her head. "You say weird stuff sometimes, Harley. No, wait, you say weird stuff all the time. But I love you. I really do. You know that." She smiled then turned her attention to her pink minivan still crashed on the side of the road. "Oh, I wish that tow truck would get here for my van."

"It'll be here soon."

Tina's giant model cupcake still lay in the middle of the road, its fallen cherry at its side.

"What about Rosie?" Harley asked.

"Oh, she's comin' with us."

"I was afraid you were going to say that."

CHAPTER 5

*T*he ride into work wasn't a quiet one.

Thump. Thump. Thump. Whoosh!

Tina had threaded a pair of Bungie ties through the truck's open windows, affixing Rosie haphazardly to the roof. Now the cupcake bobbed and crashed with each bump in the road, letting in every manner of cold wind.

Thump. Thump. Thump. Whoosh!

Tina was singing along to *Hits of the Eighties*, a radio station on her cell phone, calling it therapy for what she'd just witnessed.

Harley turned the truck onto Main Street, passing the Mad Hatter tea shop, the Spice Up Your Life spice shop, and the Holy Grounds coffee shop. She stopped in front of Tina's bake shop, Tina's Treats, and put the truck into park.

Tina hopped out of the Chevy and standing in the open doorway said, "I need you to promise me to be ready at six sharp for the historical society meeting tonight. Everybody and I mean everybody important is going to be there, and I need to make a good impression for my business."

"I promise."

Tina neatened her jack-o'-lantern sweater and dropped her cell-phone in her skirt pocket. "And answer your phone every once in a while. Being off-grid is actually not cool, especially when you're always late."

Though this was probably true, Harley did not acknowledge Tina's remark, only said, "I'll pick you up at five forty-five."

After waving goodbye to Tina, Harley headed down the narrow alleyway connecting Tina's Treats with the Henrickson family liquor store, Smoky Mountain Spirits, and parked the Chevy in the loading zone. She lifted a crate of apple brandy from the truck bed and entered the store's back room, a large, open floor plan which included a desk for her laptop, a small kitchenette for making hors d'oeuvres, and a series of shelves for extra storage. After setting the whiskey crate on the prep table, she removed a bottle of apple brandy and carried it inside the shop's public area.

The three-story brick building, constructed in 1835, had initially housed Mildred's, a department store specializing in women's clothing. Over the last two centuries, the building had transformed from a department store to a doctor's office, to a restaurant, to a pharmacy, the deed changing hands ten times before it came under Harley's grandfather's ownership twenty years prior.

Architecturally, the structure retained all of its original hard wood floors, large storefront windows, and exposed brick walls. With the natural wood shelves and stainless steel light fixtures, the shop possessed a rustic yet modern appearance, blending the town's historic roots with its modern-day attraction for tourists.

In the center of the public area, Harley's grandfather had installed a bar where customers could congregate with a cocktail sample while taking a break from shopping. Over the years, Harley had met many interesting people at the bar, many tourists who shared fascinating life stories as she served them one of her latest creations. The cocktail menu changed daily based on the season, the fresh ingredients, and her particular mood that day.

With that in mind, she set a bottle of apple brandy on the bar and studied the shelves of liquor lining the wall behind her. To make a decision, she removed a series of liquors and stationed them alongside the apple brandy. Vintage cocktail shaker in hand, she added rye whiskey, Tuaca, pear liquor, and apple brandy, finishing the cocktail with a dash of Old Fashioned Bitters.

"The Autumn Orchard," she said, naming the cocktail and garnishing it with an orange peel.

With a cocktail spoon, she gave the concoction a good stir and added the mixture to a series of plastic sampling cups. As customers perused the store, sipping an Autumn Orchard cocktail, hopefully they would feel compelled to purchase a bottle of whiskey, brandy, or moonshine.

Yet something was missing. Harley glanced around the store. Garlands of colorful leaves hung like streamers from the shelves, the storefront window showcasing copper stills and antique whiskey bottles. Just then a woman passed by the storefront window, her dog pulling her by its leash. The dog wore a black-and-yellow striped sweater with two antennae protruding from a headband on its forehead. A bumblebee dog.

Yes, of course. Halloween.

After a few moments of searching in the back room, Harley found an orange wooden bucket painted to resemble a jack-o'-lantern. She returned to the shopping area and filled the bucket with individually wrapped peanut butter cups and pieces of toffee, the perfect accompaniments for whiskey.

Harley glanced at her watch. She had just enough time to unload and stock the remaining bottles of liquor before opening the shop. Afterward, she would sit down at her laptop and print out recipe cards for the Autumn Orchard cocktail that customers could take home with them.

But a draft had seeped into the old building, sending a chill up her forearms, and she decided to build a fire in the potbellied stove. As she knelt beside the stove and added strips of kindling to the growing flames, she realized the previous night's storm had not only ushered in a cold front but a blanket of newly fallen leaves on the curb. With the fire at a crackling pace, she grabbed her broom from the back room and ventured out onto the sidewalk, sweeping the first of many autumn leaves.

Through the glass door, Harley could see Dr. Patrick Middleton, president of the Notchey Creek Historical Society walking along the sidewalk, heading in the shop's direction. He wore a navy argyle sweater and khaki corduroys, his wire-rimmed glasses pushing back waves of salt-and-pepper hair. Presumably, he'd been coming from the hospital and was now heading back to his mansion in Briarwood. As he ambled down the street, Harley thought he looked more tired than usual, his handsome face appearing a bit drawn.

Harley had always admired Patrick Middleton. Folks had been a bit suspicious of the handsome "yankee" history professor when he'd first moved to Notchey Creek over thirty years ago, but Harley had always considered Patrick Middleton a good man, an honest man, one who'd surprised her with his disaffected manners and his down-to-earth gentility, refreshing for one so educated and for one so wealthy. Patrick had never been judgmental of the region, not once, never believing the false stereotypes some placed on Appalachia, saying that it was a cultural backwater whose people were uncouth and uneducated, that its society was a marginalized and bleak one, secluded from the greater world by the mountains.

No, Patrick had taken an immediate interest in the area, and one could often find him on Main Street, engaging with locals from all walks of life, touched by the beauty of a people so devoted to their land, to their history, to the hard work of their hands. "And what beautiful things those hands can make," Patrick said each time he bought a hand-woven basket, a piece of earthenware pottery, a home-made quilt, or a hand-crafted rocking chair, all of which he placed in his home or gave as gifts to northern relatives.

It wasn't long after Patrick Middleton had settled in his old estate in Briarwood and had restored it to its original integrity that the townspeople began to see the qualities Harley had recognized in Patrick when she was a child. And then the town warmed to their newest resident, finally adopting him into their hearts, their community, their shared way of life. And once someone was in, they were family. They were loved forever.

Harley watched Patrick as he paced down the sidewalk, a troubled expression on his ordinarily pleasant face. Just then a hunter green Range Rover slowed to the curb alongside him, and Arthur Johnson, a prominent contractor in town, lowered the driver's side window.

"It's true, then, is it?" Arthur said, a scowl on his face.

"Pardon?"

"The land. You've decided not to sell."

Patrick narrowed his eyes, then dropped his gaze to the sidewalk. "So I see you've heard."

"Yes. And from someone else besides you. You didn't even have the decency to tell me?" Arthur's hands gripped the steering wheel, his knuckles turning white. "But you promised that land to me."

"And I've changed my mind."

"Just like that? Over thirty years of friendship and this is how you repay me. By turning the most lucrative construction project this town has seen in years into a history museum!"

"I have to be going, Arthur, I'm sorry."

Arthur idled the Range Rover alongside Patrick. "Listen, I don't think you understand. I want that land. *Desperately.*"

When Patrick did not respond, Arthur punched the gas pedal, and the Range Rover revved forward, the tires shrieking as it reentered traffic on Main Street. Harley watched as the vehicle sped past Patrick, who was peering down at the sidewalk as he walked, his mind lost in troubled thought.

Snort.

Snort. Snort.

To Harley's left, past the hay bales and pumpkins and buckets of chrysanthemums, lay Matilda, her leash tied to the leg of a patio table, her body splayed across a bed of dirt and shredded flowers.

With a groan, Harley knelt beside the pig and pulled a note from beneath her collar. In hurried handwriting, Aunt Wilma had written: *Hair emergency. Pig sick. Take to vet.*

But Matilda didn't appear to be sick, and she'd felt well enough to destroy Mayor Montgomery's prized flowers.

Hoping she might be able to clean up the mess and replace the flowers before anyone noticed, Harley reached for her broom and commanded Matilda to rise. It was then she heard Mayor Ruby Montgomery and her Chamber of Commerce president, Alveda Hamilton chattering down the sidewalk, heading in her direction.

Mayor Ruby Montgomery, the widow of coal magnate, Walter Montgomery, always wore wool pantsuits worthy of a Communist dictator. She was a powerful woman to behold, her statuesque figure still athletic and slim from riding her bicycle into town each day. To finish off her look, the town's best stylists coiffed her brown hair in a pageboy and painted her nails in a perfect French manicure.

Alveda Hamilton, on the other hand, reminded Harley of Miss Prissy from *Looney Tunes*. Petite and emaciated, Alveda's matching sweater sets and loafers dwarfed her tiny figure. In the face, she was bird-like, with squinty eyes and a long, pointy nose, a pair of glasses resting on her beak.

From what Harley could hear, it sounded like Alveda was in the middle of sharing a piece of gossip. "Well, I heard she's been seeing him in secret. Having little engagements at his house late at night."

Ruby, who seemed to be half-listening, continued her patrol down Main Street, surveying the decor.

Alveda continued. "And I don't doubt it one bit, Ruby. That girl's always had a thing for him. Even when she was a little girl she would moon over him. And him old enough to be her daddy." She shook her head. "She's always been too beautiful for her own good, Savannah has. I've always said that. And Patrick Middleton? Well, I suppose every woman in town has been after him at one time or another. He is handsome, I do have to admit. And he has all of that money he inherited. Of course, Michael Sutcliffe has money too, and he's twenty-five years younger."

"Now Michael I do feel sorry for," Ruby said at last. "Losing his parents so young and now this. Why he ever became engaged to someone like Savannah Swanson I will never know."

The chatter stopped. Both women froze on the sidewalk. Harley looked up to find Alveda and Ruby with their hands clamped over their mouths, staring at Matilda.

"My flowers!" Alveda screamed.

At her baseline, Alveda Hamilton was a high-strung woman, and when she became agitated, her high-pitched voice jumped to falsetto. "Harley Henrickson! You awful girl. It's that pig again! It's that old rotten pig of yours!"

Harley swallowed a lump in her throat and jerked Matilda to her side.

"Do you know how much time it takes the Chamber of Commerce to plant these flowers? Do you? How much love and devotion goes into each and every bloom? It's all volunteer work, you know. *Our* volunteer work."

Alveda scowled, the grooves in her face becoming more pronounced as she took in Harley's appearance and demeanor.

"But you wouldn't know about that, would you, Miss Lonely Hearts? It's no wonder you can't get any dates. With a crazy pig like that and looking like you do all the time. This is not *Green Acres*. We do not have pigs congregating on Main Street." She shook her head. "You've always been a strange bird. Always had your own ways. You know what I'm going to do? I'm going to call Jed Turner. Yes, that's what I'm going to do. He can deal with you. I'm sick of trying. Besides, he needs to know what goes on down here when he's not around. I—"

Just when Harley thought all was lost, Alveda clamped her mouth shut and stared over Harley's shoulder at someone approaching from behind.

CHAPTER 6

The man's shadow grew more substantial with the sound of his footsteps as he approached the three women. He wore a red flannel shirt, the sleeves of which had been cut out, exposing a pair of protruding biceps in a black motorcycle vest. On his bottom half, a pair of ripped jeans covered his long muscular thighs, black combat boots laced up to his calves. While Harley could spot no tattoos, she assumed there were at least a few beneath his clothes. By her estimation, he was probably somewhere in his early thirties.

Fewer assessments she could make about his face. A baseball hat covered his dark wavy hair which was tied loosely in a ponytail down his back. A matching beard obscured most of his face, but beneath it, she detected high cheekbones and a prominent jawline.

The man's dark blue eyes seemed to take in the scene before him with amusement: the two furious women, the redneck girl, the unapologetic pig, and the trail of dirt and petals littering the sidewalk. A slight smile crossed his bearded face, then quickly disappeared.

"This shop open?" he said, motioning to Smoky Mountain Spirits in the foreground. His voice spoke of late nights, whiskey, and cigars.

With quiet reverence, Alveda Hamilton stared up at him, her mouth agape. Even Ruby appeared startled. Confused by their reactions but thankful for the interruption, Harley nodded that the shop was indeed open.

He marched in that direction, leaving a fawning Ruby and Alveda in his wake. Alveda Hamilton scuttled along behind him like a chicken, balancing her purse on her elbow. "And I hope you'll come to Pioneer Days this week," she said. "Your presence would mean so much to the community."

But he'd already disappeared inside the shop, the bells clanging behind him.

All decorum fell from Alveda's face, her former coquettishness replaced with bile. "As soon as he leaves," she said, pointing toward the shop, "and not a second after, I want this mess cleaned up, and I want those flowers replaced. And if I ever see that awful pig near my flowers again, I'm calling Animal Control."

Ruby Montgomery, who typically treated Harley with cold civility, approached and in a stern voice said, "Clean up the debris and replace the flowers by noon today or you will be fined and your business will be banned from participating in the festival."

Repentantly Harley nodded and led Matilda inside the shop. With the door closed and the incident behind her, she exhaled in relief and rested her back to the door.

The man stood in the back right-hand corner of the store, perusing the whiskey collection. Before Harley headed his way, she led Matilda over to the potbellied stove and tied her leash to one of the load-bearing pillars, assuming the pig couldn't possibly bring the pillar and the entire store to the ground. Harley patted Matilda on the head, then caressed her silken ears, an effort to comfort them both, it seemed. It had been a terrible day. As soon as the man left, she would close the shop temporarily, take Matilda to the vet, then back to the farm.

From a distance, Harley watched the man as he studied the whiskey bottles in quiet thought.

He seemed relieved to be there, in the quiet of the shop, in the comfort of its bottles, in the warmth of its stove. Once again, she surveyed the ripped jeans, the motorcycle vest, and the trucker hat. He was a bit rough looking, she supposed, but no more than some of the hillbillies who blew through town on the weekends, their beat-up pickup trucks leaving a trail of exhaust on their way to Pigeon Forge. No, Harley guessed he was merely a long haul truck driver or perhaps a Hell's Angel. She predicted he would buy a bottle of whiskey or scotch, and after a wordless transaction, he would be on his way.

Instead, he started laughing. It was not a jolly laugh, a guffaw, or even a giggle. It was more of a gravelly chuckle as if he had not laughed in some time.

"I apologize," he said, clearing his throat. "It's just that I'm rarely surprised, but that outside…well, let's just say I wasn't expecting it." He laughed again. "That bird woman," he said, referring to Alveda Hamilton, "does she always get her feathers up like that?"

"She does around me I guess," Harley said. "I seem to have that effect on people.

"It's because you're not a cookie cutter," he said, "and that's all right."

"So," Harley said with a smile, trying to turn the conversation away from her, "are you just coming off a long haul?"

He turned from the shelves and seemed to look at her for the first time. His dark blue eyes lit up ever so slightly and a subtle smile formed on his bearded face. He did not answer at first; his gaze moved over her appearance, from the camouflage hat and the pigtails to the thick-lensed glasses, the overalls, and boots.

"Are you?" he said in that whiskey and cigar voice.

Harley realized she must've looked as rough to him as he had to her. And she'd felt rough too, had felt rough for some time. Recalling the events of the last several years, she nodded and said, "Yes, I guess you could say that."

His expression adopted a look of understanding and in a lowered voice he said, "Me too."

Harley perceived a certain coolness about the man, an understated coolness, as if he chose to dress this way, that he could do better and could afford better but he chose not to. She, on the other hand, wore whatever was easy and clean and comfortable, putting hardly any thought into it. There was no style to it. No understated coolness. Some called her hopeless, others pitiful.

"So, what's the best whiskey you've got?" he asked, returning his attention to the shelves of liquor.

"Single barrel," she said.

"Can I try some?"

"Sure."

Harley motioned to the bar, and he followed behind her, taking a seat on one of the stools, and resting his bulbous arm muscles on the counter. She placed a tasting glass in front of him and filled it with a shot of single barrel whiskey.

He lifted the glass to his lips, and with his mouth slightly open, his eyes closed, he drew in the aroma of caramel, vanilla, and char. His face relaxed for the first time, his features drifting into the softness of what Harley could only interpret as nirvana. Eyes still closed, he drew a sip and rolled it over his tongue, as if he were in a pleasant dream, and Harley expected him to moan at any moment. Instead he opened his eyes, his features falling back into their somber seriousness.

"You got a bottle I can take with me?"

Harley nodded in ascent, then realized she did not have any single barrel in stock at the store. "I can get some to you by this afternoon, if that's okay."

A brief look of disappointment, then, "Good enough."

He raised the whiskey taster to his lip once more, and as he did so, Harley noticed a series of hard callouses across the fingertips on his left hand.

"You make this?" he asked.

Harley nodded that she indeed had.

"So how does somebody get into the whiskey-making business?"

She considered for a moment, then said, "Well, I guess for me it was family. We've been making whiskey for centuries, even before our ancestors immigrated from the British Isles to Western Pennsylvania in the eighteenth century. Then with the Whiskey Rebellion in the 1790s, we made our way down the Appalachians to East Tennessee and settled here in the Smokies. The mountains provided much-needed privacy, and the spring water was perfect for distillation."

"And what about Prohibition?" he asked, looking at her with sincere interest.

"Well, let's just say it was the only thing that kept us from starving during the Great Depression."

He seemed to appreciate this piece Henrickson family history and said, "Interesting history this region has. I've always thought so."

"So you didn't grow up around here, I take?"

He hesitated. "Only for a short time. I spent a lot of my early life all over. In foster homes mostly." Her question seemed to have touched a vulnerable place in the rough-hewn man, and he lowered his eyes to the bar and changed the subject. "So when you're not making whiskey, you're raising pigs?"

"Well, there's only the one pig. Matilda." Harley looked to where the pig was still napping by the potbellied stove. "My granddaddy gave her to me years ago."

"Interesting present for a kid."

"Granddaddy said I needed a friend...and I guess he was right." Realizing how pitiful this sounded, she turned away from him to hide her embarrassment.

"Well," he said, "don't feel bad. I've never had many friends either. Not real ones anyway."

Before she could respond, he added, "You're more of a reader I take than a socializer anyway."

His assessment of her was correct. Never having attended college or graduate school, books had formed Harley Henrickson's education, her education and her comfort. Even as an adult, she still turned to the row of books above the bar when things were slow at the shop or when she needed a moment of gravity, something they always managed to give her.

"Well," he said, studying his calloused fingers absently, "sometimes the worlds we find in books are better than what the real world has to offer."

The man was a walking contradiction, and Harley liked him for it.

She pointed to the row of hardback books lining the top shelf of the bar and to the copy of Charles Dickens's *Great Expectations*. "That book...that book is my favorite."

He gazed at the book's worn spine, his expression relaying one of somber understanding and agreement.

"So what do you do?" Harley asked, returning the topic back to him. "For a living I mean?"

"I..." He paused, seeming to ponder the best approach to answer this question. "I'm a musician," he said at last.

"And you play the guitar?"

He gave her a suspicious look, and she followed up with, "I saw the callouses on your fingers."

"Ah," he said with an expression of relief. "Yeah, I guess I have built them up over the years."

"So, are you playing in some of the local clubs around here?" she asked. "I know Bud's Pool Hall has live music most nights, and my Uncle Tater knows the owner really well. I could have him set up something for you."

The hint of a smile curved his lips. "That would be kind of you. Thanks." He reached for his wallet. "Now, how much do I owe you?"

"Nothing." She smiled. "Consider it a welcome gift. And I'll deliver it this afternoon."

"Thanks, Harley Henrickson," he said. "You're a good kid."

Harley wanted to ask him how he knew her name but was interrupted by the ringing of the shop bell.

"Excuse me just a second," she told him. "I'll be right back."

Harley headed toward the front of the store where two men stood, searching the place with a sense of urgency. One of the men had hair as blond as straw and skin as tanned as dried tobacco, both having spent a lot of time in the sun or salon. He wore tight, distressed jeans, a black long sleeved shirt, unbuttoned to display his bronzed chest muscles beneath. The other man was quite his opposite. His black hair was styled into a Mohawk, and what little skin peeked from his head-to-toe black clothing was pale and smooth like a mannequin's.

"Oh, lord, there's a pig in here," said the blond, catching sight of

Matilda on the floor. "Why am I not surprised in this godforsaken town?"

His companion did not seem to appreciate the commentary, and beneath his breath said, "Take it easy, Marcus."

When Harley approached from the back of the store, Marcus took in her appearance then broke into laughter. "Look coming here, Stevie," he said. "It's one of the extras from *Deliverance*." He hummed a bar of "Dueling Banjos" and laughed at his own joke.

Stevie, however, did not laugh. He inclined his Mohawk head toward Harley and smiled, exposing a row of perfectly straight, white teeth. "Good Morning," he said. "We were wondering if you might be able to help us. We're looking for someone."

When Harley didn't answer, Marcus said, "Oh, don't pretend like you don't know who we're talking about. We know he's in here. Somebody saw him come in." He turned to Stevie. "You know, he probably took one look at Deliverance here and ran for the hills."

Harley glanced over her shoulder to the bar where the man had since disappeared. "I haven't seen anyone," she said.

As soon as she said it, she caught sight of Matilda in her peripheral vision. The pig had risen from her place on the floor and was walking toward the two men. She idled sheepishly before Marcus, hovering over his feet with her mouth slightly open. Harley had only seen the pig this way a few times before and every time she had...

Blech!

Vomit projected from Matilda's mouth, congealing in a pool over Marcus's feet. "My boots!" he was yelling, staring at his feet in horror. "Two thousand dollars! That's what I paid for these." He reached down as if to scoop some of the vomit from his boots, but then thought better of it. He glared at Harley, as if he expected her to clean it up, and she stood placid, expressionless. Her passivity seemed to anger him even more, and he opened his mouth to spew more curses when Stevie interrupted, tugging at his elbow.

"Let's go, Marcus. We'll get you cleaned up back at the resort. Come on. We have more important matters to deal with."

A few malicious glares more, and the still-fuming Marcus turned away, cursing under his breath, something about an ignorant hillbilly girl and her disgusting animal. The stream of insults filtered out onto the sidewalk, only silenced by the clang of the shop door.

At the bar, the stool where the man once sat was empty, his whiskey glass still stationed on the counter. There was something else there too. A piece of paper. In surprisingly neat handwriting, it read: *Muscadine Farms.* Beneath it were five one-hundred-dollar bills.

But she did not have long to ponder this because the shop door opened yet again, but this time it was Sheriff Jed Turner.

"Smells like puke," he said, making a face of disgust. Then, his eyes roamed over Harley, and he added, "and poop."

But Harley did not engage. She walked past him, trying to locate another towel she could use to clean up Matilda's vomit.

Following behind her, Jed had his muscled arms flexed on his hips, his biceps at the best angle for admiring eyes, for which at the moment there were none. He looked about the shop in the smug way only Jed Turner could muster. "I got a call from Alveda," he said to Harley's back as she mopped up Matilda's vomit with a towel. "Said you and that pig of yours have been destroying property on Main Street...been involved in some disorderly conduct."

Harley kept her head lowered, continuing to mop.

"Might I remind you that we've got a festival starting here tomorrow morning? A *big* festival. With lots of people and lots of money pouring in. And I tell you what, you are being nothin' but a problem for me. First, you're finding drunks in the ditch and saying they've witnessed a murder. Then you and that pig of yours are tearing up flower beds on Main Street and harassing —"

He crossed the room and stood over her. Harley could feel his eyes glaring into her shoulder blades. "Harley, are you listening to me?"

No answer.

"Harley Henrickson, you are the most infuriating woman. Listen, I don't want to hear anything about you from here on out. You got it? You lay low. No more of you and that pig disturbing the peace, especially not during this festival."

Harley lifted herself from the floor and met his gaze. "Did you find anything out?" she asked. "About the homeless man we found in Briar-wood Park this morning?"

"You mean the drunk one?"

Losing her patience, Harley turned her back to him and started toward the bar.

"Okay, yes, Harley, I did make some calls," he said.

"But I thought you said he was 'just some old drunk.'"

"Well, he probably is."

"And? What did you find out?"

"Well, he was at the shelter last night, like you guessed…but only for supper, they said. He ate, then said he was going to Bud's Pool Hall."

"Bud's?"

"Yes. I asked if it was because he wanted to drink, and they said, 'no.' He said he'd given up drinking. Said he was supposed to meet someone there."

"Who?"

"Don't know."

Interesting, Harley thought. Who would the man have known in Notchey Creek? Was it an old friend, an acquaintance, or someone he was meeting for the first time? And had the person been responsible for his inebriated state that morning? Or perhaps, she thought, they could at least tell them who he was and why he was in Notchey Creek.

Before she could ask any more questions, Jed's cell phone rang and he answered it. "Sheriff Turner." As he headed for the door, Harley could still hear him talking. "Uh huh. Yes, Alveda, I spoke with her. No, Alveda, she and that pig aren't going to terrorize the community anymore. What? No, they're not going to ruin the festival either. Okay. Okay. Bye."

Then the shop door slammed shut behind him.

CHAPTER 7

The distillery was quiet when Harley arrived later that
afternoon. She was happy to see Uncle Tater had risen
from bed and was sitting in the barnyard, assembling a moonshine
still. When he heard her truck rumble into the drive, he lowered the
wrench to his side and saluted her with his beer bottle.

Uncle Tater always looked amused, like he'd just heard a good joke,
an expression that matched his lackadaisical approach to life. He
reminded Harley of Papa Smurf but dressed in a flannel shirt and
overalls, with his white hair tucked in a John Deere hat.

As she stepped outside her truck, he said, "Well, if it ain't my
favorite truck and my favorite gal both come to see me."

Harley smiled, heading across the barnyard in his direction.
"What's the still for?"

"Pioneer Days," he said, tightening a copper coil with his wrench.
"Patrick Middleton asked me to make it. Like the ones they would've used
back in the 1800s. I figured I'd set it up outside the store down yonder."

"Ah, that's great, Uncle Tater," Harley said, wanting to promote any
worthy endeavor. "I bet it'll be a big hit at the festival."

"Well, we'll see, I reckon." He rested his wrench in the grass and took a sip of his beer. "Hey, what're you doin' out here at this time of the day? I figured you'd be down at the store."

"I had to bring Matilda back from the vet and pick up a bottle of single barrel for a customer."

"She doin' all right?"

"Just another upset stomach."

Tater shook his head. "I'm surprised that old pig is still alive the way she carries on." He thought on this a moment and chuckled. "But I reckon folks say that about me too, and I'm as fit as a fiddle." He took a sip of his beer. "Well, why don't you join me for a beer in The Shed after you're done with your business."

Harley agreed, then headed toward the distillery.

Inside, she found Aunt Wilma at her desk, reading *The Notchey Creek Telephone*, a gossip magazine that posed as the town's newspaper. A wig worthy of an Oompa Loompa peeked above the newspaper's pages, and Harley feared what lay beneath that wig. Wilma was sensitive about her hair, and she would be undoubtedly cranky about the failed permanent. But to Harley's surprise, Wilma lowered the newspaper and grinned.

"Ain't it marvelous, Harley?" she said. "I tell you what. I done myself a favor with that old failed permanent. If my hair hadn't fallen out, I wouldn't have got this here wig. And if I hadn't got this here wig, I wouldn't have known how beautiful and low-maintenance it is. You see, all I gotta do is put it on when I wake up, and I'm done. Purdy as punch."

"I'm glad you're enjoying it," Harley said. *What a relief.*

"That pig all right?"

"She's okay," Harley said, scanning the shelves of whiskey behind Wilma, then grabbing a bottle of single barrel.

"I know you're awful proud of that new batch yonder," she said. "Though you won't never brag on nothin' you do. Who's wantin' it so soon?"

"Just somebody who came into the store."

Harley tucked the bottle under her arm and headed back toward the front door. Before she could make her escape, Wilma said, "Oh, did you hear the big news?"

Harley paused in the doorway.

"There's a big rock star in town. Can you believe it? There's a story about him here in the paper. Front page. *The Telephone* says he and his quote 'entourage' is stayin' up yonder at the Muscadine Farms while he looks at properties in the area. And he's rentin' out the entire place, can you believe it? Lordy, that must be costin' him a whole lotta money." She rustled the paper and continued reading. "'Left the lights of L.A.,' it says, 'for the quiet refuge of the Smokies.' Wants to do some kind of work on a solo album... 'in private,' it says."

I doubt he'll get that.

Wilma pulled a magnifying glass from her desk drawer and angled it over the newspaper, squinting at the accompanying photo. "Now, that ain't bad," she said, gliding her tongue across her bottom lip. "No, sister, that ain't bad *at all*. Of course, he'd be even better lookin' if he'd cut that old long hair and shave that scruff off his face. I swear I don't see why a man like that's got to ruin his looks by havin' hair and clothes like that."

Harley opened the door to leave, and Wilma added, "His name's Beau Arson or somethin' or another. Awful name if you ask me, but apparently he's the lead guitarist and singer for some hard rock band or another called Assault. Real famous, apparently." She shrugged. "Of course, I ain't never heard of no Assault or no Beau Arson neither. As you know, I don't listen to much but Mr. J. Bazzel Mull and the Sunday Mornin' Gospel circuit. But all the young people around here's heard of him, and there's quite a write-up about him in today's paper."

When Harley showed no reaction, surprised, thrilled, or otherwise, Wilma added, "Well, I guess you ain't never heard of him neither then."

No, but I've met him. "See you later, Wilma."

Not waiting for a reply, Harley ventured out into the morning sun, smiling as the distillery's door slammed shut behind her. The air felt a bit warmer now, and she hoped for temperatures in the low sixties.

After resting the bottle inside her truck, she decided it was time to pay a visit to "The Shed," the red tin outbuilding where Uncle Tater held court. She didn't usually visit The Shed at this time of day, but wanted to ask Tater something.

She found him inside, lounging in a green plastic lawn chair beside a small cooler, with his boots propped up on a giant spool of copper cable. He held a remote control in one hand and a longneck beer in the other, his eyes dancing with the flickering light of a flat screen TV. A collage of license plates lined the wall behind him, and a long-abandoned hornet nest peeked from the corner of the ceiling.

"Come on in, honey," he said. "Have yourself a seat on the couch yonder."

"The couch" was a long vinyl car seat Tater had disemboweled from an old minivan.

Like most things in The Shed, he had acquired it from Floyd's Junkyard. "Wanna beer?" he asked, patting the cooler beside his lawn chair.

"Not yet, but thanks."

"Well," he said, picking up his remote, "you're lucky. You arrived just in time for *The Golden Girls*." Tater grinned as the opening credits for *The Golden Girls* appeared on the screen." He turned up the volume.

"'Thank you for being a friend,'" he sang along. "'Travel down the road and back again. Your heart is true, you're a pal and a confidant.'"

"Tater," Harley said over the music, "can I ask you something?"

"Yeah, what's that, honey?"

"Have you seen anyone new in Bud's recently?"

"What kind of individual are you talkin' about?"

"A man, probably middle-aged or older…dark hair, ratty clothes."

"That sounds like half the county."

"But this man had scars on his face…several…like he'd been in an accident or something terrible."

"Scars, scars," Tater said, scratching his chin. He took a sip of beer and burped. "Hmm. Seems like I did see a feller like that last night."

"Did you talk to him?"

"Nope, but—"

The Shed's door flew open and Tater's best friend, Floyd Robinson, stepped inside, a Hardee's bag in one hand and a six-pack of Pabst Blue Ribbon in the other.

"Well, there's old Winnie Cooper, ain't it?" he said, smiling at Harley.

"Floyd," Harley said in return, pleasantly.

Floyd Robinson, proprietor of Floyd's Junkyard, was a large, burly man in Dickies and loafers. With his bulbous red nose and happy demeanor, he reminded Harley of Mr. Hamburger from *Popeye*, but with a shock of white hair. He thumped down into the beanbag beside her, and she wondered how he was ever going to get up from it again.

"Did I miss *The Golden Girls*?" he asked.

"Naw, you ain't missed 'em. And it's one of your favorite episodes. 'The Men of Blanche's Boudoir,'" Tater said with panache.

Floyd unwrapped his cheeseburger and took a bite, smacking his lips. "Yep, I reckon that's one of my favorites."

"Uncle Tater," Harley said, "you were telling me about the man you saw in Bud's."

Both men looked over at Harley, seemingly surprised that not only was she talking, but that she was asking questions.

"Oh, yeah, that," Tater said, taking a sip of beer. "Well, he was goin' around the bar yonder askin' questions of folks."

"What kind of questions?"

"About folks in town mostly," Floyd said, his mouth full of cheeseburger.

"Sure was," Tater said. "But who he really wanted to know about was Patrick Middleton. Why I don't know, but he wanted to know where he could find him."

"Said he was supposed to meet him there," Floyd said.

"And?"

"Well, I reckon somebody give him Patrick's address because the next thing anybody knew, he was gone. Just like that."

"What time was this?"

"Aw, about eight, I reckon."

"And you haven't seen him since?"

"Nope."

Harley was about to ask another question when Floyd began pointing at the TV screen in excitement.

"Oh, look yonder, we're comin' up to my favorite part."

Blanche was on screen presenting a calendar to Sophia, Dorothy, and Rose. "The Men of Blanche's Boudoir," she said. "I'm surprised you were able to walk in October," Sophia added.

Floyd's laughter burst through The Shed, rattling the tin walls and inflating the beanbag. Patting his belly and catching his breath he said, "That Blanche. She's a good un."

"Naw, not for me," Tater said. "I'm more of a Dorothy fan. Takes charge. Knows what she wants."

"Well, you'd have to get you one of them step ladders for your dates."

"What do you know about dates, Floyd? I bet you ain't had one in thirty years."

Floyd laughed, this time only rattling the bean bag. "Well, I have me a right mind to ask old Hazel Moses out. She's about the only person in town I know who's been single about as long I have."

"That's because she's been pinin' for Patrick Middleton for thirty years. It seems like everybody's interested in him lately."

"Aw, Tater, you know Patrick ain't gonna get with her."

"She don't know that."

"Well, she ought to know it. Heck, he would've made a move by now if he was interested."

"I heard he likes 'em young," Tater said. "And blonde. Hazel's right purdy, I reckon, but she ain't young."

"And she definitely ain't no blonde," Floyd added.

Harley glanced at her watch and rose from the minivan seat, satisfied with her visit to The Shed. If anything, Tater and Floyd were a wealth of information.

"Where you headed off to?" Tater asked.

"An errand."

"Yeah?"

"And then to the historical society meeting."

"You mean the 'full of horse poop meeting'?"

Harley couldn't help but laugh. "Yeah, that one."

"Well, you better take a shovel with you, you hear?"

"Will do," Harley said, forcing back another laugh.

After leaving The Shed, she walked back to her truck, pondering the homeless man's behavior in Bud's Pool Hall. Why had he been searching for Patrick Middleton? She stopped when she spotted Wilma standing beside the truck's passenger side door.

"I need you to take that pig in and get her weighed," Wilma said, motioning to Matilda in the truck bed. "For Pioneer Days. I think we ought to enter her in that Prize Pig contest. I think she's got a good chance of winning. And that prize money's twenty-thousand dollars, Harley. You know what we could do with twenty-thousand dollars? We could make repairs to the distillery, buy us some more barrels. Heck, we could even build Matilda her own little house at your place. With heat and air and a refrigerator."

Harley considered. While their whiskey business was no longer in bankruptcy, they were still a long way away from being successful. The money would certainly come in handy. And though Matilda was precocious, she was objectively a large and beautiful pig.

Harley nodded in consent, and Wilma clapped her hands together in excitement. "Alrighty! You're to drop her off at six o'clock tomorrow mornin' at the festival grounds, you hear? And I figure she can stay with you tonight, bein' as you live in town."

The last time Matilda had stayed at Harley's house, the pig had chewed through the laundry room wall and eaten her hardback copy of *The Fall of the Roman Empire*. Nonetheless, they did need the money.

Harley got inside her truck. "6 a.m., it is."

"You won't regret it, Harley. I promise you won't."

Harley was about to make her escape when Uncle Tater ran out of The Shed, flagging her down with his beer bottle. "Hold up there, Harley honey. I need you to haul somethin' for me if you don't mind."

He pointed to an antique toilet in the back of his orange 1976 Ford pick-up truck. Harley was not a historian, but she knew the toilet must date back to at least the 1860s.

Wilma huffed. "You mean that old toilet?"

"Opha Mae Shaw wants it," Tater said. "Says it's got hysterical value. Says she wants to plant some flares in it for Pioneer Days."

"I don't care if it's got historical value or not," Wilma said. "That ain't no flower pot."

"Opha Mae's the creative type, Wilmer. And I reckon it ain't no worse than that cupcake Harley's got perched on her roof yonder." He moved his gaze from Rosie, the cupcake, then back to The Shed. "Floyd, get your butt out here!"

Seconds later, Floyd emerged from The Shed, his cinder block legs wobbling in his Dickies. Before Harley knew it, the two old men were loading the antique toilet in the back of her truck, stationing it alongside Matilda.

Tater took in the scene and grinned. "Well, Harley, I reckon that old Mr. Dickens of yours would be right proud. You got your own 'Olde Curiosity Shop.'"

"And it's mobile," Floyd said with glee.

CHAPTER 8

$\mathcal{T}$he last rays of autumn sun peeked through the canopy of trees as Harley's truck climbed the winding road to Muscadine Farms. On over thirty acres of rolling farmland and surrounded by the Smoky Mountain foothills, Muscadine Farms was a hidden, yet famous gem.

Featured in numerous travel and food magazines, the resort was a private refuge for affluent guests who spent over a thousand dollars per night fishing, hiking, and hunting in the Smokies while enjoying the best wine and cuisine in the Southeast. But there was nothing pretentious about the place. The owners, Laura and Max Abner, were locals who'd become a successful businesswoman and chef, respectively.

As the Chevy climbed the hill and parted the clearing, Harley spotted the resort's signature red barn and its two adjoining white farmhouses, serving as a dining hall and inn, respectively. A cornucopia of pumpkins, gourds and hay stalks lined the buildings' perimeters and the paths connecting them with the inn. The parking lot, usually open to the public, had been cordoned off with a makeshift fence, and behind the fence stood an enormous bald man in leather chaps and a matching vest, gold rings hanging from each of his pierced ears. He reminded Harley of Mr. Clean.

His gaze moved from Rosie, the giant cupcake, to Matilda, the giant pig, then to the toilet, which compared to modern toilets, was also a giant. Harley stopped her truck beside him and rolled down the window. Even more displeased with her looks, it seemed, he crossed his arms at the chest and gave a smug look.

"What?" he barked.

"Good Afternoon, sir, I'm here to see Mr. Arson."

"No fangirls allowed."

Harley held up the bottle of single barrel whiskey for him to see.

He gave a definitive shake of his head. "Oh no, not this again. Listen, Olive Oil. Girls have tried to bribe me with a whole lot more than that to see Beau. I've been tested more than Jesus in the desert."

Harley tried again. "He came by my shop this morning and asked me to deliver it to him." She showed him the note Beau had left and the one-hundred-dollar bills.

As the man stared at the note and money in disbelief, she added, "Look, I really have no interest in seeing him. I just want to drop this off. If you could just make sure he gets it, I'll be on my way."

Mr. Clean considered this for a moment, leering at Harley with skepticism. He grabbed his walkie-talkie and began speaking. "Yeah, I've got some teenager out here, says Beau asked her to deliver a bottle of whiskey to him."

He stopped talking for a minute and examined Harley. "What do mean what does she look like? Um, well, let's see. She's got these big Sally Jessy Raphael glasses from the 90s, dark brown Pippi Long-stocking braids, and a camouflage hat. Looks like she could've been on *Heehaw*. Yeah. But not one of the hot ones in the short dresses that hung out in the cornfield. No, more like, 'I caught me a possum in the woods yonder, and after I skin it, I'm gonna fry it up for my supper.'"

Nice, Harley thought. *Just what every girl wants to hear.*

There was laughter, then undecipherable talking on the other end of the line. "Yeah. Yeah. Okay."

Mr. Clean rested the walkie-talkie at his side. "You're expected inside."

Harley tried to hand the whiskey bottle to him, hoping he would just take it and she could be on her way.

"Nope," he said. "I have orders that you're to deliver it personally."

He eyed the pig, the toilet, and the giant cupcake. "But I ain't parkin' this freak show on wheels."

Silence.

Mr. Clean grunted, then eyed the antique toilet in the truck bed. "Love the port-a-potty," he said, making a face. "Dang, how old's that thing? At least the 1800s, I bet."

Time passed. The engine hummed.

"Well, I don't care if Abe Lincoln dropped a deuce in that toilet, I still ain't parkin' this rattle trap."

Time passed. The cupcake wobbled.

"Hey, is that a pig you've got back there? Dang, that thing's huge."

Time passed. The toilet rattled.

At last, Mr. Clean, acknowledging he wouldn't win the quiet game with Harley Henrickson, motioned behind him to the barn. "You're a strange duck, aren't you?" he said. "Okay. Park it back there behind the building where nobody can see it. And when you get inside, I don't want you botherin' Beau, you hear? Trust me, you ain't his type." Then, under his breath, he added, "I ain't sure whose type you would be. Jeremiah Johnson's?"

He chuckled to himself, then pulled back the fence and motioned for Harley to drive past. As she moved to do so, he placed his hand on the door. "Hey, what's your name anyway?"

Harley kept her eyes fixed ahead and put her foot on the gas, forcing Mr. Clean to lift his hand.

In the rearview mirror, she could see him watching her progression toward the barn, a perplexed look on his face.

"My name's Boonie," he called after the truck. "Boonie Davenport."

Harley parked in the back corner of the staff parking lot, got out of her truck, and headed toward the front of the inn where Boonie

Davenport now stood, guarding the front entrance, his muscled arms crossed at his chest.

"Now remember what I said," he told her, opening the front door. "No teenage fangirl nonsense. It gets old after a while."

Inside, the chatter of voices, the clink of cocktail glasses rose in a symphony toward the vaulted wooden ceiling, only outdone by Metallica's "Enter Sandman" blaring from the speaker system. At the room's center, a fire crackled in the majestic stone hearth and the mahogany tables were packed with people Harley had never seen before, decked out in leather skirts and halter tops, expensive clothes made to look cheap.

There was no sign of Beau Arson. Harley decided she would give the whiskey to the first person she found, then leave. That person turned out to be Laura Abner, who co-owned Muscadine Farms with her husband, Max.

Laura, who was always meticulous with her grooming and appearance, looked as if she'd just woken up. She had her ginger hair tied into a messy bun and her print dress was stained and wrinkled. The lines and dark circles around her eyes suggested she hadn't slept in days. She rushed past Harley, carrying a tray of cocktails, and nearly crashed into the younger woman.

Since when did Laura act as a cocktail waitress? Harley wondered.

"I'm so sorry, Miss," Laura said, rebalancing the tray. When she looked up and recognized the girl was Harley, she said, "Harley? Harley Henrickson? What a surprise to find you here." She leaned in and lowered her voice to a whisper. "You better leave while you still have the chance."

"He's that bad, is he?" Harley asked.

"Who? Beau Arson? I wouldn't really know. I don't get much of a chance to interact with him. No, it's all of his people. They're so rude and demanding and they surround him like a fortress, Harley. Nobody gets to that man without going through all of them first. And they refused my waitstaff, don't you know? They said for 'security reasons.' Said they couldn't trust them around Beau. So, now I'm doing all of the servicing and Max all of the cooking."

"Goodness, Laura," Harley said. " I'm so sorry. But why are you putting up with it? You all are so successful as it is."

"Oh, Harley," she said with a sigh. "That man is richer than Croesus." She paused in thought, then almost laughed. "He doesn't look like it though, does he? More like a bouncer at a dive bar. But anyway, you're right. We don't need the money, per se, to run things as they are…we're doing great…but you see, we want to add another building to the inn. Demand has gotten so high. The money he's paying us will cover that plus another barn for the livestock and another garden for our produce."

"So, how much longer are they going to be here? Do you know?"

"Indefinitely, from what I understand. He's working on a solo album, they say, and looking at properties in the area."

"So he's planning on living here permanently then?"

"I don't know about permanently. People like him have multiple houses all over the world. But he does plan on having some sort of residence here. How often he'll ever be here is yet to be seen."

"But why here? Why Notchey Creek?"

"He was born around here apparently, and the place has special meaning for him."

Harley remembered Beau Arson having said he'd lived in Notchey Creek for a short time but had spent the remainder of his early life in foster homes.

"Well, good luck, Laura," she said. "Just keep thinking about that new addition to the inn and the barn for the horses."

"Thanks, Harley."

Harley handed Laura the whiskey bottle. "Could you please see that this is delivered to Beau? He came by my shop this morning and ordered it. I promised I'd get it to him by the end of the day."

"I'll see what I can do," she said, taking the bottle and placing it on the tray of drinks.

"Thank you."

Laura continued past the bar and called over her shoulder, "I'll see you, Harley."

Harley headed back outside, thankful for the silence of the parking lot. Being in there had been like being trapped in a dark cave, one populated by primitive creatures who fed off cocktails and heavy metal. She wondered if they would all turn into vampires at nightfall.

Thankfully, now the only sound was that of her boots hitting the pavement as she made her way back to the truck.

But wait.

She paused in the parking lot, training her ear to listen. She looked around the dark lot but she could see no one.

But I know I heard something.

Then it came again.

Voices. Male voices rising in anger.

Harley crouched to the pavement and crept behind a pickup truck, then alongside a sedan. Peeking over the sedan's hood, she spotted Beau Arson and Patrick Middleton by the barn. Beau no longer wore his trucker hat or sleeveless flannel shirt, just the leather vest and ripped jeans, his wavy dark hair released from its ponytail and falling past his shoulders, his bare, muscled arms resting by his sides. Patrick wore the same argyle sweater and corduroy trousers she'd seen him wearing on Main Street that morning.

"But Beau, please," Patrick said. "I'm so sorry. I know I should've told you. It was my own cowardice. My own shame. I admit it. But you see why I didn't tell you then, and why I have to tell you now?"

Beau shook his head and deflected his gaze to the ground, mumbling something Harley couldn't hear.

"I will make it up to you," Patrick said. "I promise I will. You'll see."

Beau jerked his body away from Patrick, turning his back to the older man. "Go home, Patrick," he said. "Go home before I kill you."

Before Harley could see what would happen next, she heard someone yelling at her from behind. "Hey, who's there? Who's that out there?"

Harley swung around and spotted Marcus glaring at her from across the parking lot.

She ducked behind a row of cars and began crawling back toward her truck. Then Matilda began snorting at her from her pen in the truck bed. "Shh," Harley whispered. "Shush, Matilda, shush."

Marcus was yelling at her again. "Oh, it's you, Deliverance," he said, quickening his pace across the parking lot. "I should've known it'd be a weirdo like you out here creeping around."

When Harley reached her truck, she secured Matilda's pen in the bed, and jumped in the driver's seat, slamming the door behind her. She fiddled with her keys and jammed them in the ignition, saying a prayer the truck would start.

Harley gasped with relief as the ancient Chevy roared awake, then jerked the gear into drive, tearing through the parking lot toward the entrance. It was then she spotted Marcus ahead, standing in the road, his blond hair glowing in the truck's headlights. He was trying to block her path, and if he did not move soon, she was going to hit him. She punched the brakes and the truck jerked to a halt.

Snap!

The Bungee cords!

The giant cupcake!

Rosie flew from the truck's roof and struck Marcus in the face, knocking him to the pavement. The giant cupcake lay alongside him, its red cherry kissing Marcus's perfectly coiffed forehead. He had his hand clamped over his nose, his eyes squinting in pain as he yelled a few choice words at Harley.

With the truck's window rolled down, Harley idled past him and murmured, "Sorry."

"You broke my nose," he said with a groan.

From the truck bed, Matilda was snorting and kicking at her pen with glee.

Once past a crumpled Marcus, Harley punched the truck's gas again, zooming out of the parking lot and leaving the giant cupcake trembling in the middle of the road. In her rearview mirror, a crowd of people had gathered on the front veranda, watching her escape with rapt attention, manicured hands over painted mouths.

CHAPTER 9

"I can't believe you just left Rosie."

Tina crossed her arms in the passenger seat and glared out the windshield. They were traveling down Main Street on their way to the historical society meeting.

Darkness had settled over the small town, the streetlights guiding the last of the pedestrians as they headed home from the restaurants.

"Well," Tina said, "we're going to have to think of a way to get her back."

Luckily for Harley, Tina's curiosity soon trumped her anger, and she changed the subject. "What's he like?" she asked.

"Who?"

Tina rolled her eyes. "Oh, come on, Harley. Beau Arson, of course. What did he say when he was at the shop? What did he do?"

"Well," Harley said, "he drank some whiskey."

"I swear," Tina said, "gettin' information from you is like tryin' to get blood from a turnip." She sighed. "So what happened after that?"

"Then I offered to get him a gig at Bud's Pool Hall."

Tina squealed with laughter. "You didn't?"

"I did."

"Oh, Harley!"

"Well, I didn't know who he was."

"Can you imagine Beau Arson at Bud's?" she said, still laughing. "Oh, it's too much!"

"Well, he did seem kind of excited about the prospect, and he did thank me for the opportunity."

"Only you," Tina said, laughing and shaking her head. "Only you." Her laughter finally settled, and she asked, "So is he sexy? Like he is on TV?"

"I'm really the wrong person to ask."

Another eye roll. "Oh, yeah, I forgot. You're like the one person in the whole world who doesn't own a TV." She crossed her legs in her wool miniskirt and placed her hands on her lap primly. "Well, what does he look like in person then?"

"A truck driver."

Tina eyed Harley in the driver's seat, her earnestness turning to teasing. "So do you," she said. "Except instead of a semi, you'd be driving a bookmobile."

They both laughed, and Tina said, "Well, there's not much of a chance there anyway. For anybody. He's a confirmed bachelor. He's famous for it. Strings of girlfriends and who knows what else, but no commitment. Ever."

Harley couldn't say anything about Beau Arson's lack of commitment. Relationships had never been her forte either, but for an entirely different reason. No one wanted her.

She turned down Briarwood Avenue, the truck's headlights illuminating the town's oldest and most beautiful homes. Briarwood was home to the town's first families, the barons of coal, timber, copper, and limestone, who'd built the long row of elegant homes overlooking Notchey Creek. And like a mecca of the small southern town, Briarwood drew crowds of pilgrims. Pedestrians, trick-or-treaters, and Christmas carolers flocked to the sidewalks on the weekends, all to enjoy the neighborhood's well-lit streets and its general curb appeal.

During the holidays, the Notchey Creek Historical Society hosted their holiday home tours in Briarwood, where visitors could roam about the grand old homes freely, enjoying the antiques, the multiple fireplaces as they sipped mugs of hot apple cider. The tours did well each year, well enough to garner thousands of dollars, the proceeds of which were given to the historical society.

Patrick Middleton's home, a three-story brick mansion dating to the 1790s, had once served as The Lamplighter Inn, a layover destination for patrons traveling by stagecoach to the Mississippi. Admiring the warm light that poured from the home's windows, Harley imagined how welcoming the place must have been to those travelers of long ago, their bodies tired from the bumps and turns of stagecoach travel.

Harley and Tina were among the first people to arrive, as there was only one other car parked in front of the house, an old green Volvo belonging to Hazel Moses. She'd obviously volunteered to help Patrick set up things for the meeting, Harley thought, and if Uncle Tater and Floyd were correct, she was using the opportunity for some one-on-one time with Patrick.

Harley pulled her truck into the driveway and parked in front of the carriage house, which in recent years had been remodeled into a garage. She assumed Patrick hadn't been the one to remodel it, as he did not drive, and she couldn't remember him ever having owned a car.

"I wonder why Patrick never drives," she said, turning off the truck's engine. "He either walks or bikes or takes taxis everywhere."

"Maybe he likes the exercise," Tina said, though it was clear she had no interest in furthering the line of inquiry. After all, she had food in the truck bed and it was growing colder by the second.

They unloaded the trays of food from the truck bed, Tina making faces at the antique toilet as she did so.

"What's up with the toilet?" she asked.

"Uncle Tater."

No further explanation was needed. Harley and Tina hoisted the trays to their chests and made their way down the stone pathway toward the entrance. Jack-o'-lanterns lined the front porch, flickering candlelight streaming from their carved faces, some smiling, some scowling at the two women as they passed. Beside the jack-o'-

lanterns, a large black cauldron filled with candy waited for trick-or-treaters.

Tina smiled. "I just love Briarwood, don't you?"

Through the bay window, two Tiffany lamps illuminated Patrick's den, an oversized room made cozy by wall-to-wall bookshelves, plush leather chairs, and a crackling fire. One could often find Patrick Middleton lounging in one of those leather chairs, cradling a glass of bourbon in his hand as he enjoyed a leather-bound book. However, Patrick wasn't in his den that evening. He was likely in the kitchen with Hazel Moses getting things set up.

"You don't have to ring the door bell," Tina said. "He knows we're coming."

Balancing the tray of food with one arm, Harley tried the door handle and finding it unlocked, pushed it open. Once inside, the warmth of the crackling fire, the welcoming aroma of woodsmoke, and complete silence met them. Harley wondered if Patrick and Hazel were out back on the veranda. Perhaps Patrick had decided to host the meeting there instead, but it was a bit cold outside for that.

Harley and Tina exchanged glances and walked through the long foyer leading into the kitchen. They stopped when they heard voices.

A man and a woman.

As they drew nearer to the kitchen, Harley could hear the voices were low and serious, almost to the point of whispering.

"No," Patrick said softly. "Please, Hazel, no."

Harley peeked around the corner and into the kitchen. Patrick and Hazel were standing in front of the kitchen sink, their chests nearly touching.

Patrick held Hazel's raised hand in his as if she'd tried to touch his face and he'd stopped her midway. Even from the hallway, Harley could sense the hurt Hazel was feeling, the reddening of her face as her eyes welled with tears.

"But why?" Hazel asked, her voice shaking. "Why not me?" She was crying now, her words coming out in sobs. "Am I not pretty enough, not young enough, not smart enough?"

Patrick gently squeezed her hand. "No, Hazel, it's not you," he whispered. "It's not you." He pulled away and his eyes met hers again. "I love her," he said. "And I think...I mean I know I will always love her. Always. Until the day I die."

Hazel ripped her hand from Patrick's, her tear-streaked face glaring at him. "It's your little blonde, isn't it? The one you're always pining over."

"Oh, please don't bring up Savannah again. You don't believe any of that nonsense they're saying about us, do you?"

"Not Savannah," she said. "The other one. The one whose picture you're always gazing at."

"Hazel, I—"

"Oh, you think I don't know? Don't know about your obsession? How you long for her? Pine for her? God, it's so disgusting."

"Hazel, I'm not sure I know what—"

"Oh, I know you, Patrick Middleton. I've known you for thirty-two years. How your mind works. What type of woman does it for you." She brushed away her tears. "I'm glad you suffer over her. Just like I've suffered over you."

"Hazel, I—"

"Happy Halloween!"

Tina rounded the corner, giving her best fake smile.

A stunned Patrick and Hazel pulled away from one another, struggling unsuccessfully to regain their composure. But after a few seconds, Patrick seemed thankful for Tina's interruption and smiled at the young caterer with relief. Hazel turned her back to them in shame, pretending to scrub dishes in the sink.

"Tina," Patrick said, extending his arms in salutation. When he noticed Harley, his face lightened in surprise. "Harley? Harley Henrickson? Is that you? Why I haven't seen you in a good long while." He extended his arms and hugged her. "Our smart, smart girl. How have you been? Personally, I mean."

"I've been okay, I guess, Dr. Middleton," Harley said, returning his smile. Regularly, she would've asked him how he'd been doing, but she knew the answer to that question. Terrible. In one day he'd had heated arguments with Arthur Johnson, Beau Arson, and now Hazel

Moses. How he kept his composure was an act of amazing willpower.

"I was so sorry to hear about your grandfather's passing," he said. "He was such a good man."

"That he was. And thank you for saying so."

"You know, Harley, I've always thought it was such a shame you couldn't go away to college like you wanted. That you couldn't fulfill all of that amazing potential you had."

"I made the only decision I could."

"The food's gonna get cold," Tina said, interrupting them as she rested the tray on the center island. "Had a mishap with my van. Had to use Harley's truck."

"Well," Patrick said, placing his hands together, "let's get everything set up. The others will be here shortly."

CHAPTER 10

$\mathscr{I}$t was 7:15 and the monthly board meeting of the Notchey Creek Historical Society was in progress. For many years the meetings had been held at the public library, but Patrick Middleton, concerned about lagging attendance rates, had changed the venue to this home instead. He'd hoped that the promise of wine and appetizers would entice board member attendance, and as Harley looked down the long mahogany table, filled with board members swilling down Patrick's wine, she realized his predictions had proven correct.

She regretted Patrick having talked her into joining the meeting and envied Tina who was still in the kitchen, preparing the main course of bourbon beef stew and buttermilk biscuits. While she had nothing against any of the members personally, she preferred to keep a low profile and sensed a conflation of egos gathered there.

Awkwardness permeated the space. At the opposite end of the table, Hazel Moses sat with her head down, presumably nursing her emotional injuries. Seated to Hazel's left was Pearl Johnson, petite and slim, vigorously recording meeting minutes on a legal pad, her gray-blonde head bobbing up and down as she scribbled with a pencil. Harley had always been fond of Pearl Johnson. In the summers following her mother's death, Pearl had babysat Harley when her grandfather was busy at the distillery. Those summer days at the Johnsons' house had been a blessing she would never forget. Pearl had always been kind and respectful of Harley's quiet ways, and for this, she was grateful.

Beside Pearl, sat her husband, Arthur, fiddling with his blue silk tie and cufflinks. He lacked Pearl's warmth and nurturing qualities, but he was an astute businessman. In his early seventies, Arthur was the most successful of all of them, having built a very lucrative contracting business in town. Tonight, however, he seemed angry and withdrawn, presumably from his altercation with Patrick on Main Street that morning.

Savannah Swanson, a former Miss Tennessee, and classmate of Harley's sat on the other side of Patrick. Harley hadn't seen Savannah since she'd moved back to Notchey Creek the year prior, and she wondered if Savannah would treat her as cold and indifferently as she had since they were children. Though it was chilly outside, Savannah wore a red mini dress and red heels, her upper thighs exposed for Patrick under the table. Beside her, Ruby Montgomery gave a disapproving glare as Savannah crossed, then recrossed her tan legs.

Balancing out the two women was Iris O'Shaughnessy, proprietor of Celtic Memories on Main Street. From what Harley had gathered, Iris was to give a presentation on Samhain, the Celtic precursor to Halloween. Now, however, they were discussing the controversial new history museum.

"But why build it there?" Ruby Montgomery asked. "Why not have it right in town? Renovate one of the old buildings downtown?"

"Because," Patrick said, forming his hands into a steeple, "there isn't room for the pioneer village in town. We discussed this, and we all agreed, did we not, that the village was a mandatory part of this endeavor?"

"It's just a history museum," Ruby said with a huff.

"A living history museum," Patrick said. "And visitors need to interact with history. They need to examine how the pioneers lived centuries ago. It's one thing to read about history on a plaque inside four walls. It's quite another thing to interact with it in nature through the structures, the tools their ancestors used."

The rest of the Board watched as verbal barbs volleyed back and forth down the long mahogany table. Patrick was used to trading barbs with Ruby Montgomery, but no one was ever sure who would win.

Ruby shook her head. "I just don't agree with the building's location, Patrick. Simple as that. We could save a good deal of money by placing it in an existing building downtown."

Harley examined Ruby Montgomery. She was a powerful woman to behold, still statuesque and lean at the age of seventy. Her brown pantsuit, made of expensive wool and outfitted with shoulder pads, spoke of a female CEO, and it seemed Ruby felt of herself that way too. As wife to the late Walter Montgomery, heir to the Montgomery coal mining fortune, she was a formidable adversary.

"I understand your point," Patrick said, taking a more diplomatic tone, "but if we've gone to so much effort, if we've secured permission from the city, the state, for this endeavor, shouldn't we create it exactly how we planned?"

"How you planned," Ruby said, tucking a section of her auburn page boy behind her ear. "You."

Ruby had accomplished many things as Mrs. Walter Montgomery. The pension program for families of fallen coal miners, the scholarships for their children, the daycare for their working wives were all products of Ruby's dynamic personality. But that forceful personality was also her hubris. Harley wondered how much more she could accomplish if she were less abrupt, less judgmental of others.

Patrick sighed and stacked the papers in front of him. "The blueprints have been finalized, Ruby. The construction will go ahead as planned."

"And what about the Sierra Club?" she said, pointing a French manicured finger at him. "I'm the president of that club, and they're protesting, you know? And the ecologists at the university. They're saying that by building it in the nature reserve, we would disturb the natural habitat out there, killing the flora and fauna, uprooting the beavers from the creek. And I agree with them. Wholeheartedly."

Patrick shook his head, tapping his pencil against the table as he looked at Ruby. "If it were up to them, we would never be able to build anything. Progress would stall, and we'd all be living in the trees like monkeys."

"Well, that's fitting," Ruby said.

Beside Patrick, Savannah Swanson once again crossed her legs in her red mini dress. A good portion of her upper thigh was exposed for Patrick's enjoyment, and he forced his gaze to her hairline. "Yes, Savannah?" he said.

"Patrick," she said, using a tone Harley considered too familiar, "we need to discuss Pioneer Days, remember?"

At twenty-six, Savannah Swanson was a former beauty queen who was engaged to Michael Sutcliffe, heir to the Sutcliffe timber and real estate fortune. Harley wondered how long the engagement would last after hearing the gossip surrounding Savannah and Patrick Middleton. If Savannah lost Michael Sutcliffe, she would also lose his wealth and social-standing, a loss her social climbing parents would resent. And if there was anything in the world Savannah Swanson had always wanted, it was her parents' approval.

"We need to discuss a performer for Pioneer Days," she said.

Loretta Lynn had been the previous year's performer, Harley remembered, and she would be a tough act to follow.

"How about Dolly?" Pearl Johnson said, lifting her attention from her notes.

"She's busy with the opening of that new ride at Dollywood, remember?" Ruby said.

"Oh, yes, that's right."

"Well, there's Kenny Chesney," Iris O'Shaughnessy said. "He's from East Tennessee, isn't he, and he's often willing to help out the local communities."

"But I think he's on tour right now," Savannah said.

"Well, then, who?" Ruby said, glancing at her watch, already impatient the decision had taken that long.

"Well, I have an idea." Savannah recrossed her legs and cupped her knees with her hands, exposing an inch of cleavage in her low-cut dress. "How about Beau Arson?"

As soon as Savannah had said the words "Beau Arson," Patrick Middleton sprung from his seat, spilling wine down the front of his trousers. "Not him," he said.

Every member of the table except Harley stared at Patrick in surprise.

"And why not?" Ruby said. She couldn't care less who the performer was, of course. She just wanted to disagree with Patrick.

A flustered Patrick seemed to be searching frantically for a response. "Um…well, isn't his music inappropriate for this? I mean, that band of his, Assault, isn't it a bit loud, don't you think for this kind of festival?"

"Well," Ruby said, "I will say he isn't the most charming person in the world. I had the pleasure, I mean displeasure of meeting him this morning on Main Street." She glared at Harley across the table. "He completely disregarded Alveda and me. Completely rude and without any class."

"But who cares about that?" Savannah said. "He's a worldwide sensation. Women love him. Men want to be him. Think of all the publicity and money this would garner for the festival."

"Perhaps," Patrick said, but he was shaking his head as he said it. His face had gone pale. "But there's no certainty he'd agree to do it. Why would he?"

"Well, I think we have a good shot," Savannah said, "with him living here now. It'd be a good way for him to get in good with the community."

"I've never heard of him," Arthur said, still not making eye contact with Patrick.

"Well, let's just take a vote and get it over with," Ruby said. "And besides, we have other matters to discuss. Iris still hasn't given her presentation." She raised her right hand, simultaneously leering at Patrick. "What say you, Patrick?"

Patrick rose from the table and retreated to the fireplace, turning his back to them while he dried the wine from his wet trousers. He looked over his shoulder, and frowned when he noticed everyone had raised their hands but Harley. And like a buoy in a dark ocean, the drowning Patrick looked to her to save him. "What say you, Harley?" he asked.

Harley Henrickson spoke for the first time. "Beau Arson came to Notchey Creek for one reason. For privacy. We should give him that."

"What do you know about it?" Ruby said.

"See, Harley agrees with me," Patrick said. "It isn't a good idea."

"But the two of you are outvoted," Ruby said.

"And so we are," Patrick said despondently. He lowered his head, watching the flames in quiet contemplation, and then as if he were making a deal with the devil, he whispered, "So be it."

"Great!" Savannah said. "I will personally make sure he gets the invitation."

"No, no, I will do it," Patrick said. He returned to the table, seeming to hate them all, wanting to be rid of them all. But somehow he managed a smile, though Harley knew it was one of defeat. "I must be the one to do it."

"Well, let's get on with the meeting, shall we?" Ruby Montgomery said. "We're running out of time."

A half hour later they'd reached the end of the agenda. Three bottles of wine sat empty on the table and speech was starting to slur from the alcohol and abundance of hot air permeating the room. They'd discussed Pioneer Days, the membership drive, the ratty old volumes of books needing replacement at the library. The majority of the books were *Firefox* novels, chronicling the traditional folklore of the Southern Appalachians. The entries dealt with the daily chores of Appalachian pioneers, including log cabin building, hog dressing, moonshine distillation, and mountain medicine.

At last, it was time for Iris O'Shaugnessy's presentation on Samhain.

"I will make it brief," Iris said, seeming to float rather than rise from her seat. She looked at Ruby. "I know some of you are very pressed for time this evening."

Iris was a regal, handsome woman, but not in a conventional way. Her attractiveness was expressed in the comfort she had with herself, in her long, gray hair that fell past shoulders in a single braid, in the expression lines of her middle-aged face, tanned from countless hours spent in her herb garden.

She began by passing around a wooden amulet, about the size of a silver dollar, depicting a tree overarched by a crescent moon.

"As you know," she said in her calm, soothing voice, "it is now late October, a month after the Autumn Equinox, a time that was known as Samhain to the ancient Celts. Herdsmen would gather in their cattle and farmers would harvest their fruits and vegetables, hopeful that the sun's nourishing light would not abandon them during the dark winter months ahead. So too was it Hallowmas, a time when spirits were believed to enter the earthly realm through the between places, where water meets land, where mountain meets sky, where spirits rise from ancient waters to walk freely about the earth until dawn."

Harley and Patrick were enraptured by Iris's presentation, but it seemed to hold no interest for the remaining historical society members: Ruby Montgomery released a yawn, Pearl Johnson excused herself to the restroom, Arthur Johnson slept, Savannah Swanson played on her cell phone, and Hazel Moses stared at her folded hands, still nursing her wounds.

Iris continued. "And when our Scots-Irish ancestors settled these mountains in the seventeenth and eighteenth centuries, they brought those beliefs with them, appropriating them to our Appalachian land-scape. You see, they believed that during Samhain, spirits would come down from the Smoky Mountains at dusk, and carried by the evening mist, they would haunt the Tennessee Valley until dawn. People would flock to the rivers and creeks and streams, hoping they might reunite with those they'd lost, those they'd loved if only for one night. It was an opportunity to say all of the things they'd wanted to say in this life, but had never been given the chance. Then, when the night was over, and the sun would begin to rise, those spirits would leave just as they'd come, the mist ushering them back to the mountains once more."

Patrick interrupted. "And when they reached the top of those mountains," he asked, "would they be welcome in heaven?"

Iris shook her head. "No, I'm afraid not. It was considered like being in limbo for them, you see. The mountains were like a stairway, of sorts, but one that only led to nothingness. No wings. Not for them. Not yet. Just more climbing."

Harley hadn't heard the last of Iris's statement. Her attentions were focused elsewhere. Nested alongside the dining room table, a series of large windows looked out onto Notchey Creek. The evening drizzle had settled for a moment, and a veil of mist clung to the forest and hills surrounding Patrick's mansion.

The valley, as it sloped into a hollow beneath the mountains, was, she had to admit, the perfect place for a ghost to dwell. A whole village of spirits, floating about the muted landscape, unseen, unhindered until the sun would rise and the mist would usher them back to the Smoky Mountains once more.

Harley imagined the mist rising over Notchey Creek, and with it, the sun peering into the line of trees beyond the pasture, to the dark places where the spirits hide, among the roots, the craggy excesses, afraid of light, of discovery. Up through the Appalachian foothills they would flee, chasing after that mist, that ghostly promise. They would dash through canopies of brilliant maples, touching leaves of amber, gold, and rust, until they reached the abiding silence of the mountains. The thinning air would be like a drink of cool mountain stream water for tired spirits about to make their annual ascent, stack by stack, up those blue-gray mountains to the between place, where the mountains meet the sky. This time they would reach paradise, this time they would lay their weary souls to rest.

But as the mist reached the tip of that mountain, it would dissipate like its promise into nothingness, forming a lavender ribbon at the crest of the heavens. And from that mountaintop, those spirits would look down into the valley, as Sisyphus had peered down the mountain knowing his fate, one of toil, one of false hope, and then they would prepare themselves for yet another journey.

"But aren't we all like that?" Harley asked, vocalizing her thoughts before she realized it. "Aren't we all like those spirits in the legend? Trapped in a limbo of sorts, reliving our memories, our pasts, day after day. And so we craft wings, we build golden staircases, whatever it takes to find peace, to find freedom."

Patrick turned and gazed at her intently. "So, you're saying we're haunted in a sense?"

"I suppose haunted is a good word for it." She paused for a moment, collecting her thoughts. "I do believe in ghosts, Dr. Middleton, but not the kind the ancient Celts believed in."

"Yes," Iris said, returning to her seat. "Yes, I think I understand very well what you mean, Harley. You're referring to the ghosts we create in our minds."

Harley rested her elbows on the table and gazed at Iris and Patrick inquisitively. "Do you think conscious awareness is a gift or a curse?"

"Well," Iris said, "I suppose it's what separates us from the animals. Makes us human. But on closer thought, it sounds like it could be a curse...at least in some ways. That our memories can be a curse."

"Some memories," Harley said, "but others may be all we have left of our past, of our loved ones. And those memories, good or bad, can come to us either bidden or unbidden. All we have to do is experience a particular sound, an aroma, a sight, and they come back to us as if they'd only occurred yesterday."

Harley breathed in deeply and closed her eyes. A memory was forming, a brief return to a sunny afternoon from her childhood. She was seated on her mother's lap in one of her grandfather's chairs. Her mother's voice was soft and gentle as she read a book to her, and she smelled of warmth and safety and lilacs. Always lilacs.

She thought of the ghosts of Notchey Creek, and as she imagined the creek coursing through the region's land and its history, she realized it did not matter to her whether the creek was haunted or not because she knew she would never find her mother there.

"Well, for me," Patrick said, pulling Harley from her reverie, "memories are a curse. They will always be a curse."

Then he rose from his seat and slapped his folder down on the table, bringing the others to attention. "Now, if there isn't anything else, I will call this meeting adjourned." He motioned toward the kitchen. "Tina has prepared bourbon beef stew and buttermilk biscuits for dinner...or supper, rather...and a pumpkin pie for dessert. Help yourselves."

A sound interrupted them, a noise so jarring Harley flinched in her seat. Hazel Moses looked up for the first time, and Arthur Johnson nearly fell out of his chair.

"What was that?" Savannah asked.

"It sounded like glass shattering," Hazel said, pointing. "In the living room."

"It's probably just trick-or-treaters," Ruby said. "Didn't you leave any candy out for them, Patrick?"

Patrick ignored Ruby and stood, the members forming a single file line behind him as he exited the dining room.

A cold draft whistled in from an undiscovered location in the living room. Upon closer inspection, they could see where the window had been shattered. On the floor, lying in a bed of broken glass, was a rock, a note attached to it.

Patrick removed a handkerchief from his pocket and lifted the rock, all of the meeting attendees looking over his shoulder.

STOP NOW OR FACE THE CONSEQUENCES, it read.

CHAPTER 11

"They've been coming for a while."

Patrick Middleton took a sip of his wine and gazed into the fire crackling beside him, the whites of his eyes glowing like orbs from the flames. He appeared tired and stressed, but composed.

There was a chill in the night air, and Patrick had given Harley his jacket, which she'd since draped across her shoulders. The surrounding outdoor kitchen was fully lit, the bistro lights strung across a giant arbor covering the outdoor dining and living areas. Inside the historical society members were helping themselves to bowls of stew and biscuits in the kitchen. Low rumbles of conversation and intermittent bursts of laughter seeped through the cracks of the back door.

"The notes," Harley said, "like the one tonight?"

Patrick nodded. "They always say the same thing."

"Maybe it's the protesters sending them. About the new history museum."

"I only wish it were that," Patrick said, diverting his gaze to the night sky. His voice dropped to a near whisper. "I only wish."

He didn't sound convinced, Harley thought, and she had the uncertain feeling he was holding something back. Patrick seemed haunted by something. Guilty. Then there was the argument he'd had with Beau Arson that afternoon and his mysterious connection to the man they'd found in Briarwood Park.

Harley turned to him. "I'm sure after the building is constructed and the museum is open, they will forget it over time. It will be yesterday's news. The grudges will pass with time."

"Do you believe that?" Patrick asked. "Do you believe that all grudges pass with time? Or do you believe they only fester, magnify, and feed resentment?"

Harley considered. "I suppose it depends on the person who's angry and what caused their anger to begin with. Some people tend to hold grudges, others don't."

Patrick stared at her in earnest. "Emotions are powerful things, Harley. Don't underestimate them. And over time those emotions are shaped by our memories of the perceived insult. They can mutate with each replay of the event until the memory carries no resemblance to the actual event. 'The memories of men are too frail a thread to hang history on.'"

"Thomas Still?" Harley said.

Patrick nodded. "Thomas Still."

Harley shifted her weight in the patio chair, trying to figure out the best way to approach the question she needed to ask. "Patrick, I need to ask you something, and I hope you won't think I'm being too nosy."

"You, Harley? Never. What is it?"

"Well…we…Tina and I found a man this morning…in Briarwood Park. He was in the ditch beside the creek…disoriented…and he was speaking gibberish. We tried to help him, but he ran off into the woods."

Patrick sprung forward in his seat. "What did he look like?"

"Middle-aged. Dark hair, tattered clothes, lots of scars on his face. He had a pair of dog tags around his neck."

"And you say he was speaking gibberish?" Patrick's voice grew desperate, his hands grasping the arms of his chair. "What did he say? Could you understand any of it?"

"He said something about a boy. He said he needed to know what happened to 'that boy.' He said the boy was 'innocent.'"

A perplexed expression crossed Patrick's face. He shook his head slowly, gazing down at the fire in thought. "Innocent? But whatever could he mean?"

"I don't know," Harley said. "I was hoping maybe you could tell me. He'd been looking for you, apparently. At Bud's Pool Hall last night."

"Last night? Well, he must've gotten it wrong then. We were supposed to meet at Bud's tonight, not last night."

He rose from his seat and threw the fleece blanket in his chair. "I'm sorry, Harley, but I have to go. I need to...."

"But who is he?" Harley called after him.

Not answering, Patrick rushed inside the house, bypassing the others and heading straight for his office, where soon after, the lights came on.

Harley sat back in her seat, pondering what had just occurred, trying to wrap her mind around the puzzle. A stranger arrived in town, a stranger no one seemed to have ever seen or known. The man had supper at the homeless shelter, then said he had a meeting with Patrick Middleton at Bud's Pool Hall, a meeting Patrick never attended. So the man got directions to Patrick's house instead and presumably went there. But he never made it, or at least Patrick never encountered him. Then she and Tina found the man in the ditch the next morning, delirious, speaking of a boy, a boy who was innocent. But the man's mentioning of the boy, in and of itself, hadn't seemed to surprise Patrick. It was the man's assertion that the boy had been 'innocent' that surprised Patrick. Before Harley could ponder further, Tina appeared on the back porch, wiping her hands on her apron.

"You about ready to head out? I've got another event in the morning."

Harley nodded, then glanced at her watch. It was getting late. She rose from the chair and folded the blanket before placing it neatly on the arm. Inside, the historical society members were gathered around the table, and Tina was in the process of packing up.

"I'm just about ready," she said.

Harley and Tina said farewell to everyone and traveled down the long entryway. As Harley moved to open the front door, she caught sight of someone in the front yard, the figure coming forth from the shadows with the porch light.

A young man, tall and slender, with neatly styled blond hair stood beneath the oak trees, his boyish face reddened with anger. He wore a burgundy cashmere sweater and dark jeans, with a plaid Barbour scarf wrapped loosely about his neck, a Rolex watch glittering in the streetlights. Harley recognized him, but not from ever having met him. Over the years she'd read about him in the society pages, from his fabled boyhood to his adolescence, and now his early adulthood. Orphaned as a child and then raised on a trust fund by Arthur and Pearl Johnson, his legal guardians, who had subsequently sent him away to the world's most elite boarding schools.

Michael Sutcliffe. Heir to the Sutcliffe timber and real estate fortune. When he'd come into his inheritance five years prior, he'd visited Notchey Creek on occasion, checking in at Briarcliffe, the Sutcliffe's ancestral mansion. But he'd only started living there recently since he'd become engaged to Savannah Swanson, the town's beauty queen.

Harley watched as Michael's gaze traveled from one lit window in Patrick's house to the next, his teeth biting into his lower lip. When he caught sight of her, he disappeared into the shadows once more.

"Tina, did you see that?"

"See what?" Tina said, peering over a stack of Tupperware containers.

Footsteps sounded behind them, and Harley turned to see Arthur and Pearl Johnson walking in their direction, their coats draped over their forearms.

"What is it Harley?" Pearl asked, looking at her with concern. "You look like you've just seen a ghost."

"Someone was out there just now," she said, "standing underneath the trees."

Arthur hurried past them and pushed open the door. He stood on the porch, his eyes darting about the front yard. "Well, there's no one out here now."

"It looked like…like…"

"Who?" Pearl asked.

"Oh, no one," she said, deciding not to mention Michael Sutcliffe's name. "I probably just imagined it."

"Well," Pearl said, "why don't you let us walk you to your truck?"

"Please do," Tina said with a sigh of relief. "That'd be great."

CHAPTER 12

*H*arley pulled into the gravel driveway of the home her grandfather had purchased for her at the age of eighteen. Known as "The Sunshine" of 1920s home models, the buttercup-colored cottage had a small, slumped porch with two white rocking chairs and an accompanying swing stationed before large double-paned windows. Several old oak trees lined the yard, canopying the house with their branches.

Uncle Tater called the home her "bootleggin' house" because it and the identical homes lining the street were constructed during the Prohibition Era, a time when many Notchey Creek residences concealed makeshift stills in their cellars, the liquor an economic necessity for ailing families during the Great Depression, a secret trade hidden in the quiet folds of a small southern town.

By Uncle Tater's calculations, Harley's house would've been the perfect hideaway spot for Al Capone, as no one would've thought to look for him in Notchey Creek. And as with all areas of Notchey Creek with an illustrious history, Poplar Street became known as Bootleg Boulevard. She climbed the rickety porch steps, the sound of dead leaves crunching beneath her feet as she crossed the porch and unlocked the deadbolts, securing the door behind her with double clicks. The floorboards creaked beneath her feet as she made her way through the dark house, tossing her keys on the antique table.

When the windows and doors were all locked, she made a fire in the stone hearth and collapsed into her wingback chair by the fire. Flames popped and sputtered in the fireplace, casting shadows on the living room's dimly lit walls. She heard a snort come from the floor, followed by a wet tickle on her big toe, then Matilda plopped down at her feet in front of the fireplace.

"Hey, there, Matilda," she said, petting the pig's head. "How's my girl tonight?" A few minutes passed and Matilda grew restless, her eyes looking toward the kitchen in search of supper.

"Come on," Harley said, rising from her chair. "Let's see if you've eaten all of your food." Following Matilda into the kitchen, she opened a container of slop from the farm and poured it into Matilda's bowl.

"Now, what should I have for supper?" she asked, looking around the kitchen.

She unwrapped a bowl of Tina's bourbon beef stew, and while the stew was reheating on the stovetop, she made a Manhattan on the rocks with Tennessee whiskey, sweet vermouth, and bitters. Moments later, she was nestled back in her chair, the stew and Manhattan resting on the table beside her. She savored each bite of stew, the aroma of browned sirloin, bourbon, and bacon heavenly.

After she finished, she rested the bowl on the side table and opened the book she'd been reading for Halloween, *The Legend of Sleepy Hollow*. But even Washington Irving's atmospheric story of two men vying for the same woman couldn't free her mind of the day's events.

She found her curiosity was nagging at her, so she drew her laptop from her bag and rested it across her thighs. After opening it, she typed *Beau Arson* into the internet search engine. The webpage exploded with hundreds of hits, Harley's eyes assaulted by a barrage of photos of the famous rock musician, performing during concerts, on album covers, and alongside countless Grammy awards and Platinum records.

Beau wasn't one to smile for the camera, and from Harley's brief encounter with him at the store, he seemed to be one who never smiled at all. He had a brooding expression, and his dark blue eyes, with their depth of feeling, suggested layers of character far beyond what his public persona relayed. His wavy dark hair, styled in various fashions over the years, had remained long, with a tendency to pull it into ponytails down his back. He never dressed up, not even for the Grammy Awards, wearing his typical outfits of old t-shirts, ripped jeans, and boots.

Harley scrolled down the page, then paused at another photo, one entirely different from the rest.

There he was on the screen, in his crashed 1970 Dodge Challenger, his long hair falling over his face, not entirely hiding the cut above his right eye. He wore a Black Sabbath t-shirt and gray flannel pajama bottoms, and no shoes, as if he'd sleepwalked from his bed to his car.

That image of him, bruised and bloody and disoriented, had appeared on the front pages of newspapers and magazines from *Rolling Stone* to *People* to *Newsweek*. Beau Arson, trying to deflect the camera flashes with his helpless hands, his face gripped in despair, a moment of private anguish publicized for the world to see.

According to the tabloids, he had gone for a midnight joyride, and helped by a cocktail of drugs, prescription and otherwise, he had crashed his car into a guardrail in east Los Angeles, nearly costing him his life.

It was as if Beau Arson, musical prodigy and frontman for the hard rock band, Assault, had been asking for death, praying for a release from his life. He was the man who had been given everything, they said, yet seemed to care for nothing in it.

There were rumors of a nervous breakdown, panic attacks, and aberrant behavior. There were references to the Greek mythological character, Icarus, the boy who'd fashioned himself a pair of waxen wings, hoping to reach the heavens, only to fly too close to the sun, his wings melting, his beautiful body plummeting back to earth, to his death. Beau Arson's life of excess had finally caught up with him, they theorized. He had flown too high this time, his wings melting as fast as they had carried him to the heavens, to stardom.

Weeks later, authorities dropped any substance abuse charges, finding Beau had been sober during the accident and had merely been trying to escape the paparazzi. The press frenzy subsided, the rumor mill stopped circulating, and Beau Arson disappeared.

There had been gasps in the media when he'd left his band, Assault, packed up all of his things, left Los Angeles, and moved to Tennessee, to the place where he was born, where he now lived in an undisclosed location near the Smoky Mountains.

And here he is, Harley thought. *But why?*

She closed the laptop and returned it to her bag. It was midnight, and her mind and body were exhausted. Removing her glasses, she rubbed her tired eyes and prepared for bed. It was then she realized she still wore Patrick Middleton's jacket. She slid her arms from the sleeves, and as she went to fold it up, something fell from the pocket.

A photograph.

Yellowed and faded from age.

And pictured was a woman, with shoulder-length flaxen hair, her skin glowing from a summer tan, her cheeks burned at the apples.

She was beautiful.

Based on the woman's hairstyle and clothing, Harley guessed the photo was at least thirty to forty years old. Who was this woman? And why had Patrick had her photo in his pocket? The woman was too young to be Vivian Middleton, Patrick's late wife. And Vivian Middleton had been a brunette.

Another thought crossed Harley's mind.

"Your little blonde," Hazel had said to Patrick earlier that evening. But was this the blonde Hazel had been referring to? Hazel had been jealous of this person, of that Harley was certain, and Hazel had said Patrick stared at this woman's photo night after night.

This must be her. Patrick had said he would love her until the day he died. Was he talking about his late wife or this woman? Perhaps she had been Patrick's secret lover or an unrequited love. After all, Patrick had been a widower for over thirty years, and it wouldn't have been unreasonable for him to have found someone else. But what had happened to this woman? Where was she now? And better yet, was she even still alive?

Harley's mind fluttered with assumptions. Deciding to give it a rest for the evening, she tucked the blonde girl's photo back inside Patrick's jacket pocket. There were so many secrets just beyond her grasp, and she intended to find them out. She would visit Patrick first thing in the morning.

CHAPTER 13

*T*he next day came early for Harley Henrickson. She rose at five, delivered Matilda to the festival grounds at six, and dropped off Tina at her bake shop at seven. By the time she headed to Patrick Middleton's house at seven-thirty, she'd only managed to take a few sips of coffee from her travel mug, hoping to clear the fogginess from her mind.

The previous night had been a restless one. The rain, beginning as a relaxing drizzle at ten, had advanced to a torrential downpour by midnight, pelleting the tin roof like bullets. And as the rain beat against the roof, so too did Harley's mind beat with unanswered questions, as she twisted and turned in her bed.

When she reached Patrick's three-story brick mansion, she parked her truck in the driveway and sat idle before the carriage house, finding the engine's vibrations and the cabin's warmth comforting.

Bags of leaves were stacked in front of Patrick's carriage house, while new leaves littered the paved driveway, waiting to be collected by Angus Pruitt, the renowned local gardener who'd tended the Briarwood properties for over fifty years. Angus had recently planted a fresh bed of colorful chrysanthemums in the front yard, their colors gleaming in the bright autumn light. And above them, on the front porch, the series of jack-o'-lanterns still scowled and smiled and booed at Harley. The bags of leaves and the sagging jack-o-lanterns were the only things detracting from the home's magazine perfect image, a flawless image Patrick Middleton, too, had maintained during his years spent in Notchey Creek.

Harley opened the truck's driver's side door, shivering as a swell of crisp autumn air sent a chill up her arms.

Just then Patrick's front door flew open, and his housekeeper, Ira Jenkins, ran from the house, nearly falling down the porch steps.

"Oh, Harley!"

Ira had been in Uncle Tater's graduating class, and she hadn't changed much over the last forty years. She still wore the same printed cotton dresses, her formerly black hair now white and coiffed high in a beehive, resembling a McDonald's soft-serve cone.

"What is it, Ira?" Harley said, jumping out of her truck. "What's happened?"

Ira threw herself into Harley's arms, her weight nearly knocking the younger woman to the ground. "It's Patrick!" she said. "He's...he's..."

Harley pulled away from Ira and cupped the housekeeper's elbows with her hands, searching her face. "He's what?"

But Ira was stuttering so severely, shaking so terribly, she couldn't form the words. She clamped her hand to her throbbing chest and pointed to the back of the house. "The creek! Harley, the creek!"

Trying to control her own emotions, Harley guided Ira back to the truck and grabbed a quilt from the cabin, wrapping it about Ira's shoulders. "Why don't you just wait here, Ira," she said. "I'll go take a look around back and then call the police. But I need you stay here and stay calm, okay? Can you do that for me?"

A shaking Ira nodded and muttered, "Yes." Then her terror turned to tears that ran down her face.

With Ira tucked safely and warm in the truck, Harley passed the side of Patrick's house and entered the backyard, still engulfed by a blanket of low hanging fog. The wet ground clung to the bottoms of her boots, bits of grass and dirt collecting in the heel. She could hear the creek babbling in the distance, and trod down the hill in its direction, mustering more courage than she had.

She froze on the creek bank.

It was there, through veils of early morning mist, she could see Patrick Middleton lying flat on his back, his body ebbing with the currents of the creek now his tomb. He appeared a bit like the Lady of Shalott, she thought, his pale hands floating alongside him, his gray-black hair falling in waves beneath the water's surface as his eyes stared at the heavens in horror.

There was something else.

Patrick was clutching something in his right hand. A small wooden object, flat like a coin, about the size of a silver dollar, a tree and a crescent moon carved on the surface. It appeared very old, centuries old perhaps.

Harley crouched down to inspect the object closer.

It was the coin Iris O'Shaughnessy had brought to the meeting the night before.

Samhain.

WITHIN THE HOUR, Patrick Middleton's house had been cordoned off by yellow police tape, and several police officers guarded the perimeter. Groups of people milled about on the sidewalk and in the street staring up at the three-story brick mansion. Many wore track suits and tennis shoes as if they'd been out for a morning walk or had just rolled out of bed and stumbled down the street in search of the excitement.

They were gathered in clusters as people do for parades and festivals, but there was a hushed resonance hanging over the crowd that morning, audible only by slight murmurs and whispers. Clouds of condensation billowed from the clusters of people as they stared at Patrick Middleton's home, the location of so many home tours and professional meetings and dinner parties, now and forever marked as a site of horror.

At the approach of Sheriff Jed Turner's truck, two patrol officers directed people away from the driveway, allowing Jed easy passage.

Stationed at the edge of Patrick's backyard, Harley took in the scene. One of Jed's deputies had already questioned her, and since Patrick's death appeared, at least to the police, to be a clear case of accidental drowning, the deputy had told her she was free to go.

Cold air whistled into her chest as she watched Jed get out of his truck. She pulled her coat to a close at the chest, and tried to hear what was being said.

"Sir, I'm glad you're here," a deputy said, opening the truck's driver's side door for Jed.

"Is the medical examiner here yet?" Jed asked.

"On his way," the deputy said, then cocked one thumb over his shoulder. "Everyone else is down by the creek."

They walked somberly past the house like two men in a funeral procession, past Patrick Middleton's outdoor kitchen and down the hill. They had since removed Patrick's body from the creek, and several police officers were huddled around it. At Jed's approach, the crowd of police officers parted like the Red Sea and looked at him expectantly.

"Looks like a clear case of accidental drowning," one of the officers said. "Must've slipped on one of those rocks by the creek."

"Such a terrible, terrible thing," a soft voice said beside Harley.

She turned to find Pearl Johnson standing there, a saddened expression on her face.

She'd not slept much the night before either. The rims of her eyes were still pink from tears she had shed earlier. "Patrick was such a nice man," she said, "and such a good neighbor to us."

Pearl wrapped her arms around Harley's shoulders and squeezed her. "And what about you? Are you doing okay? I heard you're the poor soul who found the body."

"Ira and I did," Harley whispered.

"Oh, Harley," Pearl said, wrapping her in a full hug, "I am so sorry that you of all people had to see that."

Harley released herself from the older woman's embrace. "Pearl, you live next door to Patrick. Did you see or hear anything last night?"

"I'm afraid not. Not a thing. Arthur and I are early-to-bed, earl-to-rise types of people. We were asleep by nine, I'm afraid, and Patrick's house was quiet and peaceful then, like always. Nothing out of the ordinary."

Pearl took Harley's hands in hers. "Why don't you come inside the house? Get warm. Have some coffee. Jed can find you if he needs you."

Harley hesitated for a moment, then glancing back at Patrick's body in the wet grass, she agreed. She needed warmth and comfort in any way she could get it, and Pearl had always been able to provide that for her.

CHAPTER 14

*H*arley and Pearl entered the Johnsons' nineteenth-century Tudor-style mansion, the home just as impressive as Patrick Middleton's next door. And Harley knew the home's beauty was in large part due to Pearl's efforts.

Pearl Johnson was an industrious woman. While she and her husband, Arthur, could afford to hire people to keep up their expansive home, Pearl chose to do a lot of the work herself: polishing the silver and crystal; waxing the long hallways of mahogany wood floors; dusting the intricate woodwork; resealing the kitchen's marble tiles; and recovering the antique furniture. It was a full-time responsibility, one Pearl had accepted with vigor over the last fifty years. She and Arthur had spent their entire marriage restoring the old historic home, and now that they'd accomplished their goal, they liked to show off the fruits of their labor, hosting many dinner parties and club gatherings there.

"Of all days," Pearl said, shutting the front door behind them, "today is our wedding anniversary."

And despite being exhausted, Pearl must have risen early and prepared breakfast for Arthur. The aroma of eggs, bacon, toast, and marmalade jam emanated from the kitchen ahead. "You know, I've been making the same breakfast on this day for the last fifty years. Can you believe it?"

Pearl wiped her feet on the entry rug, brushing loose leaves from her shoes before hanging her coat on the rack in the foyer. She continued down the hallway to the kitchen where Arthur was seated at the kitchen table, enjoying a last bite of toast as he read the morning paper.

"I met him when I was only eighteen," Pearl said, a wistful tone in her voice. "That seems so young now. I'd just moved to town and had started working at the library as an aide. Arthur had just finished college and was working for Sutcliffe Real Estate. He would come into the library on the weekends."

She glanced over her shoulder at Harley and smiled mischievously. "And I guess you could say that when he wasn't checking out books, he was checking out me at the front desk. And over time and multiple stamps to his library card, we kindled a romance, a whirlwind romance, I guess you would call it, and we were married just a few months later."

Harley glanced into the kitchen, watching Arthur as he finished the last of his breakfast. Even from where she was standing in the hallway, she could tell that behind his newspaper, behind his expressionless face, he seemed preoccupied with Patrick's death. She imagined the two of them had been awake for hours, discussing the tragedy that had occurred next door, still disbelieving it could've happened to a man they'd known so well. Patrick Middleton had been a good friend of theirs, and not only had he been a good friend, Patrick also had been Arthur's best friend for the last thirty years.

But something had disturbed that friendship as of late. Patrick's decision to deny the Briarwood land for Arthur's shopping complex and to purpose it for a history museum instead.

In the kitchen, Arthur looked over the top of his newspaper. "Pearl, honey, is that you?"

"Yes, darling, it's me. And I've brought Harley home with me."

"Well," Arthur said, resting his newspaper on the kitchen table beside him, "bring her in here. Let's get her some breakfast."

Pearl smiled warmly at Harley. "There's still a bit of eggs Benedict and toast left if you'd like."

"Thank you," Harley said, "but I'm afraid I don't have much of an appetite. A cup of coffee would be nice though."

Pearl smiled. "You've got it."

They entered the kitchen, and Arthur greeted Harley with a hug before pulling out a seat for her at the table. Arthur Johnson had a kind face, framed by a head of gray, thinning hair and a pair of honey brown eyes that smiled behind wire-rimmed glasses. His friends often teased him, saying he could play the grandfather in a Werther's Original commercial. Based on his appearance alone, it was hard to believe he might've had something to do with Patrick's death. But Harley had seen the hatred in his eyes, the anger in his voice when he'd confronted Patrick on Main Street the day before.

"Have a seat now, young lady," he said. "I didn't get a chance to really talk to you last night. How are you doing?"

"I've been better, Mr. Johnson, to tell you the truth."

"Yes," Arthur said with a sigh, "it's been weighing on all of our minds, weighing on mine, weighing on Pearl's, all morning. We just can't make sense of it."

Pearl placed a coffee mug on the table next to Harley and filled it with coffee. "Cream and sugar?"

"No, I'll just go with black today." She turned to Arthur and paused a moment, collecting her thoughts. "Mr. Johnson, I..." She took a sip of coffee and gazed at him over the mug. "I understand Patrick denied your company the rights to the Briarwood land for your proposed shopping center."

All politeness fell from Arthur Johnson's face. His smile straightened into a grimace. "Where did you hear that?"

"Just talk," Harley said, holding her composure. "Around town." She did not mention she'd seen Arthur and Patrick arguing over the issue on Main Street the day before.

Arthur pulled back from the table and rested his shoulder blades against the back of his chair. "Already around town then, is it?" He sighed and shook his head. "Figures. And yes, to answer your question, Patrick did promise the land to my contracting firm. Everything was set to start. Then all of sudden, I hear he's decided to keep the land and use it for a living history museum. A living history museum! I mean, we'd been friends for over thirty years, and that's how he was going to repay me."

Rising from the table, he threw his napkin down on his plate. "But I suppose it matters very little now, does it? The shopping center will go forward as originally planned." He removed his suit jacket from the back of the chair and guided his arms through it.

He started to leave, but then stopped and took Pearl's hand in his. "Happy Anniversary, sweetheart," he said. "You know I'd do it all over again."

Ignoring Harley, he made his way out of the kitchen, then over his shoulder said, "I'll be home by five for dinner. Send the police to my office if they need to question me. Although there's not much to say. We were at home together all night, weren't we, dear?"

"Of course, darling."

Moments later, the front door opened and closed, followed by the rumble of the garage door opening. Arthur's Land Rover passed by the front of the house and disappeared down Briarwood Avenue.

Pearl rested her back against the kitchen counter and smiled, looking wistfully past Harley to the front door. "He's been such a good husband to me over the years. Arthur has."

She began clearing dishes from the table and placing them in the sink. "Eric Winston is back in town," she said, rinsing a plate then drying it with a kitchen towel. "And he's grown into such a handsome man, though there's no surprises there, of course. And still so very smart. I just saw him next door. He's the new medical examiner, did you hear? He finished up his fellowship at Yale, worked a few years in New Haven, and now he's returned home. Oh, I know his parents must be absolutely thrilled. It's all they ever wanted for him, you know. To become a doctor. To move back and be close to them."

Eric Winston. She thought of how he'd impacted her life as a child, had left such an indelible impression, one she would never forget. And now he had returned home to all of them, after all of these years.

It must be terrible that his first case was that of his childhood next door neighbor, Patrick Middleton, a man he'd probably known very well.

Pearl turned from the sink and gazed at Harley in a way she hadn't seen since she was a child as if Pearl recalled the sad little ten-year old girl she'd been, the sad little girl who'd just lost her mother.

"Grief is a terrible process," she said. "You and I both are well aware of that." She tilted her head to one side and in earnestness said, "You take care of yourself, Harley, please? Don't let Patrick's death send you back to that dark place again."

Pearl turned back to the sink, this time raising a juice glass from the soapy water and scrubbing it. "Those summers you spent with us, Harley, when you were a child were so special to me. As you know Arthur and I never had children of our own, so those summers meant a lot."

Harley, too, had loved her time at the Johnson home, playing in their expansive backyard, splashing her feet in the creek, reading beneath the ancient oak tree that towered over the lawn.

Without speaking, she rose from the table and wrapped her arms around Pearl, burying her face in the older woman's shoulder. "Me too," she said.

CHAPTER 15

*W*hen Harley stepped outside the Johnsons' front door, a chilly gust of wind greeted her, sending her wool scarf alight. The outside world smelled of dead leaves and damp earth, and as the cold air kissed her face, she felt her cheeks color.

The police had cleared the scene at Patrick's house and the crowds of onlookers along with it. Now only the yellow police tape remained, fluttering in the wind, demarcating Patrick's property from the remainder of Briarwood.

Gazing up at the gunmetal skies, Harley watched an army of dark clouds rove across the horizon, sending gusts of wind through the front yard's maples, the bright, brittle leaves rustling in agitation. All morning long, the sky had carried that same melancholy expression, as it if it, too, were mourning Patrick Middleton's death.

Harley pulled her coat tighter and glanced at her watch. On any other day, she would've closed the shop in honor of Patrick's memory, but with Pioneer Days about to begin, the Chamber of Commerce had made opening the store imperative.

Having a good fifteen minutes left, she decided to meander through Arthur and Pearl's backyard for old time's sake. Rounding the side of the home, she walked along the tree line separating the property from Patrick Middleton's next door. Harley was familiar with the Johnson property, having spent several of her childhood summers there after her mother had passed away. The one-acre backyard had been quite a magical place to behold, even for an eight-year-old country girl with rolling farmlands at her disposal.

But it was the oak tree that had made the back yard truly special. The grand old dame towered to a height of over two hundred feet in the center of the yard, its majestic limbs decked out in a palette of gold and rust, canopying a good section of the surrounding lawn and flowerbeds. What things that tree must have seen throughout the course of its long life, Harley thought, so many decades of history, of progress, of goodness, of evil. She bet if she were to peer inside the tree's trunk, the many rings would blind her, each circle marking a piece of history, a season of the tree's life.

For sentimentality's sake, she took a seat beneath the oak tree, resting her back against the trunk, just as she had done so many times as a child. A whirl of autumn wind met her, and she pulled her legs to her chest, resting her chin on her knees. She gazed across the lawn and into the distance. At dawn, the morning mist had risen, making its daily pilgrimage back to the Smoky Mountains. The creek, after having seemed so diabolical the night before, babbled happily in the distance, like a biblical character touched by Jesus, thankful its night-time demons had been exorcized once more.

Harley's gaze ran along the creek, scanned the tree line, then passed over into Patrick Middleton's back yard. The lawn was littered with yellow police tape and a trail of muddy footprints left by the police and the EMS. Just beyond the creek and over a small grassy slope stood a weeping willow, lonesome, its limbs canopying a patch of moss. There, on the patch of moss, stood a young man, his eyes staring listlessly toward the creek.

Eric Winston.

He'd remained behind at the scene, Harley supposed, to collect his thoughts.

Time had changed him, or what she could remember of him, his boyish features chiseled into a grown man's face. His blond hair had darkened considerably to a sandy brown, trimmed in a style worthy of a young professional. He had dressed in a hurry that morning, just a thin Burberry raincoat haphazardly thrown over a navy sweater and wrinkled khaki trousers, protective covers shielding the scene from his shoes. Though his eyes were circled with fatigue, he was even more handsome than she remembered.

HARLEY WAS eight years old the first time she met Eric Winston. School had let out for the summer, and she was spending one of many days at Pearl Johnson's house. The first hot day had struck the region, bringing with it a veil of humidity that hung steaming in the air like a sauna. Seeking relief from those dog days of summer, she'd found shelter beneath the cool bows of her favorite oak tree, her bare feet splayed in denim overalls, a book in her lap. For hours she would sit and read beneath that tree, the June bugs serenading her with hidden songs among tall strands of Johnson grass.

Most days she would have the entire Briarwood neighborhood to herself, except for when Angus Pruitt, Briarwood's famous gardener, would appear from time to time, his gray head popping up from a garden hedge to snip at a wayward limb, or at other times when he would drone by on his lawnmower. But for the most part, Angus and Harley respected one another's privacy, and when they would by chance encounter one another on the lawn, they would wave politely and go about their respective businesses. Angus Pruitt was a kindred spirit of sorts, Harley had decided. He seemed to go about his gardening as she went about her reading: quiet, solitary, and meticulous.

And that was exactly what she needed to be that summer. Pearl had offered to play with her - board games, t-ball, jump rope - whatever she had wanted, but Harley said she just wanted to sit beneath that brilliant oak tree and read her books. "Each person has his or her own method of mourning," she'd overhead Pearl telling her husband, Arthur, "and that is Harley Henrickson's method."

And that is all Harley did do day after day that summer. She read, she thought, and she mourned. And in many ways, that old oak tree had mourned her mother's death right along with her, had listened to every quiet prayer, every silent sob, every angry cry she had elicited to whatever power might listen. And by summer's end, the tree and Harley both had a new ring to add to their trunks, the sign of a shared experience that had left an indelible mark on both.

Those sultry summer days passed one after another, July into August, and Harley had grown accustomed to the symphony of sounds in her secret garden: the chirping of birds, the scampering of squirrels, the croaking of frogs, the creek babbling in the distance. The woodland creatures had become like a second family to her. She had even taken to naming several of them: Squabby Squirrel, Robby Robin, Frank the Frog, Minnie Minnow, Rupert the Rabbit, and Theodosius. He was the slug. She figured she might as well name all of them, being as they were her only friends.

But then someone else began appearing in Harley's little domicile that summer, interrupting the not-so-quiet ecosystem.

A boy. A boy in the yard next door.

From what Harley had heard about Eric Winston, she knew he was about six years older than her and from a wealthy family in town. He was at the top of his class at the private school he attended in Knoxville, and like his father, a prominent surgeon in town, he would attend Yale and become a doctor. The Winstons had big plans for their young scholar.

That summer, Harley watched Eric a lot, not because he was handsome, or because he read a lot, but because he seemed to have a wounded heart. And wounded souls she understood. Harley wondered what his story was, why he always seemed so sad. Harley knew why she was sad. She knew she would never see her mother again, would never rest her head on her mother's shoulder, would never feel her mother's soft touch as she brushed her hair from her forehead, would never feel her lips on her cheek as she kissed her goodnight. And her mother would never read to her again.

But why Eric Winston? He seemed to have the whole world at his disposal, yet he seemed to care for nothing or no one in it. He never smiled, he never laughed, he never cried. He was just listless. The one thing he would do that summer was take long walks along the creek bank, day after day, his eyes focused and narrowed on something in the creek below him, something invisible. He would trace the water with a branch and intermittently flip rocks to look beneath them or lift the marsh to search for something underneath.

On occasion, he would pick up an object from the creek bed for a closer look, and after examining it for several seconds, he would drop it back into the water once more. At last, tired from his wanderings, he would lie beneath a weeping willow tree and read a book, a grown-up's book by the looks of it, one with small text, thick binding, and an ancient man staring from its tattered cover. Moments passed then his body would relax, and his handsome features would soften into a dreamlike trance.

Harley decided she would start leaving presents for him underneath the weeping willow, little things to brighten his mood. First, she left an apple, then a string of daisies, followed by a shiny river stone, then a cork from her grandfather's distillery. Lastly, she left a bookmark, one she had made by cutting a pressed leaf into a heart shape and attaching it to heavy craft paper. Underneath the heart, she had written in crayon: *You are Loved.*

What Eric thought of those gifts she never knew. When he would come to the tree to collect them each day, Harley would duck behind the hedgerow, hiding from his sight and any reactions he might have had. But, in the end, it mattered very little what his reactions had been. She knew she had done the right thing. She had helped someone who was hurting, hurting like her.

Those peaceful days passed one after another in that fashion, the two of them acting as amiable and silent companions, aware of, but not acknowledging the other.

Too bad it was all about to come to an end.

Away from school, away from the playground, Harley thought she would be safe from the evils that had tormented her at school each day. But somehow, some way, they had found her, had discovered her shelter, her secret hiding place. And when she looked up from her book one afternoon, she found Kevin Grazely and Spider Buttle standing over her, wicked smiles across their freckled faces.

Harley sprung from the tree's bow, only to find her collar ripping at her throat, whiplashing her body backward into Kevin Grazley's chest. Kevin, big-boned at eleven, held her suspended by her t-shirt as Spider Buttle, skinny and rat-tailed, tore her book from her arms and hurled it into a nearby mud puddle.

"You're such a freakin' nerd," Kevin said.

Harley kicked Kevin in the shins and took a running slide across the lawn after her book, skidding her knees on the grass. As she blindly slopped through the mud, searching for her book, she could hear the distant chime of the ice cream truck two streets away, its trills matched by the cries of children racing toward their favorite time of day.

Cries came from Harley's mouth too, but for another reason.

Kevin and Spider had pushed her face-forward into the mud puddle, her eyes stinging with mud. "Haha! What a stupid dork," Kevin said, standing over her.

"Yeah," Spider said, "and she's even uglier with all that mud on her face!"

With her knees and palms scraped with blood, her face covered with mud, Harley pulled *The Giving Tree* from the puddle and stared at it helplessly. A swell of hot tears ran down her cheeks. The book's green cover had been reduced to swamp, its pages congealed to pulp.

She fell to the grass and hugged the book to her chest, rocking her body back and forth. *The Giving Tree* had been the last present she'd received from her mother, the last gift given to her before her death. Kevin Grazely stomped his foot down in the puddle and splattered mud on her face and overalls.

"Yeah, try to read your stupid book now, you stupid weirdo."

Harley charged at Kevin, and raising her right fist, popped him in the eye. He cried out in pain, his hand cupped over his left eye.

But Spider, seizing on Harley's distraction, ripped the book from her arms. He held it out in front of her and howled with laughter, "What're you gonna do now, weirdo?"

A red-faced Kevin grabbed the book from Spider and ripped the soggy pages out, throwing them at Harley's feet.

In defeat, Harley fell to the ground, taking the torn pages in her hands, burying her face in the book's remains.

"Haha! Haha!" they laughed.

Silence fell over the backyard.

A long silhouette stretched across the lawn beside Kevin and Spider, their eyes raising to towering heights.

A deep voice, deeper and more grown up than Harley had ever imagined, said, "Beat it. And if you ever come near her again, you'll wish you'd never been born."

Kevin and Spider stood frozen, with their mouths agape. The three children stared up at the boy with the golden hair, the teenage boy who was even bigger than he'd appeared from a distance. There was something in his manner, something hard and cold and worldly. Realizing this was a fight they could not win, Kevin and Spider sped across the Johnsons' yard and jumped their bikes, speeding down Briarwood Avenue.

Harley wiped her eyes on her t-shirt and squinted into the blazing sun, eclipsed by the shadow of the boy's face.

The boy extended his hand to her and lifted her tiny body from the ground. He wiped a row of sludge from her cheek and smiled. "You okay, kiddo?" he asked in his deep, grown-up voice.

"Yes," Harley said, trying to hold back more tears.

"Please don't cry."

"I'm sorry," Harley said, her voice shaking. "Granddaddy says I'm a big girl now. That I'm not supposed to cry anymore. He says that if I cry anymore I'll run out of tears."

"You know," the boy said, lowering himself to Harley's level, "a very wise man once said, 'we need never be ashamed of our tears, for they are rain upon the blinding dust of earth, overlying our hard hearts.'"

"But what does it mean?" Harley asked, sniffling.

He brushed a tear from her cheek and smiled. "It means it's okay to cry."

"Really?"

"Yeah." Though his eyes were rimmed with sadness, they were surprisingly kind. "You were a very brave little girl just now. I saw you. I saw how you stood up to them. I saw how you fought back. And they wouldn't have beaten you, not if they hadn't taken something you loved."

Harley swallowed a sobbing breath. "My book."

"Shh...shh," he said, wiping another tear from her cheek. "Hey, look, I've brought something for you." He extended his arm out, revealing a hardback book bound in leather.

"*Great Expectations*," Harley read aloud, gazing at the front cover. She looked up at the boy with curiosity. "But what is it?"

"It's a story about an orphan who has big plans for his life."

Harley gazed at the boy thoughtfully. "I'm an orphan. I mean... well, I used to be a bastard...but now...um, I guess I'm just an orphan."

The boy closed his eyes for a moment, lines forming between his brows. He gently shook his head then slowly opened his eyes once more to meet hers. "You may be an orphan, little thing, but your life is destined for greatness. Just like mine."

"But the kids at school are so mean to me."

"Now, now," he said, patting her on the head. "There are always going to be bad people like those kids who try to run you down, who try to make you feel bad. And they won't be happy, not until they've done just that. Until they've hurt you. That's where they get their power, you see, and you can't let them have it. You just ignore them, okay? Remember, you're a very smart little girl with a big, big heart. And you have an amazing future ahead of you, too big for any of them to consider. You have to keep your power, Harley Henrickson, your pureness of heart, you promise me? Don't ever let it go, okay?"

Harley wondered how he knew her name, but instead of asking, she nodded, and looking up with wide-eyed wonder, said, "Okay."

He rose back to his towering height and stretched his long limbs. "Now, you keep enjoying those books of yours. Sometimes they're just what we need during tough times. Sometimes they're better than what the real world has to offer."

Harley nodded. She'd never met a boy as wise and gentle and mature as this one. "I will keeping read them," she said. "I promise."

The boy smiled, looking down at her. "You know, one of these days when you're all grown up, you're going to look back on all of this, and you're going to wonder why you even cared what any of those stupid, mean kids thought of you."

"Really?"

"I promise." He gazed down at her intently. "So what do you want to be when you grow up?"

"A writer," Harley said without hesitation. "I want to write books. I want to tell stories."

"And you will. I have no doubt about that."

Harley smiled at the mere idea of his predictions for her future.

"All right, kiddo," he said. "I'll let you get back to your reading. Goodness knows you've had too many interruptions today already."

Then he stepped out of the blazing sun, his golden hair catching the sunlight in waves, his kindness having saved an eight-year-old girl in more ways than he could have imagined.

"Wait," Harley said, calling after him.

He looked over his shoulder and waited expectantly for her to speak. "How does it end?" she asked. "The orphan's story."

"I don't know," he said, smiling. "I haven't finished the book yet. Why don't read it and let me know how it works out for him, okay?"

"I will," she said.

"And don't forget about me, you promise, Harley Henrickson?"

Harley held the copy of *Great Expectations* to her chest and watched the boy disappear among the trees in the backyard.

"I won't. I won't ever forget you."

CHAPTER 16

"*H*arley Henrickson?'

Eric Winston stood before Harley, his handsome face gazing down at her with concern. Above him the last of the fall leaves rustled in agitation, seeking escape from the tree's limbs as they reached toward the brooding sky.

"You are Harley Henrickson, right?" His voice was calm and soothing and kind. If Eric Winston were to ever retire from medicine, Harley thought, he could record self-help books for relaxation.

Harley repositioned herself on the grassy bank, trying to reclaim her equilibrium. "Yes," she muttered. "Yes, I'm Harley."

Eric inclined his head toward her, and his voice filled with caring, he said, "It's okay, Harley. I understand you're the one who found Patrick's body, and it's perfectly normal to feel shaken after what you've just witnessed. I'm assuming you and Patrick were friends and then having to find his body makes it even more tragic. I'm so very sorry."

His calm demeanor, the genuineness of his concern disarmed her at once. "Yes," she said. "Yes, it was horrible."

"I'm sure. You know, even after all of the cases I've had, each one still seems new to me, each one still seems to haunt me afterward.

They're never just bodies. Not for me. They're people, people who had lives and families and loves. When I see a hand, it's not just a hand, but a part of a person that held loved ones, favorite books, those special cups of coffee in the morning."

In the act of comforting, Eric placed his hand on Harley's shoulder, and when it made contact, a surge of electricity ran up her neck and ignited her ears.

What a strange sensation, she thought. Strange and thrilling and entirely out of her control. She felt herself blush and hoped Eric hadn't noticed.

He removed his hand from her shoulder and extended it to a handshake. "I'm Eric Winston by the way," he said. "I don't know if you know this, but I grew up next door to Patrick. He and my parents were very good friends. And now I'm back in town as the new medical examiner."

"Everyone is so glad you're home," Harley managed, but she was disappointed Eric hadn't seemed to remember her.

"I only wish it were under better circumstances," he said. He looked toward the creek where Patrick's body had once been, then back to Harley. "I was wondering if you might have a minute to help me out."

"Of course."

"Thank you. You see, they removed Patrick's body from the creek before I was able to see it, to examine it. They took photographs, of course, but it's not the same as seeing it in person and..." His voice trailed, but then he continued. "Jed is a good man and a good sheriff, but I'm assuming he hasn't had much experience investigating suspicious deaths. He and his officers might not be abreast of proper protocol. Anyway," he said, drawing a pair of shoe covers from his pocket and handing them to Harley, "if you could just accompany me to the creek for a minute, and answer just a few questions, it would be a great help."

After affixing the shoe covers to her boots, Harley followed Eric down the hill toward the creek. "Just watch your step," he said kindly.

When they reached the bank, he asked, "Now, when you found Patrick this morning, was his body facing up or down?"

"Up," she said, "and with his eyes open. He was staring up at the sky and he had this horrified look on his face...as if he'd just seen a ghost."

"A ghost?"

"Yes. Well, maybe not a ghost, but something had definitely frightened him. It's almost like he was in the middle of a bad dream, a nightmare, like he'd sleepwalked from his bed to the creek." Her gaze, focused in concentration on the water, snapped back to Eric. "Do you happen to know what time Patrick died?"

Eric considered. "Sometime between midnight and two a.m. That's my best estimate anyway. And that's what I'm having so much trouble with, Harley. I keep asking myself, 'Why would Patrick have been down here at that time of night?' It just didn't seem normal for him. From what I understand, he was a nine o'clock bedtime sort of person."

He paused in thought for a few moments and lowered his voice. "And why was he still wearing his pajamas? He didn't even take the time to get dressed before coming down here. He didn't even put on his glasses. Glasses he always wore." He shook his head. "None of it makes any sense to me. It's almost like you said, that he sleepwalked down here. "

He looked to Harley for an explanation and she said, "Samhain. I think that's why he was here in the middle of the night."

"Samhain?" Eric said, rolling the term around in his mind. "What is that exactly?"

"A Celtic holiday. A precursor to what we know as Halloween. I didn't know what it was either until last night. There was a meeting at Patrick's house for the historical society. Patrick had asked Iris O'Shaughnessy, the owner of Celtic Memories on Main Street, to give a presentation on Samhain. I suppose he thought it would be appropriate since it was Halloween."

She collected her thoughts and continued. "You see, the ancient Celts believed that at midnight, on just one day of the year on

Hallowmas spirits would descend from what they called the 'between places,' such as bodies of water, mountains, etcetera...and they would enter the earthly realm, and there they would dwell until dawn the next day. Then, at midnight, on that very day, the Celts would gather at the between places, hoping to see their lost loved ones."

"And you think Patrick took this Samhain legend to heart? That he came down here to meet someone he'd lost?"

"Possibly. Look, I know it sounds crazy, Eric, and Patrick wasn't a suspicion person, not usually anyway, but he hadn't been himself lately. He seemed, at least to me, deeply troubled by something. Like something or someone was haunting him. But there's another reason I think he was here because of the legend."

She continued. "When I found him this morning, he was holding something in his hand. A wooden coin, about the size of a silver dollar, a coin with an engraving of a tree and a crescent moon on the front. It's the symbol for Samhain, and it was same coin that Iris brought to the meeting for her presentation last night."

Eric removed a sealed plastic bag from his pocket and held it up for her to see. Inside was the still-damp coin. "Is this it?" he asked.

"Yes."

"I found it on the creek bank a little while ago. It must've fallen out of Patrick's hand when they removed his body from the creek." He contemplated this for a moment and said, "Patrick was a widower of over thirty years. Were you aware of that?"

"Yes."

"And did you know that he lost an infant son, not long before he moved to Notchey Creek?"

"A son? No, I never knew he had a son."

"Indeed," Eric said with a sigh. "My parents were close friends with Patrick. They're the ones who told me. It's a very tragic story, I'm afraid. Apparently, both his wife and his child died on the same day while she was giving birth to the baby. That's why he moved here initially, to get away from the memory of it all, to heal his wounds."

His voice adopted a thoughtful tone. "You know, I always thought it was strange he never remarried, that he never had more children.

You'd think he would've wanted to, to make up for such a great loss. But my parents said that Patrick was one of those people who mated for life, that he'd known his wife since they were both children, that they'd married young, and that she'd been the love of his life. He never had eyes for another woman. Not one. So, maybe, if your theory about Samhain is correct, he was here to see her."

No, Harley thought. *He wasn't here to see her.* He'd made peace with his wife, his child. It was the other one. The one whose picture he gazed at night after night. She removed the blonde girl's photograph from her pocket and held it out for Eric to see. "I think he was here to see her."

Eric studied the photograph, then raised his brows. "But who is she?"

"I'm not sure. Last night, Patrick loaned me his jacket to wear after the meeting, and I found her picture inside the pocket." She paused. "Did your parents ever mention Patrick having any other loves other than his wife? Anyone he dated, even briefly?"

"No," Eric said, shaking his head. "Not one. And you would think that if he were that infatuated with this woman, whoever she was, someone would've known about it."

"Exactly." Harley looked to the creek and to the place where she'd found Patrick's body that morning. "Eric, did you see any indications of a struggle? Any evidence that someone might've pushed Patrick into the water or held him down?"

He considered. "Not as far as I can tell. No vegetation is disturbed. There aren't any markings in the grass or dirt along the creek bank to suggest a struggle." He looked at her in earnest. "Do you think he might've been murdered?"

"I don't know," she said. "It's always possible, isn't it?" She didn't mention the various altercations she'd witnessed between Patrick and multiple members of the community.

"I'll know more, of course," he said, "once I've had a chance to examine the body more closely, to see if there are any self-defense wounds, bruises, or lacerations under his clothes." He glanced at his watch. "Well, I better get to the morgue. Is there somewhere I can find you, if I have any questions?"

"Sure," she said. "At my shop. On Main Street. It's called Smoky Mountain Spirits."

"I know the one."

He reached forward, and gently taking her hand in his, he said, "Stay safe, Harley Henrickson."

CHAPTER 17

When Harley went to unlock Smoky Mountain Spirits that morning, she found Hazel Moses beneath the awning, her dark bobbed hair stuffed in a fedora and her clothes covered by a navy raincoat.

"I didn't want anyone to recognize me," she said, her gaze darting up and down the damp sidewalk. "I'm not ready, you see, to talk to them, to answer their questions. There's already been so much talk about Patrick and me as it is. I just need something strong to drink. I just need time to think."

"Why don't you come inside, Hazel," Harley said, holding the door open. "And rest for a minute at the bar. I can hold off opening the shop for a bit to give you some privacy."

A grateful smile crossed Hazel's lips, and she said, "Thank you."

After Hazel handed Harley her hat and raincoat, she hung them on the coat rack beside the door and ushered Hazel to the bar where the retired school teacher took a seat.

"I need something strong," Hazel said. "Strong and warm and comforting."

"I know just the thing."

Harley started the electric kettle, and when the water had come to a boil, she poured it into a mug and added a lump of sugar, a shot of whiskey, and a squeeze of lemon juice.

"A hot toddy," Hazel said with a smile, as Harley placed the steaming mug before her. "You know my mother used to make these for me when I wasn't feeling well. And I always did seem to feel better after drinking one of them." She took a sip, nodded that it was indeed good, and still holding the mug to her lips said, "Of course, I don't know if it was actually the toddy that made me feel better or if it was just the fact that my mother had made it for me, that she was still sitting beside my bed, comforting me as I drank it."

"It was probably a bit of both," Harley said. "My grandfather used to make them for me as well."

Hazel rested the mug on the bar and studied the toddy's rising steam in deep thought. After a few moments, she said, "I know you and Tina must've overhead what happened between Patrick and me last night. I know how pitiful I must've seemed to you."

"You didn't seem pitiful," Harley said in a sympathetic tone. But her heart had broken for Hazel, the pain and embarrassment she'd felt.

"I want you to know, Harley, that I'm not some crazy, lovesick, middle-aged woman. I want you to know that the feelings I had for Patrick, they weren't just some silly infatuation. They were special, at least to me...built slowly over a very long time, as we became friends, as we worked together."

Harley rested her elbows on the bar and leaned closer to Hazel, letting her know she was listening to her, understanding her.

"I never should've stayed here. In Notchey Creek. I never intended to, you know, never intended this to be my life. I never thought I'd wind up as an old maid school teacher in a small town, chasing after a man who clearly never wanted me. Then pitied by everyone else." Her voice began to crack and she swallowed hard, steadying herself once again. "I had dreams once," she said, "plans for myself. I was going to move away to New York or Chicago or Los Angeles. I was going to become a famous writer for a magazine, or perhaps an editor." She lowered her voice to a near whisper. "Of course, that never happened, did it?"

"Why did you stay here?" Harley asked in a gentle tone.

"My mother. You see, not long after I started high school, she became ill. She'd developed Lou Gehrig's Disease. She couldn't keep her job at the woolen mill, couldn't do much of anything with her hands or her body anymore. It was so heartbreaking watching her debilitate, watching the disease eat away at her body. She'd always been such an active woman. So talented with her hands. Knitting. Sewing. Quilting." She cleared her throat, then ran her fingers through her dark hair. "By the time I graduated from high school, my mother had been reduced to an invalid."

Hazel took a sip from her mug and hugged it to her chest. "It was only the two of us by then. My father had left us when I was only five. Just up and left without a word. We never saw him again. So I began working full-time, took college courses at night, worked during the day, supporting the two of us until I graduated with my teaching degree, and became an English teacher. I chose teaching because it gave me the evenings, weekends, and summers off to care for my mother."

She took another sip of her hot toddy and continued. "And that took up just about all of my time for a while, which was a good thing. My work, my mother's care. But then she passed some five years after that, and I was left alone in that house, in that same house I'd grown up in, sleeping alone in the same bed I'd slept in since I was a child, in that same bed I still sleep in today. And I was lonely, Harley. So very lonely. I wanted to get married, you see, to have a family, create something whole to replace what I'd lost. But I was always so picky when I was younger. I wanted something better for myself, something better than what the men in this town had to offer.

"My friends said I wasting my time, wasting my best years, my most attractive years, waiting for the perfect man, the one I'd created in my mind, the one they said didn't exist, would never exist. But I knew he did. Somewhere. And I knew I would find him eventually. I knew that if I waited, if I was patient, if I was a good person, a good teacher, he would come. So that's what I did, Harley. I waited. And I waited. Day after day. Year after year."

She gazed at Harley over the rim of her mug, and said, "And then Patrick Middleton moved to town. He was handsome and smart and cultured. Everything I'd ever wanted in a husband. And I thought he'd been sent just for me."

Hazel smiled in reverie. "That's why I joined the historical society, you know. To meet him. And when he asked me to help him type up his manuscripts, to do some proofreading work, I thought my dreams had come true. Of course, he would fall in love with me, I told myself. Of course, he would see we were meant to be."

Her voice began to falter, and she drew her hand to her face, pushing back an emerging tear. "When he didn't show any interest initially, I thought it was just because he was mourning his late wife. Sometimes it can take a long time to get over a lost loved one. I decided I would give him the time he needed and comfort him in the meantime. But over the years, I realized it wasn't his wife he was mourning. It was someone else."

"The blonde girl," Harley said.

"Yes." She repositioned herself on the bar stool. "Sometimes when I was at Patrick's house, I would find him staring at her picture when he thought I wasn't looking."

"Did you recognize who she was?"

"No, I'm afraid not. It was too far away. And as soon as he would hear me coming, he would tuck her photo back inside the desk drawer or in his pocket, like he was ashamed."

"And he never spoke of this woman? Never mentioned her?"

"Never. And I didn't ask. I was afraid to. It's like she didn't exist, Harley, that he didn't want anyone to know she existed."

"That's so strange."

"Yes, and if that wasn't bad enough, I started hearing rumors about Patrick and Savannah Swanson. At first, I thought it couldn't possibly be true. I mean, Patrick was old enough to be her father, and he didn't seem like the type to go for someone so young, even if that someone was as beautiful as Savannah. And she was already engaged to Michael Sutcliffe by then. I figured the Sutcliffe wealth would keep her from doing anything stupid, anything that would ruin her chances with Michael. But then I started seeing her at Patrick's house at night sometimes..."

Her voice trailed off and she looked up at Harley. "Not that I spy on Patrick. It's just that I like to take walks in the evening."

"Of course."

"Anyway, the thing with Savannah finally convinced me I needed to make a move. I needed to tell Patrick how I felt about him. Maybe if I told him, I thought, he would see that we were perfect for each other, had been perfect for each other the whole time, just as I'd realized the first time I'd ever laid eyes on him. But it never happened, of course. He made it so clear last night. So very, very clear. Not in all those years did he ever feel anything more than friendship for me." She banged her fist on the bar. "Nothing!"

Hazel dropped her face to her forearm and broke into sobs. "Oh, I'm so glad he's dead, Harley! I'm so glad he's dead! Now I can be free of him!"

Harley rushed around the bar and wrapped her arms around Hazel, rocking her in the bar stool. "It's going to okay, Hazel," she said. "It's going to be okay."

Hazel cried into Harley's shoulder, moistening her flannel shirt with tears. "But I didn't kill him. I wanted to. Oh, how I wanted to. I wanted him to hurt just like he'd hurt me."

Harley released herself from Hazel's grasp and pulled a handkerchief from her pocket, placing it in Hazel's hand. Then she grabbed the kettle and refreshed the hot water in Hazel's mug.

"Do you believe me?" Hazel asked, wiping the tears from her face with the handkerchief. "Do you believe I'm innocent?"

"I'm not the one you have to worry about, Hazel. The police are going to question you."

"Yes," she said, "I was expecting that."

"They're going to ask you where you were last night. What you were doing."

"Well, I was at home most of the night. I even went to bed early, and that's the truth. But I found myself tossing and turning in my bed, thinking about what had happened between Patrick and me. So I got up and I went downstairs. I sat at the kitchen table and I wrote him a letter, apologizing for how I'd acted, hoping maybe at some point we could be friends again."

"And?"

"I decided I didn't want to wait until the next morning to give the letter to him. I wanted to do it then. So I got dressed and I put on that same hat and raincoat hanging over there," she said, pointing to the coat rack, "and I walked to his house."

"What did you see?"

"Well, when I got to his driveway, I noticed the living room lights were still on, and the curtains had been drawn. It was odd, I thought, for Patrick to be up at that hour. He always went to bed so early. I thought he might've accidentally left them on before he'd gone to bed. But that didn't seem right either. So I walked up to the front porch, and I peeked through the gap between the curtains."

"And what did you see?"

"Patrick was sitting in his leather chair, and he was talking to someone, someone who was sitting across from him."

"Who was it?"

"I don't know. The chair was facing away from the window. It's that tall leather chair, you know, the one by the Tiffany lamp."

"Could you hear what they were saying?"

"No. Patrick installed top of the line everything in that house, including all of those windows."

"Do you remember anything else? Anything different about Patrick. About the room?"

"Patrick seemed fine. It seemed as if the two were just having a normal, pleasant conversation." She paused in thought for a moment. "I do remember something out of place though. Something that hadn't been there at the meeting last night."

"Yes?"

"A bottle of whiskey. One of your bottles actually. It was on the table beside Patrick along with a half-filled glass. One of the ones he was always drinking from…with the curved lip."

"A Glencairn."

"Yes. Yes, I think that's what he called them."

"And the person who was with him. Could you tell if they were drinking too?"

"I believe so. I mean there was a glass beside the chair."

"Then what happened?"

"I don't know. I heard a car pull in the driveway and I left."

"Did you see who it was?"

"I believe it was Ruby Montgomery. At least it was her Lexus. And you know how she drives. Aggressive. Even when she's pulling into someone's driveway."

"Did she go inside?"

"I assume. She parked the car and got out of it. And there was one other thing," she said. "Not something that happened last night, but about a month ago."

Harley waited for her to continue.

"I've been going through old newspapers in my attic, ones my mother had kept over the years. She never did throw anything away, my mother. I thought I might go through them, see if they could be of some value for the historical society.

"Well, I was working my way through some of them one Saturday. I had them piled up on the dining room table when Patrick walked in. He'd just stopped by to say hello, he said, and to pick up some of the manuscript pages I'd typed for him that week. I told him about the newspapers, how I'd found them in the attic, and was sorting through them to see if there might be anything I'd like to keep. He said he thought that was a great idea, and he began looking through them himself for fun.

"After a little while, I asked him if he wanted anything to drink, and he said, 'Yes, a cup of tea would be fine,' and I went into the kitchen to get it. When I came back into the dining room, his eyes were glued to one of the newspapers, transfixed, like it was the most interesting thing he'd ever read. I'd never seen that expression on his face before. It was so strange. And he didn't even answer when I asked if he wanted some lemon with his tea."

"What was he reading in the newspaper? Could you see what the article was?"

"No, unfortunately, I couldn't. And when I asked him, he tucked it under his arm, said he had to get going. Then he took it without asking. Just left without even saying goodbye."

"Do you remember the date of the newspaper? The issue?"

"No, Harley, I'm sorry I don't."

She noticed the disappointment on Harley's face and added, "But I do remember the one I'd been reading just before that one. It was from thirty-three years ago. During the Fourth of July festival. I assume it would've been around the same time. You see, mother had stored all of the newspapers chronologically in the attic. She was like that."

"Thank you for telling me all of this," Harley said, placing her hand over Hazel's. "I appreciate it."

"I thought I had to tell somebody," she said, rising from the bar stool. "Other than the police, that is. And, well, I trust you, Harley. I know you aren't a gossip. I know you value people's feelings. Keep their secrets."

"Here," Harley said, "let me show you out."

Harley made her way toward the front of the shop with Hazel following behind her. When they reached the coat rack, Harley took Hazel's raincoat and helped her guide her arms through the sleeves before handing Hazel the fedora hat.

"Thank you," Hazel said. She tucked her dark bobbed hair into the hat and pulled a pair of sunglasses from the pocket, perching them on her nose. "Maybe I can get home without seeing anyone I know." She looked through the windows where people were starting to pass by with regularity. "Looks like they're already gathering for the festival tomorrow."

Harley unlocked the shop door and held it open for Hazel. As she passed through, Harley touched her arm. "Patrick did love you. I know he did in the best way he could. You were a true and dear friend to him. A friend he needed all those years. I know it's not quite the type of love you wanted, but it's no less special, no less true."

The expression of hurt tightened Hazel's features again, then softened into a frown of complacency. "I wish that were true, Harley. I wish I could see that. But right now all I can feel is that he didn't care anything for me at all. That I was just someone to type his manuscripts, bring his coffee. Old trustworthy and reliable and nondescript Hazel. That's all I was."

She drew her raincoat to a close at the chest then scurried down the sidewalk, her petite figure disappearing among the pedestrians on Main Street.

"You will come to see it in time, Hazel," Harley whispered. "I know you will."

CHAPTER 18

*A*s Harley closed the shop's front door and turned the entrance sign to *OPEN*, a black Mercedes SUV pulled up to the curb, with the giant model cupcake, Rosie, attached to its roof. Rosie's cherry had been reaffixed to her mound of icing, and the dirt cleaned from her pink foil. In truth, she looked the best Harley had ever seen her.

Stevie, the man with the black Mohawk who'd been at the shop with Marcus the day before, stepped outside the SUV and neatened his leather pants.

"Ah," he said, looking at Harley with a smile, "just the person I came to see."

"Stevie." Harley came out to meet him on the sidewalk. "But I didn't think you all would..."

"Bring her back?"

"Yes."

He smiled again, revealing a row of perfectly straight, white teeth. "Well, after yesterday, this old girl's pretty famous in our circle."

He unsnapped the ties holding Rosie to the luggage rack, then lifted her from the roof before carrying her over to Harley. "Where would you like her?" he asked.

"Let's take her to the back for now," Harley said, holding the shop's door open for him, "and I'll deliver her to Tina later."

"Sure thing."

When they'd safely deposited Rosie in the storage room, Stevie followed Harley back inside the shop area to the bar.

"This place is pretty cool," he said, looking around. "Is it yours?"

"I inherited it from my grandfather."

"Nice."

"Would you like something to drink while you're here? A cocktail? A glass of water?"

"I'll just take some water if that's okay. And do you mind if I sit for a minute?"

"Please do," she said, pointing to the row of bar stools. "Take your pick."

He removed his black leather jacket and rested it on the bar before taking a seat across from her.

Harley placed a glass of ice water in front of him. "How is Marcus?" she asked.

"Well, his nose is fine…a little bruised, I guess, but his ego…well, that's another story."

"I am really very sorry."

"I'm not." He took a sip of water and returned the glass to the bar. "Marcus needs to be taken down a notch every once in a while. It's good for him."

"Is he going to press charges?"

He shook his head. "Nah, I think he'd be too embarrassed. I mean getting clocked by a giant cupcake. Are you kidding me?" He laughed. "Besides Beau wouldn't let him press charges even if he wanted to. He knows what Marcus is like."

"He does seem like he's insecure about something."

Stevie looked at her over the rim of his glass. "You're very perceptive. And yes, that's probably why he can be difficult."

"So why does Beau put up with him?"

"That's a good question." Stevie folded his arms at the chest, then rested them on the bar. "And the answer says more about Beau really than it does Marcus. You see, we go way back, the three of us, me and Marcus and Beau. We went to Juilliard together. Took all of the same classes, had all of the same friends…even shared an apartment at one point." He smiled in reverie, thinking back on what were now 'the good old days.' "And of course, like every other guy our age, we wanted to be rock stars."

He laughed and repositioned himself on the bar stool. "Anyway, long story short, Beau became successful, beyond successful, and we didn't." Thinking on this for a moment, he gazed down at his folded arms and said, "But then again, I always knew he would. Ever since the first time I ever heard him play." He looked up at Harley. "Have you ever heard him? I assume you must've. I mean, who hasn't?"

"I don't really listen to much."

"He's incredible, Harley. I mean, the man has a gift. A true prodigy. And can you believe that before he went to Juilliard, he'd never even had a music lesson? Not one. He learned to play by ear."

He took a sip of water from his glass. "And I think that's part of Marcus's problem, his 'insecurity,' as you put it. Even though he loves Beau, I think he's always been a little jealous of him. Of his talent and the fact he made it big and we didn't. And Beau never even graduated. He dropped out after our first year." He shook his head, as if he were still awed by Beau's meteoric rise from music school drop out to international superstar.

"And you obviously kept in touch after Juilliard," Harley said.

"Oh yeah. You see Beau's not one to make new friends. He doesn't trust them. He only lets in people who knew him before he became famous, people who knew him back when he was just a broke foster kid. So he hired us as his managers." He shrugged. "It's not quite what we dreamed of for ourselves, but the job has a lot of perks. Definitely better than anything we could've gotten playing at dive bars and coffee shops."

He hoisted his weight from the bar stool. "I better head back. Things got a little crazy at the resort this morning."

He guided his arms through his leather jacket and pulled it to a close. "You know all those people you saw at the resort yesterday?

Well, Beau sent them away this morning. Every single one of them."
He pulled his car keys from his pants pocket and held them in his
right hand. "But I guess they weren't really his friends anyway, were
they?" he said, walking toward the entrance. "They were ours. But
still, he's never done anything like that before. Never seemed to
bother him until now."

"Why do you think he did it?"

"Don't know. He just said he wanted to be left alone. Then he
locked himself in his room, and I haven't seen him since."

"Stevie," Harley said, following behind him, "did Beau ever
mention anyone by the name of Patrick Middleton?"

"Patrick Middleton," he repeated, seeming to search his mind for
the name. "That's that professor he was friends with, right? The rich
one. Gosh, I think Beau's known him since he was a kid. Said he used
to help him out back then. And if I'm not wrong, he's the one who
paid for his tuition at Juilliard."

"Paid for his tuition?"

"Yeah. Beau didn't have any money. Not back then anyway. He
wasn't a trust fund kid like me and Marcus. Didn't have rich parents
to help him out. Everything that poor kid got, he had to work for, or it
was given to him by that Patrick Middleton guy."

"Stevie," Harley said, touching the back of his shoulder. "There's
something I need to tell you…about Patrick Middleton."

He turned around and waited for her to speak.

"He died last night. His body was found this morning outside
his house."

Shock fell over Stevie's face. "No wonder," he said, running his
hands through his Mohawk. "No wonder Beau has been acting so
weird. He must be devastated. I'm assuming his death was from
natural causes, right?"

"They're not sure yet," Harley said. "They've initially ruled it an
accidental drowning, but the body hasn't been fully examined."

"I really hate to hear that."

"I wanted you to know because the police will be coming to see

Beau, I suspect. To ask him some questions. They'll figure out he and Patrick were acquainted."

He followed her train of thought. "Well, Beau was at the resort all night. I can testify to that. We don't let him get out of our sights much, as you know. It's not safe. There's no way he could be involved. Besides, he loved that guy. I'm sure of that."

"What makes you so certain?"

"Because I know Beau. He's a loyal guy. Once he loves you, he's loyal to the very end."

"That's good to know," she said. "I mean about their relationship."

He nodded in agreement and passing through the shop door said, "You take it easy."

"Goodbye, Stevie."

On the way to his Mercedes SUV, Stevie passed Ruby Montgomery on the sidewalk, the shoulder-padded mayor eyeing him with disapproval. Stevie, apparently accustomed to raised brows and judgmental looks, offered a cheerful greeting as he got into his car.

Ruby Montgomery barked a "humph" in return, and after neatening her gray pantsuit, she stepped inside Smoky Mountain Spirits.

CHAPTER 19

"This town is being overrun by hooligans," Mayor Ruby Montgomery said as she blew through the shop's door, a whirl of leaves entering with her. "It's that Beau Arson character. Word is getting around that he's here, and they're all congregating like those zombies on that TV show. I swear," she said, dusting off her shoulder pads, "if it weren't for all of the publicity and money he's bringing in I'd…"

"What?" Harley asked.

"Well, I don't know what I'd do. But I'd do something. Anyway, I'm not here to discuss Mr. Arson or his minions, I'm here to speak with you about the festival."

"I'm listening," Harley said.

"I need to know your plans, Miss Henrickson. You never submitted your proposal to the Chamber of Commerce as you were supposed to, and Alveda didn't want to deal with you. She begged me to meet with you instead."

"Well," Harley said, "it's pretty simple. Uncle Tater will host a moonshine demonstration out on the sidewalk."

"Not offering samples, I hope."

"No. We couldn't offer samples even if we wanted to. The moon-shine would not have had time to age. It would taste terrible."

Ruby heaved a sigh of relief.

"Then," Harley said, "Wilma will be inside the shop, greeting customers and serving cocktail samples."

Ruby held up her index finger. "I'm not sure Wilma True is the best person to represent this business or this festival. Her grammar is atrocious and her fashion sense leaves much to be desired."

Harley Hernickson rarely grew defensive with Ruby Montgomery or with anyone else for that matter, but this time she did. "Aunt Wilma may not have mastered the finer points of English grammar or of fashion," she said, "but she has mastered one thing: The art of conviviality. She is pleasant and warm and genuine and kind, traits that are far more endearing and difficult to hone than the superficial ones you mentioned. She will represent this business in the way I've intended for it to be represented, in the way my grandfather intended it to be represented. Without pretense and with a sense of welcoming. When people enter this shop, I want them to feel like they can be themselves, to be comfortable, to be treated like family."

A stunned Ruby Montgomery stared at Harley, speechless. She'd never raised the young woman's ire to this degree before, and she seemed to flounder in her response to it. After a few moments, she cleared her throat, and as if she were figuratively stepping off her high horse, lowered herself to one of the bar stools. "I apologize," she said, resting her hand to her forehead. "I've just been so stressed out with this festival. So much is weighing on it."

"Your reputation as mayor being the first," Harley said.

She glanced up at Harley, an injured expression on her face. "Yes, that is one of the reasons, but you don't have to put it that way."

Realizing her defense of Aunt Wilma had bordered on unkindness to Ruby, Harley reeled in her emotions and adopted a friendly tone. "Everyone is stressed out about the festival," she said. "It's okay. Every-thing will work out." *And you'll just love Aunt Wilma's new hairdo,* Harley thought.

"Oh, I don't know," Ruby said, shaking her head. "Sometimes I just get so focused on proving myself I forget...I forget the important things. And then with Patrick's death, without his help and his leadership, I don't..."

"But I didn't think you liked Patrick," Harley said, taking a seat beside Ruby. "I mean you were always arguing about your different visions for the community's projects."

"I didn't like him," she said. "It's true. I even hated him some days, but he..."

"Kept you sharp?"

"Yes," she said, her brows raised. "Yes, he did 'keep me sharp,' as you put it. I never did agree with him on anything, of course, and this latest venture, this ridiculous living history museum in Briarwood Park, well, it was the worst yet. Not only for environmental reasons, but because of the loss of community green space."

"But it's more than just green space to you, isn't it?" Harley asked. "It's something far more personal."

She nodded, seeming to crumble atop the bar stool. "You see...my father...he planted those trees. When he came home from Europe, he and his fellow GIs planted them as a memorial in Briarwood Park, the section that belonged to Patrick Middleton. My father loved nature his entire life, you see, and those trees were so important to him, and even though he worked seven days a week, he took the time to care for each and every one personally. And they're still there today, and would remain there if Patrick would've forgone that silly historical complex."

"Is that why you went to Patrick's house last night? To voice your concerns over the history museum?"

"How did you know I was at his house last night?" Ruby asked.

"Someone mentioned it."

"Who?"

Harley gave her a look suggesting her question had reached a dead end, and Ruby conceded.

"Ok," she said, smacking her manicured hand on the bar. "I did go to his house last night. And I did go to voice my concerns about the history museum."

"And?"

"Someone was already there."

"Inside?"

"No, at the door."

"Could you tell who it was?"

"No. It was dark. Then I realized how ridiculous and inappropriate it looked for me to be there too at that hour, so I left." She deflated once again on the bar stool. "Although now I almost wish that silly history museum was going forward."

"Why do you say that?"

"Patrick left no provisions for it in his will, so now it will be auctioned off to the highest bidder. And we know who that will be."

"Arthur Johnson?"

"Correct again, Miss Henrickson. I see you're still the sharpest knife in the drawer." She drummed her burgundy fingernails against the bar top. "He's always been a shrewd one, Arthur has. He's always gotten his way. Now he'll have his multi-million dollar shopping center too."

Harley turned to her with concern. "Mayor Montgomery, what do you mean by saying Arthur's always been a shrewd one, that he's always gotten his way?"

Ruby angled her body on the bar stool toward Harley. "You know Arthur's contracting business was built on Sutcliffe Real Estate, don't you? That when he started out, he was just a day laborer, working on one of their hotels."

"No," Harley said, surprised. "No, I never knew that."

"Yes. He somehow ingratiated himself to the Sutcliffe's older son, James…he was Michael's father. They became very good friends, and not surprisingly, over time, Arthur was promoted from one level of management to the next. By the time James Sutcliffe took over the business, he'd made Arthur his second in command. And then when James died so tragically, and I will not voice my suspicions of Arthur in that regard though I do have them…Arthur received James's shares of the company."

"So James had willed them to him then?" Harley asked.

"So the story goes. James was a recent widower, you see, and Michael was just a baby at the time. Arthur was his best friend. It made sense. Then the remainder of the Sutcliffe shares remained with Michael as part of his trust fund. So you see what I'm getting at, Miss Henrickson?"

"Yes," she said. "I see very clearly. Arthur Johnson became a very wealthy man after James Sutcliffe's death, and is about to become even wealthier after Patrick Middleton's."

"Indeed."

"But Pearl says Arthur was at home with her the night Patrick died. He has a solid alibi."

"That's a lie," Ruby said. "I know because when I was leaving Patrick's house, I saw Arthur's Range Rover pulling into his garage next door. He hadn't been home apparently. Not all night at least."

"And he'd been somewhere he needed to lie about," Harley added.

"So it appears."

CHAPTER 20

"*A*re you ready yet, Harley?" Tina said, scuttling through the shop's back door, bringing a current of cold wind and the faint aroma of baked goods with her. She wore a hot pink sweater, matching miniskirt, and silver stilettos with white puffs of fur on the toes. A heart of silver beads glittered from her sweater.

"Ready for what?" Harley asked. It was a little before seven, and she was turning off the lights in the storefront windows.

"The engagement party, of course. Michael and Savannah's. Don't tell me you forgot."

In truth, she had forgotten. She'd been so preoccupied with Patrick's death and the subsequent events thereafter, the party had utterly slipped from her mind. Luckily, she'd prepared for the occasion the week before, setting aside designated boxes of liquor marked *Sutcliffe Engagement* on a shelf in the storage room.

"So they're still having it then?" she asked. "I thought they might've canceled because of Patrick."

"Canceled? Oh no. I got a call from Pearl Johnson this morning, confirming. And I can't miss it, Harley. Michael's paying me and you too much money to cater this thing."

"Just let me get my things."

"Oh, and here's your uniform." Tina handed Harley one of the black-and-white tuxedo-style uniforms they used when catering events together. "I know how you love to wear it."

"I look like a blackjack dealer at a casino."

"More like Steve Urkel at the prom." Tina laughed. "Besides, it's your own fault. You should've picked the skirt combo like I did. It's way cuter."

"I thought the pants were more practical."

"You would."

After Harley closed the store, she and Tina loaded the food and alcohol in the truck bed and made the short pilgrimage to Briarwood and to the Sutcliffe's ancestral home, known throughout the region as Briarcliffe. And if Briarwood was the ruler of this small southern town, then Briarcliffe was indeed its crowning glory.

As Harley's truck climbed the hill, Briarcliffe's wrought iron gate rose through a vine of artfully groomed wisteria, the sweetness of summer's white blossom replaced by autumn's aroma of woodsmoke rising from the mansion's chimney.

Harley brought the truck to a rattling stop, her eyes squinting against the glare of the truck's headlights.

"What a beauty," Tina said in the passenger seat. "And to think Savanah gets all of this."

Briarcliffe was the town's oldest property and its most significant, a residence befitting a family of timber barons who'd later tripled their wealth in real estate, constructing luxury chalets and hotels in the Smokies. The three-story Georgian home, constructed of butter-yellow limestone, hand-hewn from quarries fifty miles north, had rows of large white paned windows on each of its three floors, and a wide veranda traveling the home's perimeter, its columns tangled with green and red tresses of tumbling ivy.

Harley smiled, gazing wistfully out the window, remembering the stories her grandfather had told about Briarcliffe from his childhood. It had been a time of innocence then, he'd said, those days before one tragedy after another struck the Sutcliffe family.

People would pack their bathing suits and swim in the creek as it traversed the property's backyard, while others would row along the peaceful, shimmering currents, pausing in a silent glide of canopying chestnut trees, dapples of warm sunshine falling warm on their cheeks. It was a romantic time, he'd said, those sleepy summer days, and he'd remembered kissing the girl who would later become his wife, Harley's grandmother, the two standing awkwardly behind the boathouse, her lips sticky and tart with traces of lemonade, her skin caressed with the perspiration of evening's first dew. She'd pulled away from him, gently, her eyes smiling, and he had placed his hand to her cheek, knowing he loved her, would always love her.

Then at nightfall, the glass solarium would come to life, illuminating the back lawn with hundreds of bulbs of phosphorescence, transforming the lawn into a veritable fairyland, a fantastic site treated with greater reverence than the most impressive of July 4th fireworks. It was a brief taste of the finer life, something the Sutcliffes had not had to share with the town, but they did, a taste that had remained on his palette long after those summer parties had ended.

At their approach, the front gate opened, and Harley's truck climbed the long drive before parking behind the house near the servants' entrance.

Pearl Johnson met them outside. She wore a beige tailored jacket and matching wool skirt with low heels, her blonde hair coiffed underneath so that it grazed her jawline. "Harley," she said, waving from the kitchen door. "Tina. You're right on time. They've just finished setting up the serving platters and stemware in the ballroom."

"Hi, Pearl," Harley said, stepping from the driver's side and straightening her tuxedo jacket.

"You still haven't found your contacts?" Pearl asked, looking at Harley's glasses with concern.

"Not yet, unfortunately. I've wanted to replace them, but I haven't had any time the last couple of days."

"Understandable. Here," Pearl said, scurrying over to the truck bed, "why don't you let me help you all carry these things in?"

Tina handed Pearl a tray of hors d'oeuvres. "Are you sure you wanna help out, Pearl? I mean, we don't want you messin' up your nice outfit there."

"It's all part of being a party planner, Tina. Even if I am only a volunteer. Anyway, I like to help out Michael anyway I can."

"Where are they anyway?" Tina asked as they walked toward the house. "Savannah and Michael. Inside somewhere?"

"Well, Michael is still upstairs getting ready, and I don't know where Savannah's gotten off to. It seems like she's always sneaking off somewhere these days." She lowered her voice to a conspiratorial tone. "Just between the three of us," she said, "I don't know if this engagement is really the best idea."

"Why's that?" Tina asked.

"Oh, I don't know," Pearl said, shaking her head. "Micheal just seems so infatuated with her. So blindly infatuated. He can't see any of her faults. Only her beauty. Her indifference to him, her apathy, her coldness, he seems to overlook. If you ask me, Savannah's just going through the motions with him. Doing what is expected of her. It's not fair to Michael."

"Have you talked to them about it?" Harley asked.

"To Savannah, no. Definitely not. And I don't intend to. I did, however, voice my concerns to Michael. After all, I've known him since he was a baby. As you know, Michael's father chose us as his legal guardians before he died. And that's part of the reason why I'm worried about him. He's vulnerable, you see. Born into all of this wealth and privilege but with no real parents to guide him on the right decisions to make. I'm not sure Arthur and I did right by him, sending him away to be educated at all of those elite boarding schools in Europe. Maybe we should've kept him here, close to us. He has freedom and money now and does whatever suits his fancy at the moment, with no thought of any future consequences. And Savannah Swanson has bewitched him, I tell you. Body and soul."

"Just tell him to get a prenup," Tina said as they entered the kitchen. "That's what a lot of the rich people do."

"Oh, if it were only so easy, Tina," Pearl said in a resigned tone.

They set the trays of food on the enormous kitchen island and began unwrapping them. "These will go on the buffet tables in the ballroom," Pearl said. "And Harley, your things will go on the bar. Here, I'll show you."

Following behind Pearl, they traveled down a long marble-tiled hallway, the walls covered in a collage of tapestries and oil portraits, the subjects of whom were watching them as they passed.

"Creepy," Tina whispered to Harley.

"Generations and generations of Sutcliffes," Pearl said, examining the long row of paintings as she walked. "Many of whom lived here or visited at one time or another."

"They're all blond," Tina said. "Not that I have anything against blonds or anything." She tossed a peroxide curl over her shoulder. Harley and Pearl were too polite to mention hers wasn't natural.

Pearl laughed. "Yes, they're known for it. The Sutcliffes. Glorious crowns of golden hair." Near the end of the hallway, Harley paused at one of the portraits, finding herself arrested by the young man's beauty, the depth of expression in his blue eyes. There was something familiar about him too, something she could not place. "Who is this?" she asked.

Pearl stopped and turned to the portrait with interest. "Oh, that's James Sutcliffe," she said, her once pleasant expression wilting to sadness. "Michael's father. He died quite young. And tragically. It happened during one of the summer parties they used to host here years ago. Your grandfather probably told you about them," she said, looking at Harley. "Anyway, James was terribly depressed after his wife died. Arthur and I tried to talk him out of hosting the party that year, but he insisted, saying it was a Sutcliffe family tradition, that he owed it to the town. He'd been drinking heavily that night, and he was walking along the cliffside out back when he fell. His body was found the next morning, his silk suit tangled in a briar thicket."

"When was this?" Tina asked.

"Oh, goodness, a very long time ago. Over thirty years ago before you all were born. Michael was just a baby at the time. I still remember how shocked we all were, how shocked the whole town was. 'A tragic accident,' the headlines had read, and 'How will we survive without our favorite son?'"

Harley imagined James Sutcliffe, handsome and young and lifeless, his fine silken suit tangled in thorns, his beautiful face bloodied and scarred from numerous briar pricks. She flinched and drew her hand to her face.

"It is tragic," she said.

Pearl nodded in agreement. "The Sutcliffe family has been tested by one trial after another, I'm afraid. What more could possibly happen?"

The darkness of the foyer, the melancholy spell of James Sutcliffe's death lifted as they entered the ballroom, the crystal chandeliers illuminating gold walls accented by ivory trim and wainscoting.

As Harley gazed around the immense room and to the vintage bar where she would serve cocktails, she couldn't help but imagine the opulent parties that must've been held there in years past, of men and women in black ties and evening gowns, sipping from champagne coupes as they danced a Waltz.

"Now this is something," Tina said with awe.

"Quite impressive, isn't it?" Pearl said. "And now that Michael is back in town, has taken his place as owner of Briarcliffe, I expect we'll be having more of these parties."

Not that we would be invited, Harley thought. *Not as guests anyway.*

"What will be you be serving tonight, Harley?" Pearl asked.

"The Seelbach," she said. When Pearl's face registered no understanding of the term, Harley said, "It's a cocktail consisting of champagne, bourbon, Cointreau, and two types of bitters: Angostura and Peychaud. I thought it would be the perfect cocktail for a celebratory occasion like tonight's."

"It does sound perfect," Pearl said, smiling.

With that, the three of them reported to their respective duties. Harley set up lines of champagne coupes at the bar, prepping each with shots of bourbon; Tina arranged a variety of heavy hors d'oeuvres on silver platters, readying them for guests as they mingled about the room; And Pearl disappeared to the front of the house, intending to greet guests as they arrived.

However, the first person to arrive in the ballroom wasn't a guest at all. It was the host, Michael Sutcliffe. He wore a dark suit and burgundy dress shoes, no tie, with his blond hair neatly styled like a businessman's on Wall Street. Though attractive in a boyish way, his looks paled in comparison to his late father's, his eyes and features lacking the same depth of expression and masculine character. To Harley, he looked like a prep school kid playing dress-up in an expensive suit.

He gazed about the room, here and there, in search of someone. Not finding that someone, he approached the bar, and not acknowledging Harley, took a champagne coupe and downed the entirety in one swallow. He slammed the coupe down and rapped his fingers against bar top, still not making eye contact with Harley. Accustomed to being treated as invisible, she merely returned to her work.

Seconds later, Pearl walked in and hurried over. "Michael," she said, her arms outstretched, "there you are. You look so handsome."

"Where's Savannah?" he asked.

"I'm sure she will be here shortly," Pearl said, trying to reassure him. "The housekeeper said she went for a walk a little while ago. She probably just needed some air before the busyness of the party."

"Needed some air?" he said. "Doesn't she know how important tonight is? She knows what this means to me." He straightened his suit in an effort to regain his composure. "I just wish she would take things more seriously. As my wife, she will have a lot of responsibilities. Social responsibilities. She'll be expected to not only be a gracious hostess at events like this, but to represent us in the community through volunteer work and serving on boards and committees." He shook his head in frustration. "She's a beauty queen, for heaven's sake. She's made for these sorts of things."

"Well," Pearl said, placing her hand on his forearm, "she did have a bit of a shock with Patrick's death as we all did."

He waved her away with his right hand, the anger returning to his face. "Oh, please don't bring him up. Not tonight."

"Well, they were friends, dear."

"Yes," he said, tightening his fist. "*Friends.*" He checked his watch. "Look, I still need to put on my tie. Make sure she's here before I get back."

Before Pearl could answer, he stormed out of the room. Moments later, Harley could hear his dress shoes as they stomped up the grand staircase to the third floor.

"Oh dear," Pearl said, turning to Harley. "It's just like I said. The whole situation is terrible. How I do feel for Michael."

I feel for Savannah, Harley thought.

"Could you please go check out back?" Pearl asked. "See if you can find her?"

"I will," Harley said reluctantly, "but I don't know if she'll come back with me."

"Please just try, Harley," she pleaded. "I can't go myself. Tina's still busy with the food and someone has to be here to greet the guests."

"I'll do it, Pearl," she said. "But just for you."

Pearl smiled with appreciation, and Harley made her way toward the line of French doors leading out onto the patio.

Darkness had settled over the immense grounds, a wave of muted green and gray lawn rolling past the solarium to the cliffside and navy sky beyond. The Smokies had many such overlooks and mountain trails, but this view was particularly beautiful, Harley thought. A brilliant harvest moon shone overhead, guiding her footsteps as she made her way down the stone path toward the cliffside. It seemed like the ideal place for a troubled mind in need of quiet reflection, and she thought she might find Savannah there.

And there she was, standing near the edge in a red flowing evening dress, her blonde hair styled in a chignon, a string of diamonds linked around her long neck. Her back was turned, but Harley could tell she'd been crying, her features etched in the same look Harley had witnessed so many years ago on her grandfather's farm. Did Savannah still remember that day as vividly as she did?

CHAPTER 21

*S*econd grade had let out for the summer, and Harley had been staying at her grandfather's and Uncle Tater's house during one of her mother's deployments overseas. It was a Saturday morning, and she'd invited Savannah Swanson over to play for the day.

Savannah had loved the farm, Harley remembered, and when she'd hopped out of her mother's red convertible that morning, she'd gazed at the rolling fields with wide-eyed wonder, not even saying goodbye to her mother before racing across the barnyard toward Harley.

The two little girls spent the entire day playing, chasing after one another across the endless fields, pausing intermittently to blow on dandelions, to chase after butterflies, or to cool their tired feet in the creek. Then after their baths, they fell among tall strands of grass, waving their arms and legs as if making snow angels, staring up at the endless blue skies and dreaming of their futures.

"What do you want to be when you grow up?" Savannah asked Harley.

"A writer. I want to write books. Tell stories."

"I want to tell stories too," Savannah said, "but I want to tell other people's stories. I want to be an archaeologist or maybe a historian."

Harley grinned with enthusiasm. "Oh, wow, an archaeologist! Can I come to one of your exhibits?"

Savannah giggled. "Of course, you can. You'll be the very first one."

Then Savannah's expression turned to sadness, and Harley looked at her with concern. "Savannah," she said. "What's wrong?"

A tear formed in Savannah's big blue eyes. "I don't want to be in the pageants, Harley. I just don't want to."

"Then don't do it then, Savannah. Not if you don't want to."

"But I have to," she said. "Mommy says so. She says I have to be pretty."

"Oh, nobody really cares about that stuff. It just seems so silly."

"Mommy and Daddy care about it. And Mommy says that if I'm not pretty, Daddy won't love me anymore. That no one will love me."

"People don't love what you look like," Harley said. "They love who you are. Your soul."

"No, Mommy says Daddy loves her because she's pretty, and I have to be pretty too."

With that, Savannah Swanson jumped up from her bed in the grass and raced across the fields, not stopping until she found the biggest mud puddle on the farm. Then she jumped into the puddle, full body, rolling around in the mud like a pig, smearing brown goo all over her face, her long blonde hair, ruining her beautiful white dress.

Harley ran over to Savannah and stood over where she lay, expecting her friend's cherubic face to burst into tears. Instead, Savannah looked up at her with a face full of joy, her smile so big Harley could see the baby tooth she'd lost recently. Then, Savannah Swanson started laughing, a big belly laugh, throwing mud on Harley in the process.

Harley jumped in the puddle after Savannah, and the two girls slopped around in the mud for the next hour or so, only stopping when Savannah grew suddenly still beside Harley.

Reality had dawned once again.

Harley searched Savannah's face, trying to figure out what was wrong. And that was when the tears came, washing away the mud from her cheeks in tiny trickles that ran down her cheeks.

"I wanna go to summer camp, Harley," she said, "I wanna play soccer. I don't wanna be in those stupid pageants."

"I'm so sorry, Savannah," Harley said, wrapping her friend in a hug.

"Do you think if I go home with this mud all over me, I won't have to be pretty anymore, that Mommy won't make me be in the pageants?"

"I don't know," Harley said. "I hope so. I really do."

Before she could comfort her any further, Mrs. Swanson's red convertible pulled into the barnyard, and the horn began honking. Harley helped Savannah up from the mud and the two girls walked slowly up the hill, hand-in-hand.

"You're so lucky, Harley," Savannah said, squeezing her hand as they walked.

Harley turned to her in surprise. "I am?"

"Yeah, because your granddaddy loves you no matter what and you're not even pretty."

At the time, Savannah's words had hurt Harley's feelings. She already knew she wasn't pretty, of course, but those words hurt coming from someone she'd considered a friend. But even at the age of seven, Harley knew Savannah had meant it as a compliment, that she truly was envious of the unconditional love she'd received.

"Are you going to come back and play sometime?" Harley asked.

Savannah smiled eagerly. "Oh, yes! Just as soon as I can. I promise I will."

But Savannah never did come and play again. Her mother took one look at her dress, her hair, her face, all covered in mud, and said her daughter would never be allowed to play with Harley Henrickson again.

The following week, Savannah was placed in the pageant circuit, and the little girl underwent a physical and internal metamorphosis, coloring her hair, wearing makeup, even miniskirts and heels. And though she was beautiful, she rarely smiled, as if she were already disillusioned with her life, with the world as it had been determined for her. And Savannah never played soccer, never went to summer camp, and never became an archaeologist.

Over the years, Savannah grew increasingly popular at school, while Harley grew increasingly less so. And Savannah seemed to forget the two had ever been friends, even making fun of Harley on occasion to fit in with the other kids. By the time they had graduated from high school, it seemed Savannah Swanson ridiculed Harley more than anyone else in school. And yet, even after all these years, Harley still hoped things might change between them.

SAVANNAH SWANSON HADN'T SEEMED to hear Harley's approach, or if she had, she did not intend on acknowledging her.

"Savannah," Harley said pleasantly, "they're looking for you inside."

Savannah turned her gaze from the cliffside and the sea of sky beyond, then over her shoulder to Harley. Not answering, she returned her attention once more to the night sky.

Ok, Harley thought. *I've done what I promised. I found her. I told her. Now, I'll just be on my way.*

She turned to leave, and Savannah said, "No, wait. Please don't go."

The two women stood looking at one another in an uncomfortable silence until at last Savannah said, "I've been meaning to come by your shop, to say hello."

Her comment, strange at best, took Harley by surprise. The idea of Savannah Swanson stopping by to say hi after years of not speaking to her was baffling.

"You see," Savannah said, "I've been thinking a lot about things lately since I moved back home...about the past. I don't know," she said, returning her gaze to the starry sky, "maybe I'm just getting more reflective, maybe I'm finally old enough to feel regret. I look at myself now, and I don't even recognize who I've become."

She turned around to face Harley, this time with a pleading expression in her eyes. "I'm sorry, Harley," she said. "I'm so sorry for how I treated you." She moved closer and underneath the moonlight, Harley could see where a bit of her eye makeup had run, bleeding at the outer corners of her eyes. "You're the only real friend I ever had...as pitiful as that sounds...and I hope that now that I'm back, maybe we can start over, maybe we can be friends again."

"Of course," Harley said, not wanting to deteriorate her already vulnerable state, "of course we can be friends again." But was this really possible?

"You were always the strong one," Savannah said, "the sensible one. Even when we were little girls. I've always wanted to be like you. I bet you never knew that, did you?"

"No," Harley said truthfully. "No, I didn't."

She wanted to tell Savannah that it wasn't her fault, that she'd been living up to other people's expectations her entire life, that she was still that carefree little girl inside.

"I've only ever wanted someone to love me," she said. "To love me for who I am on the inside. But I don't even know who that person is anymore. I've been fabricating an image of myself for so long, have been running this race for so long, I'm lost inside. Lost and exhausted. And I've hated myself for it. I've hated myself just as I've secretly hated the men who've desired me, just as I've resented women like you who do have something special inside them, just as I've hated my parents for making me the person I've become. I'm lonely, Harley. Lonely and empty and ugly."

In that moment, Savannah Swanson looked over at Harley Henrickson with that same hurt look she'd seen that afternoon on the farm when they were children.

"I'd like to just go home right now," she said, "and stand underneath the shower, allow the water to wash off all these layers of makeup, all these layers of pain, let them all wash off and go down the drain forever, let me be free of it all." She looked up at Harley. "But I can't do that, can I? I can't wash it all away, can't be free from it. This is my mask," she said, bringing her hand to her face, "has been my mask for as long as I can remember. And there's safety in it. I've grown so comfortable behind this shell, so comfortable behind this mask, that I don't even know how to step outside of it. And people who've tried to challenge me to do so, people like you...just by being who you are...I've only treated you as enemies."

Harley was speechless. All of those thoughts and feelings had been ruminating inside Savannah for all of those years, and now they had at last risen to the surface, had exploded. She wondered what had brought about this epiphany. Had it been Patrick's death? Her engagement to Michael Sutcliffe?

"I don't want to marry him, Harley," she said. "I don't love him."

"Then don't marry him," Harley said in an understanding tone. "You don't have to. You can make other choices for your life."

She shook her head. "It's not that easy. It's expected of me, you see. This is what my parents have always wanted for me, to marry into a rich family, be a socialite. And Michael is the key to that, but he doesn't love me either," she said. "He's just like them. I'm just an object to him, his idea of what Mrs. Michael Sutcliffe should be. He's infatuated with this mask I wear," she said, pointing to her face again. "And if I marry him, I'm going to lose who I am even more."

"Have you spoken to him about it? About how you feel?"

"Oh, yes," she said with a grimace. "And he's been very clear about his expectations of me. He doesn't want me to work after we're married. Doesn't want me to go back to school." She paused, and a brief expression of triumph lit up her face. "But the thing is I have been going back to school."

"To get a master's degree," Harley said, "in history."

Savannah stared at Harley in disbelief. "How did you know?"

"Well, when I heard the rumors about you spending time with Patrick, everyone thought you all were having an affair, but I didn't believe it, not about Patrick. I figured it must be because you were one of his graduate students. And then I remembered when we were children you wanting to be an archaeologist or work in a history museum."

Savannah smiled for the first time, her face caught in a momentary glow that made her appear like a little girl again. "Yes. I never quite made it into archaeology, did I?" she said. "But I'm still looking at that job in a history museum. The thing is though, Harley..."

The smile wilted from her face and the haunted look returned. "I did want Patrick," she said, turning her engagement ring around on her finger. "I did think I had feelings for him even if he was old enough to be my father. He was so different from so many other men. So genuinely interested in my academic career, in my bettering myself. It had nothing to do with my looks."

Her voice began to stutter with emotion. "I did desire him...I don't know if it was because I wanted an excuse to break off things with Michael or because..." She took a deep breath and steadied her voice. "And you were right about something else too. He didn't share my feelings. Patrick didn't. At least he never tried anything physically."

And it's best he hadn't, Harley thought. Not until Savannah had sorted things out with Michael.

"He scares me, Harley," she said, a worried tone in her voice. "Michael does. I don't trust him. I think he might've..."

"Had something to do with Patrick's death?"

She exhaled as if she were thankful to have at last told someone. "Yes."

"Why do you say that, Savannah? Why do you suspect Michael?"

"He's just so jealous," she said. "Always thinking I'm out with someone else or that I'm cheating on him. I think he used to follow me to Patrick's house when I'd go there for our meetings."

This, of course, was true, because Harley had seen him there herself.

"And then Marcy Cooper...you know her husband, Rick, works for Parks and Recreation...she told me Rick's been seeing Michael in Briarwood Park at all hours of the day and night walking around. The only reason I could think he'd be going there is to spy on Patrick and me."

"Because Patrick's property abuts the park," Harley added.

"Yes."

"And I don't know where he's been the last couple of nights," she said. "He usually stops by my parents' house for dinner or just to visit, but he hasn't been coming by. Then I don't hear from him until the next morning."

Classical music began lilting from the ballroom, and through the

French doors, Harley could see people gathering around the cocktail tables.

"I should get this over with," she said.

"Savannah, are you sure you want to do this?"

"I don't have a choice," she said. "Don't you see? I've never had a choice."

Then she headed back along the path, her dress catching on stones, her gloomy expression juxtaposed to the merriment inside the lit ballroom.

CHAPTER 22

"I'm the happiest man in the world," Michael Sutcliffe said into the microphone, smiling at the crowd of people gathered in the ballroom. Standing behind him, Savannah had reaffixed her so-called "mask," a plastered smile of red lipstick and painted eyes that stared emptily into the crowd. Michael lifted his champagne coupe in a toast, and someone called out, "To Michael and Savannah," which was responded to in kind by the audience.

The clinks of glasses were followed by sips of cocktails, and the crowd broke into small groups for the purposes of mingling. Tina wove her way through the various clusters, offering a selection of hors d'oeuvres. How she walked in those three-inch stilettos while effortlessly balancing silver platters on her shoulders was an act of athletic prowess, Harley thought.

Harley rested her tired back against the bar, happy things would be over soon, at least she hoped for herself. It was then Jed Turner emerged from the crowd, having left Cheri behind to mingle with a group of women from the Notchey Creek Gardening Club. The whippet-thin Cheri made quite a statement in her black leather slip dress and knee-high stiletto boots. As the gardening club ladies presumably spoke of proper weeding and pruning practices, Cheri smiled in rote agreeability, all the while looking over their shoulders for someone more socially desirable to speak to.

Well, at least Cheri and Jed are back together for the time being, Harley thought. Maybe Jed would be in a better mood. However, this was not the case. Jed approached the bar, and pushing aside the display of small pumpkins and gourds, rested his elbows on the counter, and heaved a big sigh of boredom. He wore a gray silk suit and blue tie, a Super Bowl ring glittering from his finger. What little the barber had left of his brown hair, made him appear like a drill sergeant.

"I need to talk to you," he said with his usual charm.

"Okay," Harley said, then continued filling rows of champagne coupes.

"Expect me at the shop first thing tomorrow."

Without saying another word, Jed made his way back to the grateful Cheri, who was by that time, up to her stiletto boots in proper pruning and irrigation practices.

"The cocktails were phenomenal," a male voice said, drawing Harley from her reverie. Eric Winston stood in front of the bar, smiling at her. Yesterday's fatigue had lifted from his face, as had the day-old stubble, and in his navy suit jacket and matching slacks, he looked more like a Brooks Brothers model than a medical examiner.

There was something of the Nordic in Eric's appearance, Harley decided. He was tall and slim with a V-shaped torso, and had chiseled, angular features, accented by striking light blue eyes. She could imagine him at an exclusive ski lodge in the Swiss Alps, sipping cognacs by the fire in between runs on the slopes. Or perhaps on a thirty-foot yacht, his white linen clothes rippling in the breeze as he worked the sails. Afterward, he would change into an expensive suit like the one he wore then and dine on lobster and brut champagne at a five-star restaurant.

And that was the difference between them.

Harley examined her silly uniform, the burden of her red glasses weighing unusually heavy on her nose at that moment. Eric Winston was of The Ritz. She was of Bud's Pool Hall.

"So what do you call this?" he asked, holding up his champagne coupe and smiling.

"It's called the Seelbach."

"Well, it sure is great," he said, before taking another sip. "I mean, who knew champagne and bourbon could make such a good pairing?"

"Adam Seger did," Harley said. "He's the one who invented it. In the 1990s."

"1990s?" Eric said, surprised. "I would've thought this was much older than that."

"That's what Seger wanted everyone to believe as well. He said he found the recipe on an old menu at the Seelbach Hotel in Louisville. He claimed the cocktail had once been the hotel's signature drink and that it predated Prohibition. And sometimes in the cocktail world, vintage is better, at least if you want to make a name for yourself."

"The things people do," Eric said, shaking his head. "And all for their five minutes of fame. Nonetheless," he said, "I'm glad he did it."

He took another sip of his cocktail and rested the coupe on the bar. "And how are you doing, Harley?" he said, his eyes searching hers with concern. "I was worried about you earlier...after what happened to Patrick. I kept thinking about you afterward, wondering how you were doing. You know, if you ever need someone to talk to, someone to listen, I'm here."

There was something about Eric Winston's easy manner, his down-to-earth gentility that put her at ease. He was so caring and genuine and so easy to talk to despite his intimidating good looks. His handsomeness seemed to matter nothing to him, as if he weren't even aware of what other people saw when they looked at him.

"Thank you, Eric," she said. "You're the first person in all of this who's taken the time to ask me how I'm doing, the first person to care. I appreciate it, and I can honestly say that I'm doing okay."

"I'm so glad. And you will let me know if you need something, right?"

"Of course," she said with a smile.

"Now, that I know you're okay," he said, taking a more serious tone. "There's something I need to tell you about Patrick." He drew closer to the bar and created an invisible circle around them with his body.

"About the autopsy?" Harley asked, lowering her voice to match his.

"Yes. And it's very troubling. You see, I found bruising on Patrick's neck and chest, consistent with having been restrained. It appears someone held him down in the water, causing him to drown."

"So he *was* murdered then?"

"I believe so. And as of this evening, Jed has changed the case from an accidental drowning to a homicide."

Hence his urgency to speak with me tomorrow, she thought.

Eric glanced around the bar area to ensure no one was within hearing distance of their conversation. "And I believe there were drugs in his bloodstream. I'm not sure exactly what yet. I've put a rush on the toxicology reports, but the drugs appear to be hallucinogenic in effect. The amount was significant." He raised his brows. "If Patrick was acting strangely, as you say, and if he did go to the creek that night hoping to meet someone, the drugs might explain it."

Yes, they would.

"And there's one other thing," he said.

Harley waited with rapt attention.

"Patrick was dying."

Harley braced herself to the bar, gripping the sides with her hands.

"He had cancer. I spoke with his doctor this morning, and he said Patrick had been diagnosed with pancreatic cancer recently. It's a terrible disease," he said, shaking his head, "and very aggressive. They call it 'the silent killer' because there's hardly any identifiable symptoms before it's too late."

"How long did he have?"

"Less than six months."

Harley shifted her weight against the bar, trying to digest the news. "Everything makes so much more sense now," she said.

"What do you mean?"

"The reason Patrick had been acting so strangely. Not selling the land to Arthur Johnson for the shopping center and deciding to build the history museum there instead. He wanted the museum to be his last legacy." She did not mention that Patrick's argument with Beau Arson had seemed confessional, nor did she mention his connection to the disoriented homeless man in Briarwood Park.

Eric's father, Dr. Peter Winston, appeared over his son's shoulder, breaking into their conversation.

"Eric," he said, an exasperated look on his face, "could you please go rescue your mother from Mrs. Petree? I have an early morning in the OR, and I need be getting home."

Dr. Peter Winston, a prominent surgeon in town, resembled an older version of his son but was less handsome and far less pleasant. The perpetual scowl he wore on his face gave him a pinched and soured look as if he were always suffering from some physical or mental ailment. In reality, he likely suffered from a general displeasure with life, finding fault with everything and everyone in it.

"Ah, Dad," Eric said, turning to see his father. "You remember Harley Henrickson, don't you?"

He offered a cursory glance in Harley's direction, and finding her wanting, returned his attentions to his son. "Eric, please," he said. "Your mother."

"Yes, Dad," Eric said, embarrassed by his father's rude behavior, "I will get her."

"I'll be in the car." Then Peter Winston made his way through the ballroom to the front of the house.

Eric returned to Harley. "Well, I guess that's all for me too tonight," he said. "If you think of anything else about the case, please stop by my office at the hospital, okay?"

"Will do."

"It was nice seeing you again, Harley."

Then he ventured off to do his father's bidding, rescuing his mother from a still chattering Mrs. Petree.

I'll have to be careful around him, Harley told herself. Already she could sense a growing attraction to Eric Winston, one she could not control. His gentle manner, his kindness, his intelligence, were all very attractive to her. He was so well-adjusted, it seemed, and so stable. He could be someone she could lean on in difficult situations. But people like Eric Winston didn't fall in love with people like Harley Henrickson.

She began boxing up the remaining bottles of champagne and bourbon and bitters, resigned to guard her heart.

There were far more critical things requiring her attention, finding Patrick's killer being the first. It was time she'd gotten serious about the investigation. Too much time had already been wasted. Her first stop the next day would be the Notchey Creek Public Library.

CHAPTER 23

"The best laid plans of mice and men oft go awry."

Harley thought of this paraphrased quote by Robert Burns on her way to the Notchey Creek Public Library the next morning. She'd intended to spend the early hours in the microfiche room, pouring over old newspapers, hoping she might locate the one Patrick Middleton had taken from Hazel Moses's house. Yet this was not to be. As she pulled her truck into the library parking lot, her phone began vibrating in her pocket, and realizing it was Tina, and realizing Tina would keep calling her until she answered, she picked up.

"Good Morning, Tina," she said.

"Where are you?"

"At the library."

"Well, you better get over here to Opha Mae Shaw's."

Opha Mae Shaw was Tina's next door neighbor.

"Why?" Harley asked.

"She wants her toilet."

"Her what?"

"Her toilet. You know that great big one you've got in the back of your truck. You think you'd be wantin' rid of it by now. Anyway,

Opha Mae came across the yard a little while ago, banging on my front door, asking me where her toilet was. She said you were supposed to bring it by here yesterday. She said yinz promised."

The realization at last dawned on Harley. "Oh, yes, that toilet. I'll be right over."

OPHA MAE SHAW lived in a white clapboard house in a neighborhood of Notchey Creek known as Hogwash Alley, made locally famous during the Great Flood of 1964. According to local legend, the neighborhood's numerous pigs were swept from their pens and carried two miles across town, finally ending up in downtown Notchey Creek, where they washed down Main Street, snorting at gawking pedestrians as they floated by.

"Where would you like this Opha Mae?" Harley asked as she and Tina lifted the antique toilet from the truck bed.

Opha Mae pointed toward a patch of grass between a plastic birdbath and a pair of pink flamingos, a horde of twenty hens pecking at the ground beneath her feet. "Right over yonder if you don't mind," she said, a half-lit Virginia Slims cigarette dangling from her lower lip.

In order to direct them better, Opha Mae headed in the bird bath's direction, her Michelin Man figure wobbling in a chartreuse muumuu and white terrycloth house shoes. "Right cheer," she said, standing by the bird bath. "At least until I can get cleaned up from the yard sale."

Tina groaned under the toilet's weight. "All right, but you're gonna have to do something about all these chickens. We can't get through the yard."

Opha Mae grabbed a broom from her front porch and began prodding the chickens' rear ends with the straw bristles. "Come on now, sweet babies," she said. "Now move for Mama, you hear?" As Opha Mae hobbled across the yard, one of her pink plastic curlers sprang from her shower cap, smacking against her cheek. She cocked the broom at the chickens. "Now don't you be makin' Mama mess up her hair, you hear? Y'all gonna get a great big old whoopin' if you do that."

A giant red rooster, tightening its talons on top of the chainlink fence, began crowing at them.

Tina snarled. "Crazy old bird. I swear that thing cock-a-doodle-dos all hours of the night and day, driving me crazy. It's circadian rhythms are off or something."

Opha Mae gunned her fist at the rooster. "You hush up now, Pecker. You're gettin' as bad as Sir Clucks-A-Lot about crowin' at folks."

Hoisting the toilet by its sides, Harley and Tina lowered it to the ground and shuffled through the grass, dodging splatters of chicken poop like landmines.

"I swear," Tina said, "those things poop everywhere. You'd think with Fud being a garbage man, they'd clean up all this chicken poop in their yard. And they're projectile too, Harley. I swear they aim their cluckety old butts right at my yard and poop right through the fence."

Reaching the patch of grass next to the birdbath, they dropped the toilet at Opha Mae's white terrycloth house shoes, nearly crushing the brown hen that stood at her feet.

Opha Mae screamed, grabbing the chicken just in time. "Lady McBawk!" she said, cradling the hen like a baby in her arms. "What do you think you're doin' sweet baby? Are you tryin' to be Mama's supper tonight? Mama's gonna pen you up, that's what Mama's gonna do." Opha Mae scuttled toward the backyard, making her way to the wire mesh chicken coop.

Harley turned to Tina. "Do all of the chickens have names?"

"Oh, yeah. Let's see, there's Mrs. McNugget, Chick-or-Treat, Professor Puffy Pants, and General Tsao. Heck, I can't even remember all of their names there's so many."

"What about the one that ruined your roses last year?"

Tina grunted. "Oh, I don't know what her name is. I just call her Mother Clucker."

Opha Mae hobbled toward them, carrying two plastic containers of petunias. "I'm fixin' to plant my flares, y'all," she said with glee.

"Here, Opha Mae," Harley said, taking the flowers from her. "Let me help you."

Harley added three pints of fall flowers to the toilet bowl and filled in the remaining space with potting soil.

"Them's is gonna be so purdy," Opha Mae said.

Tina curled her lip. "Yeah, they're ready for the cover of *House Beautiful.*"

Opha Mae smiled warmly. "Sure do appreciate y'all helpin' me out."

Harley removed a green watering can from the front porch glider and poured a stream of water over the flowers, moistening the soil. As she reached down to pat the soil, something fell from her shirt pocket and fluttered to the grass.

It was the photo of the blonde girl, the one that had been in Patrick Middleton's jacket pocket. She'd placed the picture in her pocket that morning, planning to take it to the library for identification purposes.

"You dropped something, Harley," Opha Mae said, picking up the photo before Harley had the chance. Opha Mae held the photo up to her face, studying it closely. "Well, I'll be," she said, "that's Susan, ain't it?"

"Who's Susan?" Tina asked.

"A girl who used to live in town here," Opha Mae said. "One of the youngins I had at the high school back when I was workin' in the lunch room. Sweet girl, Susan was. Got killed in a car wreck some years back. Back before y'all was even born."

Harley moved toward Opha Mae, desperation growing in her voice. "A car wreck? Do you remember when it was?"

Opha Mae looked down at the grass in thought and shook her head. "Oh, lordy, that's been a mighty long time ago. Can't remember the exact year. But I remember the day. Always will. It was Halloween night." Opha Mae smiled, looking at the photo. "She sure was a purdy gal, weren't she? That long blonde hair. Looked like it was spun right out of gold. I remember she used to walk past the pharmacy there downtown and all the men on Main Street would just a swing around and watch her as she passed by. Those purdy dresses of hers and those long, long legs."

"What was Susan's last name?" Harley asked.

"Thompson, I believe," Opha Mae said. "Susan Thompson. Her folks was Alan and Cynthia. Her daddy passed away some years back, but I reckon her mama still lives in town over yonder on Cypress."

Harley was about to ask whether Susan was seeing anyone before she died, when Opha Mae said, "Oh, and I got your costumes ready."

Harley stared at Opha Mae, a confused expression on her face. "Costumes?"

"Yours and Matilda's."

Opha Mae opened the screen door to her house and grabbed a fifty-gallon black trash bag. "Wilma ordered 'em," she said.

She removed two flour sack dresses, a long, slim one tailored for a woman and a short, wide one tailored presumably for a pig. The necklines were high enough for a Puritan church service, and the pea-green print, dappled with yellow, orange, and pink flowers, could best be described as *The Brady Bunch* meets *The Swiss Family Robinson*.

"Oh, and there's bonnets too," Opha Mae said, holding up two mustard yellow bonnets, one in each hand. "Now, what do you think about that, Harley? Ain't that somethin'? Just finished 'em on the sewin' machine."

Harley raised a brow and could hear Tina snickering beside her. "Wilma ordered those?" she asked.

"She sure did. And ain't you lucky she spoils you and Matilda like she does. Thought it'd be right cute you two havin' matchin' outfits for the festival. Kind of like twins does when they's growin' up. And since you gotta dress up anyway, you might as well 'up your cuteness factor,' as they call it. Not that you need it, Harley," she said. "I hope you know I ain't sayin' that. I ain't like some folks around town who talks about you."

"It's okay, Opha Mae," Harley said. "I understand."

"Anyway," Opha Mae said, "Wilma thought it might help Matilda win that Prize Pig contest. And Wilma says it'd be good for you to stand outside the store yonder and wave at folks as they go by. Might get 'em to come inside."

Or scare them away.

Dread crept over Harley, and as if Tina were reading her mind, she said, "Oh, I hope you don't have to wear that thing, Harley. You couldn't pay me."

As Harley worked to construct an excuse why she couldn't wear the costume, her cell phone vibrated, and Wilma, in her Oompa Loompa wig, appeared on the screen.

"Hi, Wilma," Harley said.

"You get your costume yet?"

Harley looked up at Opha Mae, who still eyed her with excitement as she held the flour sack dresses. There wasn't a productive way to avoid this without injuring both women's pride. "Yes, Wilma," she said. "I got it. And the one for Matilda too. Thank you and Opha Mae for thinking of us."

"Have you tried it on yet?"

"No, not yet."

"Well, you'll need to be wearin' it down at the store today. Festival's already started."

"Wilma, I don't know if…."

Wilma disappeared from the screen, and the line grew quiet. Harley knew beyond the silence, a disappointed Wilma was trying to hide her hurt feelings. "I was just tryin' to do something nice for you, Harley," she said, still missing from the screen. "Don't seem like you ever let me do nothin' for you. Not even when you was a youngin."

Harley couldn't take the guilt trip, and as was always the case with Aunt Wilma, she conceded. "Of course, I'll wear it. And Matilda will wear hers too. The dresses are perfect for us."

Wilma reappeared on screen, her wig titled to one side of her head. Her mouth spread into a grin. "Oh, I can't wait to see you, Harley, and wait till you get a load of my costume."

A prick of dread crept up Harley's back. "I'm sure it's lovely."

"No peekin' now," Wilma said, giggling, holding up the phone to her chin. "I'll see you at the store directly."

The call ended, and Harley returned her phone to her pocket. She stared at the flour sack dress and bonnet and decided that if she was going to do this for Aunta Wilma and Opha Mae, she might as well do it right. She took the dress from Opha Mae and slipped it over her shoulders.

"A PIG IN A BONNET?"

The festival livestock manager stared at Harley, trying to gauge the seriousness of her request. He wore overalls and a camouflage hat, a toothpick bobbing up and down on his bottom lip. He reminded Harley of Elmer Fudd.

They stood between two rows of hog pens in the back corner of the festival grounds. Inside one of those pens, Matilda lay sprawled across a bed of hay, snoring.

"Sir," Harley said, taking a conciliatory tone, "I know it's not exactly conventional, but it would really mean a lot to my great-aunt. You see, she had these costumes specially made for us."

The man examined her, raising a brow as he perused the flour sack dress and yellow bonnet. "You mean to tell me you and that pig's got matchin' outfits?"

"Yes, sir," Harley said, feigning dignity. "That's exactly what I'm saying."

He chewed on his toothpick in thought, then checked his clip-board, as if there might be a special stipulation allotted for pigs to wear period clothing. "Hmm," he said, "well, I reckon I don't see why it'd hurt. There ain't nothin' here that says you can, and there ain't nothin' here that says you can't. So until I hear somethin' different, she can wear that there dress."

"And the bonnet?"

The toothpick danced. "And the bonnet too."

"Thank you!"

Matilda had woken from her nap and joined them at the edge of her pen.

"But you're the one whose gonna be puttin' 'em on 'er," the man said. "I ain't gettin' near that pig. She's feisty."

"I can certainly do that, sir," Harley said. "Thank you."

As she placed the dress and bonnet on Matilda, securing the Velcro fasteners, the man watched with glee. "She kinda looks like that pig on TV," he said. "The one all the youngins likes. Penny Lope, or somethin' or another."

"Penelope?" Harley said, securing Matilda's bonnet. "Yes, I suppose she does."

"And I reckon you kinda look like that one on that other show. The one back in the '60s. *The Beverly Hillbillies.*"

"Elly May Clampett?" Harley said with some hopefulness.

"No," he said, scratching his chin. "I was thinkin' Granny."

CHAPTER 24

*S*eated in the Notchey Creek Public Library, Harley thought about death and about ghosts, two phenomenon she hadn't given much consideration until recently. Beyond the quiet warmth of the library, she could hear the autumn wind howling through the trees outside, smacking their limbs against the window panes, the leaves clawing at small cracks in the sills. She sat at a long mahogany table, and the microfiche being out of operation, she'd been reduced to combing through a disorganized mess of newspapers, written accounts, and diary entries, dating back more than a century.

Over the last two hours, she'd managed to litter the table with swaths of archaic texts, some handwritten in the embellished style of old, and some typed on old-fashioned typewriters with a letter or two of text missing.

Those documents once had been part of Nothchey Creek's oral history, having been spun for generations by the region's old timers before being put to paper. Those old timers must've taken great delight in rehashing the town's many tragic events from the comfort of their rocking chairs, their stories embellished with each curl of wood that fell from their whittled cedar sticks. Harley imagined their wives, seated in straight chairs beneath neighboring shade trees, smiling into their needlework as their husbands, once again, recounted those stories to anyone who cared to listen.

And when the old timers were done with their part, the stories rose with the smoke of campfires on dark, sprawling farms, igniting the imaginations of teenagers, who years later would tell the stories to their own children, tucked into beds on screened-in back porches, the crickets humming moonlit symphonies among tall strands of Johnson grass, the fireflies floating in dappled sparks among garden hedges.

Nonetheless, for Harley's purposes, it was hard to separate the weeds from the chaff in the paper melee.

With a yawn, she pulled her long dark hair into a loose ponytail and massaged the back of her neck, sore from hours of crouching and reading. At twenty-six it seemed as if she'd been reading longer than she'd been walking, but her body still ached from hours of research underneath the library's bright fluorescent lights. But she loved the comfort of the library, its familiar aromas, its polished wood tables, its worn leather chairs, the endless rows of dusty hardbacks. They brought back lingering spells of childhood nostalgia, of when she would make daily pilgrimages to the library after school.

In neighboring chairs, elderly patrons staved off post-breakfast naps with steaming mugs of coffee and large-print editions of commercial spy thrillers. Mornings in the library were generally quiet, the peacefulness permeated only by the snores from her neighboring patrons or from the sound of Hettie Winecoop's wayward library cart as it groaned its way down the aisles.

Harley watched as Hettie rolled the rusty book cart past numerous tables, collecting stacks of old books and returning them to even older shelves. Everything in the library was old, it seemed. A century prior, the red brick structure had been the philanthropic dream of Augustus Sutcliffe, a timber baron whose name was forged on most of the town's important buildings.

Architecturally inspired by a visit to Thomas Jefferson's Monticello, Augustus Sutcliffe had commissioned a domed skylight for the town's public library, one that afforded a beautiful view of the morning sun, sending prisms of light through the canopying maples.

Hettie Winecop leaned past Harley and removed a stack of books from the table. Though Harley had added to the elderly librarian's workload significantly that morning, Hettie was always pleasant, even eager to inquire about how she was doing.

"How's the research going, sweetie?" Hettie asked.

Harley rested her glasses on the table, the rims spread across the pages of an open book. "It seems like I'm finding everything but what I'm looking for, Hettie. And I've certainly read enough tales about the different people who've died in the creek over the years. Goodness," she said, "I didn't realize there were so many."

"It's true," Hettie said with half a laugh, though there was no humor behind it. "I guess there have been quite an awful lot over the years, haven't there? Of course," she said, "there's tragedy in any town's history, but it's been a bit heavy-handed in Notchey Creek, I have to admit. But that creek's awfully old, Harley. Lordy be, I bet it's older than the dinosaurs. As old as the Smokies themselves."

And from the Smoky Mountains the creek had been born, an ancient progeny flowing from a vein of the Tennessee River, furrowing through the verdant fields of Knox County, and treading south for ten miles into the rolling pastures of the Tennessee Valley. When Notchey Creek, at last, reached the small town bearing its name, it dwindled to a five-mile stretch of babbling stream, framed by overhangs of weeping willows and pebble-laden banks rich with crawfish and minnows.

"Yes," Hettie said, shaking her head, "there's been a bunch of those stories told around town over the years. Let's see, there was that one story about the two bootleggers back during Prohibition. Remember them? They were the two who shot each other in that moonlit brawl beside the creek one night. Then, to beat all, the Notchey Creek Decency League unearthed all of the change that had fallen from their pockets and, donated it to The Temperance League."

She released a raspy laugh, and a tuft of her shaggy white bangs stood on end, causing her to head to resemble a dandelion caught by a spring breeze. Harley watched as the strands came alive, moving animatedly with Hettie's words. Harley couldn't help but think Hettie bore a resemblance to Albert Einstein.

"And what about Miles Pruitt?" Hettie asked. "You remember him? He was the one that ruined that local girl back in the forties. What was her name?"

"Bessie Winfield," Harley answered.

"Yes! Bessie Winfield!"

Harley could tell that Hettie, like the old timers, found her own delight in rehashing the creek's many tragic events.

"And then when he refused to marry poor old Bessie, her father shot him. Just like that," she said snapping her fingers. "Didn't think twice about it either. And did you know that Bessie's father was the town's dentist?"

Harley feigned ignorance and Hettie said, "He sure was. Now, isn't that something? Anyway," she said, tucking her hands into her book apron, "they found Miles's body floating in the creek the next morning. Doc Winfield's spent shotgun shells were bobbing in the current beside him."

"And didn't Bessie die in the creek too?" Harley asked.

Hettie nodded. "Of a broken heart, if you ask me. They found her some weeks after Miles had died. She'd killed herself apparently. Witnesses said that her hair was floating like palm fronds on the creek's surface, and her body was surrounded by wells of bobbing cattails. Looked like she'd been laid to rest in some kind of watery tomb."

Harley began organizing the various papers into piles, and Hettie said, "I do apologize again for the disorganization, Harley. When they converted everything digitally, I guess they didn't take the time to reorganize it. I've been meaning to get to it myself, but we're under-staffed right now, and I just haven't had the time."

"It's okay," Harley said. "And you're sure there wouldn't be any old newspapers anywhere else? Some place we haven't considered?"

Hettie leaned against her book cart and put the question to thought. "Wait a minute," she said, her face lighting up. "There is someplace else." She locked the wheels on the cart and motioned for

Harley to follow her. "In one of the study rooms. Where Patrick Middleton used to work."

Eagerly Harley followed Hettie to the back of the library to a long row of study rooms, the glass windows dark, the doors closed.

"Patrick's the only one who ever really used these," she said, drawing her keys from her library apron, "and I bet all of his materials are still here."

And so they were. Like gifts on Christmas morning, the newspapers, dated for the exact year Harley needed, were stacked in chronological order on the table.

Thank you, Patrick.

"This is it," Harley said, grinning. "This is what I've been looking for."

"So glad," Hettie said.

"And you let me know if you need anything else."

She closed the study room door behind Harley and disappeared among the stacks.

Like a mental feast, Harley dug into the newspapers, spreading them across the table and paging through each one. Harley recalled the newspaper Patrick had taken from Hazel's house, dated for the week of July 4th, thirty-three years ago, then to Opha Mae's assertion that Susan Thompson had died on Halloween night the following year.

Thanks to Patrick's meticulous organization, the two dates were easy to find, and Harley separated them from the rest. Focused on the July 4th issue, she ran her finger down the front page, the stories dealing primarily with the Independence Day celebrations. Photo after photo depicted shots of the parade on Main Street, some of the attendees and others of the individual floats.

She turned to the next page, and finding nothing of relevance there, moved on to the third. About halfway down the page, she paused and stared at a photograph.

This is what entranced Patrick at Hazel's house that day, she thought, *this is what caused him to steal the newspaper.*

And no wonder.

CHAPTER 25

*H*arley stared at the newspaper photo. A man and woman were embracing in a hug on Main Street, the parade commencing behind them. They were holding hands, and the woman was grinning at the camera, but the man had his head turned so Harley couldn't see his face.

Beneath the picture, in small, bolded print it read:

Susan Thompson, a graduate of Notchey Creek High School, enjoying the parade with her boyfriend, U.S. Army Private, Martin Evans, who is on leave from Afghanistan.

Harley grabbed the November 1st issue for the following year, her gaze rushing down the front page.

Her breath caught in her throat.

Girl and Baby Killed in Tragic Car Accident off Maple Bluff

The article continued.

A mother and her baby were killed by a possible drunk driver in the late hours of Halloween night, police say. This happened on Nullichucky Road northbound near Farmer's Croft shortly before 12 a.m. Authorities speculate an unknown vehicle slammed into the back of Thompson's car on Nullichucky Road, causing it to careen down Cedar Bluff and burst into flames.

The woman's mother, Cynthia Thompson, of Notchey Creek, told The Telephone, the victims were her daughter, 19-year-old Susan Thompson, and Susan's 3-month-old son, Luke. Susan and the baby were last seen driving down Main Street at around 11:30 p.m. in Thompson's car. Cynthia Thompson is unsure why her daughter and the baby would have been out at that hour and considers it very unusual behavior for Susan.

Thompson's charred remains were found inside the car this morning, but the baby is still missing. Broken glass in the rear window suggests the baby was thrown from the car. Police are conducting searches for the baby's remains at present, but aren't hopeful given the amount of active wildlife in the area.

Harley tucked the newspapers in her bag and grabbed her keys. There was one more thing she needed to check.

PATRICK MIDDLETON'S house was dark when Harley arrived some ten minutes later, a stream of yellow police tape still tracing the perimeter. Having trekked from the library on foot, she hoped to evade any detection by neighbors or the police.

She approached the carriage house and studied the double doors. Padlocked. Assuming there must be another point of entry, she rounded the corner and stopped at the first of two five-feet high windows, flanking the back wall.

After removing a crowbar from her bag, she wedged it underneath the aluminum pane and thrust backward, prying the window open wide enough for entry. Her body at an angle, she slid one leg inside the window and finding her footing, followed with the other leg.

Darkness engulfed the carriage house, and a dank mustiness assaulted Harley's senses as she guided her head inside. She removed a strand of cobweb from her face, realizing its maker had died ages ago, entombed by walls of forgotten tools and rusted oilcans, like a long-buried secret she was not meant to unearth.

Cupping her hand over her nose and mouth, she ripped a pair of old curtains from the window. Daggers of sunlight cut though the darkness, releasing hazes of fleeing dust.

Patrick's long-held secret, the secret that had haunted him for over thirty years, that had racked him with crippling guilt, was at last revealed.

Before Harley lay a chrome fender and a reduced heap of gold metal.

CHAPTER 26

"*H*arley Henrickson, where are you?"

"Jed?"

"No, it's the Dalai Lama. Of course, it's me. Look, you were supposed to meet me here at the shop first thing this morning, and here it is 10:30, and you're still not here, and this shop still isn't open."

"Jed, it's been a terrible morning."

"Stop your bellyaching and get over here."

Click!

"NICE GET-UP," Jed said when Harley arrived at Smoky Mountain Spirits a few minutes later.

Thankfully, he was too preoccupied with the purpose of his visit to make any further comments about her festival costume.

When Harley unlocked the shop door and let Jed inside, he said, "Leave the place closed a bit longer until we've had our talk."

As ordered, Harley locked the door behind them and left the entrance sign in the *CLOSED* position.

"You got any coffee?" he asked, following her to the bar.

"I can have some brewed in a few minutes."

"Good."

Jed took a seat at the bar, and after the coffee had brewed, Harley placed a steaming cup in front of him. After taking a sip and returning the mug to the bar top, he reached inside his jacket and removed a clear plastic bag containing a whiskey bottle. He placed the bottle on the bar in front of Harley.

"Can you tell me who bought this?"

The bottle's gold label indicated it was a single barrel whiskey, and the serial number on the back would tell Jed everything he wanted to know. Harley angled the bottle so she could read the back label then wrote down the serial number on a notepad.

"I'll be back in a second," she said, disappearing to the back room. Seated at her desk, she ran the serial number through her inventory spreadsheets, then stopped when she realized the bottle had yet to be registered. There was only one bottle she hadn't inventoried, the one she had given to Beau Arson.

"Beau Arson," she said, returning to the main room, then to the bar.

Jed rolled his eyes. "I should've known he'd have something do with this."

"Did you find it at Patrick's house?" Harley asked.

"Yes." He glared at her with annoyance. "Are you always one step ahead?"

"Well, Hazel Moses said she saw a bottle of Henrickson's at Patrick's house the night he died. He'd been having a drink with someone in his living room, apparently, and the bottle was open on the table. Given that Eric thinks Patrick was drugged, the bottle of whiskey is a critical piece of evidence."

Another glare. "You've really been making the rounds, haven't you?"

"Were the drugs found in Patrick's glass or inside the bottle?"

"His glass."

"Then it might not have been Beau."

"Oh, no," Jed said, eying Harley over his coffee mug, "don't tell me even *you've* fallen under his spell."

Harley, of course, hadn't fallen under Beau Arson's spell, nor anyone else's for that matter, except for maybe Eric Winston's, and that was a hopeless cause. Nonetheless, she decided not to dignify Jed's comment with a response.

He lowered his gaze back to his coffee mug and grimaced. "What do women find so attractive about him anyway? I mean, really. The man looks like he needs a shower. And he's all Cheri's been talking about lately. Beau Arson this, Beau Arson that. Good grief, I wish he'd never even come here. Maybe it's just the money to her, but I've got money too...not anything like he does, of course, but enough."

He looked up at Harley. "Do you know she broke up with me as soon as she heard he was in town? Yeah. Said she wanted to be available just in case. And then, when he didn't pay her any mind, she said she wanted to get back together with me."

So that's what this was about. Jealousy.

Jed continued. "I think it's because he doesn't like them back. I mean, no matter who they are. Helen of Troy could throw herself at him, and he'd be indifferent. I think it's some kind of challenge for the women, you know. Take 'em or leave 'em, that's his motto. Drives them all nuts. And that brooding attitude of his...why do women go for it?"

Jed looked to Harley for an explanation, and when she couldn't provide one, he said, "Did you ever think that Beau Arson might've been the one having that drink with Patrick the night he died? And if so, he could've easily put those drugs in his glass."

"It's possible," Harley said, "but there's one big problem with that theory, Jed. Beau has a solid alibi for the entirety of the night. A hundred people can testify to it."

"How do you know that?"

"Stevie told me."

Another glare. "Is there anybody you haven't talked to? All right, spill it," he said, slapping his hand on the counter. "Tell me everything you know."

"First, tell me the drug that was in Patrick's glass."

"No."

"I can ask Eric."

"Good grief, Harley Henrickson. All right, it was Ambien."

"The sleep aid?"

"Yes. Apparently one of the side effects of Ambien can be auditory and visual hallucinations. And given the large dose Patrick was given, Eric thinks Patrick likely saw or heard some crazy things before he died."

"Things that compelled him to leave his bed in the middle of the night and go to the creek."

"Right. Eric says the dose wasn't quite enough to kill Patrick, so the killer had to drown him at the last minute instead."

"And that person must've been watching Patrick's house that night, to know that the drug hadn't killed him, that he...or she needed to finish the job."

"Correct."

"What about the Johnsons?" Harley asked. "They live next door. It would've been easy for one of them to have done it, and Arthur had a lot to gain from Patrick's death."

"You're talking about that shopping center, aren't you?" he said. "The one Arthur was wanting to build on Patrick's Briarwood land. Yes, well, I'm aware of all that too, and I questioned Pearl and Arthur about where they were the night Patrick died. They said they were home all night, that they went to bed at nine o'clock."

"Pearl told me the same thing," Harley said. "But then Ruby Montgomery saw Arthur's car pull into the garage after midnight."

"I looked into that too. Not that we can really trust Mayor Montgomery on any of this. She hated Patrick Middleton, as everybody in town knows. Something about some trees her daddy planted in Briarwood Park. Anyway," he said, shifting his weight on the bar stool as if he were about to embark into uncomfortable territory. "Arthur's whereabouts...now, that's a touchy situation."

"What do you mean by 'touchy'?"

"Well, you're right in what you said. He wasn't at home all night, that's true. But where he was...well, it's..."

"Where was he, Jed?"

He hesitated, then relented. "The Cat's Meow."

"The strip club?"

He put up his hand. "Now, that does not leave this store, Harley, you understand?"

"Of course."

"Yeah, so, apparently, Arthur has a female companion up there. Keeps him company some nights of the week. I've spoken to her. Her name's Puddin' or something like that." He stopped and cleared his throat to keep from laughing. "I'm assuming that's a stage name. Anyway, she says she can vouch that Arthur was with her during that time."

"Oh, poor Pearl."

"And that's one of the reasons you have to keep quiet about it. I'm assuming Pearl doesn't know, and it's not our place to give her the news. You know how much she adores Arthur."

"And what about Michael Sutcliffe?" Harley asked. "He's been seen outside Patrick's house at night."

"Spying on Savannah. Yeah, I know that too." He shook his head. "And I thought I had a bad case with Cheri. Poor old Michael Sutcliffe. Lovelorn over somebody who doesn't give a sneeze for him, and had the hots for somebody old enough to be her daddy. Yeah, well, Michael's lawyered up like any rich guy would do. And without any physical evidence linking him to the crime scene, my hands are tied until something more develops."

He took another sip of coffee. "Hazel Moses is the one I'm worried about, to tell you the truth. She's been crazy infatuated with Patrick for years. Everybody in town knows that. And she was seen walking to his house not long before he was killed. A woman scorned and all that," he said, before taking another sip of coffee.

"There's one other piece of the puzzle, Jed," Harley said, replenishing his coffee. "A piece I haven't shared with you yet."

"Well," he said, "go ahead. What are you waiting for?"

"Susan Thompson."

"Who?"

Harley removed the young woman's photograph from her pocket and placed it in front of Jed.

"Well, she's good looking. I'll say that."

"She died thirty-two years ago, killed by a drunk driver."

"And what does that have to do with this case?"

"Patrick is the one who killed her."

Jed nearly spat his coffee across the room. "What?"

"Yes. You see, when Patrick loaned me his jacket the other night... after the historical society meeting, I found this woman's photograph in the pocket. I couldn't make any connection between the two until Opha Mae Shaw identified her. She said Susan died in a car accident on Halloween night many years ago, so I went to the library and saw where Susan had indeed died in a car accident and had been killed by a drunk driver. Then I went to Patrick's house and looked inside his garage."

"How did you get in?"

"A crowbar."

"Okay, that's one count of breaking and entering."

"And inside the garage, I found Patrick's car. The front end was totaled."

Jed leaned toward Harley on the bar stool, his interest piqued. "So that's why he never drove. I always wondered. And now you're thinking somebody might've found out about Patrick killing this girl, this Susan Thompson, and took revenge."

"Possibly."

"But who?"

"I don't know."

Jed paused in thought. "Susan Thompson," he said. "Do you think her mama might be Cynthia Thompson? The one who lives over on Cypress?"

"According to Opha Mae Shaw, yes."

"But she must be in her eighties by now. I doubt she could've killed Patrick."

Harley didn't mention the fact that Susan's baby had been in the car with her, a baby that had never been found, a baby that might be

Beau Arson. And she would not mention it, not until she had more evidence.

"Interesting theories," Jed said, rising from the bar stool and drawing his car keys from his pocket. "Call me if you think of anything else. And stay out of trouble. You're still on Alveda Hamilton's naughty list."

CHAPTER 27

"You owe me fifty bucks."

Harley turned to find the livestock manager pointing his dirty index finger at her. She was standing outside Matilda's pen, feeding the pig her lunch. She shoved one of Aunt Wilma's Little Debbies through the pen's wires and watched as Matilda chewed it.

"Sir?" Harley said, looking at the man over her shoulder.

"That pig of yours chewed a hole through her pen last night, trying to get at a candy apple some kid dropped on the ground." He pointed to a small section of Matilda's pen that had been patched up with duct tape.

"I apologize," Harley said, "but fifty dollars for a piece of duct tape?"

"Forty-nine of that is for the inconvenience."

Harley could feel Matilda pulling at her dress through the pen's wires, and she tried to shoo the pig away with her hand. "Just a minute, Matilda," she said, patiently. "Let me finish my conversation."

"Judges say if she does it again, she'll be disqualified."

"Okay." Harley was about to concede when she looked down in horror to see Matilda had chewed a hole in her dress, a huge hole.

"I can see your granny drawers," the livestock manager said, grinning with his three teeth.

"What?"

"Your granny drawers."

Harley looked down at her dress again and shrieked. Indeed, through the gaping hole, you could see her cotton panties. To make matters worse, the panties were a pair Aunt Wilma had given her for Christmas the year before, with a slogan that read: *No Peeking Until Christmas.*

Her gaze shot up to the livestock manager in embarrassment. How much of her had he seen?

He held up his hand in a solemn swear, and in a sarcastic tone, he said, "Now, don't you worry none. I was somehow, by the grace of God, able to forgo temptation."

Harley made a face, then grabbed her dress and bunched it together in the middle, closing the hole. She needed to find something, anything to cover it. Her eyes darted about the festival grounds, searching for a solution. *One of Tina's aprons,* she thought. *Yes, that would do!*

She hurried toward Tina's shop on Main Street, leaving the livestock manager at Matilda's pen. Behind her, she could feel his eyes smiling into her back.

"And I promise," he said, snickering, "I won't peek 'til Christmas."

Pushing her way through crowds of festival goers, Harley wondered what else could happen, how she could be humiliated any more. Then, her chest collided with Eric Winston's, and she received her answer. A smiling Eric, impeccably handsome and tailored and barbered in a cashmere sweater and jeans, grabbed Harley by her elbows to keep her from falling.

"Harley," he said, rebalancing her body on the pavement, "what a pleasant surprise."

She clamped her hand over her crotch before he could notice the hole and the granny panties. "Eric," she said, forcing a smile. She was so embarrassed and nervous, she found herself dancing back and forth on the pavement as she held her crotch.

"Is everything okay?" Eric asked, searching her face with concern. "You look rather..."

Harley labored to think of an excuse, any excuse. "I'm sorry, Eric," she said, pulling away from him, "but I have to...I have to...pee."

Hurrying back through the crowds, she berated herself, wondering why she couldn't have thought of something better. *I have to pee! I have to pee! Are you kidding me?* That might've been worse than the hole in her dress and the granny panties.

At last, she made her way to the sidewalk and then to Tina's Treats. To her surprise, she found Uncle Tater's antique toilet stationed outside the shop, and Opha Mae Shaw standing beside it, adding water to the flowers in the bowl.

"Well, howdy there, Harley!" Opha Mae said, raising her watering can from the bowl.

Opha Mae noticed Harley had her hand clamped over her dress, and raised her brows. "You all right, darlin'?" she asked. "Why you got your hands over your no-no spot? You gotta go potty or somethin'?" Opha Mae looked down at the toilet bowl in consideration, then back at Harley again. "Well, I reckon I could just let you go in here, but my flares, you see."

"That's perfectly all right, Opha Mae," Harley said, rushing past the old woman and her toilet. "I think I can make it."

Inside Tina's shop, a crowd of people was lined up behind the bakery case, gaping at the assortment of cookies and cakes and pies as they pondered their selections. Tina stood behind the counter, grinning, as she pulled desserts from the case with gloved hands and wrapped them in parchment.

"Tina," Harley said, waving from the front door. "Tina, I need you for a second."

Tina handed a bag of baked goods to a departing customer and headed in Harley's direction. "What's wrong?" she asked, wiping her hands on her apron. "You look constipated or something."

"I don't have to go the bathroom in any way. I have...a problem."

Tina motioned for Harley to follow her to the bakery's back room, which housed the kitchen.

There, among the prep tables and ovens and stand mixers, Harley removed her hands from her dress and let Tina assess the damage.

She squealed with laughter. "Let me guess," she said. "Matilda."

"Yes."

"And those awful panties! They're like man repeller."

"They're comfortable."

"Well," Tina said, still giggling, "I'm sorry, Harley, but I don't really see how I can help you."

"I need one of your aprons."

Tina considered. "Well, I have a load of them in the washer right now, but they won't be dry for a while. Let me go look in the linen closet." She walked to the back corner of the kitchen and then to a wardrobe by one of the sinks. She removed an apron from the wardrobe and returned to Harley.

"Here you go," she said.

Harley's glimmer of hope diminished. The apron was hot pink and lined with black lace. A giant crocheted bun smiled from its center with a slogan beneath it that read: *Bakers Knead Hot Buns.*

"And you're sure you don't have any other clean ones?" Harley asked.

"Sorry, sweetie," Tina said, smiling. "It's this or the granny panties."

And what was worse, she was about to pay a visit to Beau Arson.

CHAPTER 28

*W*ithin the hour Harley arrived at Muscadine Farms only to find the resort wholly deserted. Not one car filled the large parking lot and Boonie Davenport's blockade was dismantled. She remembered Stevie having said Beau had sent their entourage away. By the appearance of things, the order still stood. But where were Stevie and Marcus? At least, she thought, they would've been there to keep an eye on Beau as they always had. And yet everything seemed deserted.

Harley parked her truck in front of the inn and made her way inside. Entering the dining room was like entering a cave, the entire room veiled in darkness, the crystal chandelier, acting as a sun during business hours, had retreated to the shadows of the vaulted ceiling, the only source of light coming from small candles, emanating tiny beacons of light from the center of the room, gathered around something, someone.

Beau was seated with his back turned and his head bowed, dark waves of hair shrouding his face and his bare chest as he embraced his electric guitar, transfixed in a resonant, soul-filled melody full of sustained notes with decidedly classical undertones.

Harley stood watching him from the back of the room, listening to the song's beauty, one of yearning, of sadness, reading like a love letter or a prayer. Beau's back moved in time with the slow rhythms, the golden flesh exposing a pair of wings, wings of deep indigo, flickering in the candlelight, extending the entire width of his shoulders, the feathers tapering down toward the small of this back.

Then as if he sensed Harley's presence, knew she was watching him, he looked over his shoulder and the two locked eyes. But he did not stop playing. He lowered his head once more, his body melding into the guitar, the music climbing to a crescendo before it at last filtered down to a soft melody, slowly dying to silence.

Harley Henrickson stood in wonder, her emotions still roused by the hauntingly beautiful song. How could something so beautiful, so ethereal, as if written by angels, come from such a rough-hewn man, so dark, so flawed, so human. Beau Arson had been given a gift of supernatural proportions, but what power had bestowed that gift?

Quietly she approached the room's center and stood over Beau's still-bowed head. Though his face remained shrouded by waves of dark hair, she could see he'd been mourning Patrick Middleton, and he now hid his face in embarrassment from having expressed an emotion he rarely felt but was too exhausted to conceal.

"Harley Henrickson," he said, his whiskey and cigar voice deepened by grief. He raised his reddened eyes from his guitar and met hers.

Harley floundered under his piercing gaze. He was like an old grizzly bear in a cave, one that had been awakened from a long, deep sleep in mid-winter, awakened before he was ready.

"I...I...need to speak with you about something," she muttered. "I mean...if it's okay, of course."

He lowered his gaze back to his guitar, then ran his calloused fingers along the spine. "What did you think?" he asked.

"Think?"

"The music."

Harley paused. Beau Arson always seemed to surprise her. She never knew what to expect of him, what he would say, what he would do, how he would react. She could not read him, could not predict him like so many others, and it left her unsettled. "It was beautiful," she said in truth, though she would've been afraid to say anything likewise. "Did you write it?"

He slid the guitar from his lap and placed it on a stand beside his chair. "I did," he said. "Just now."

Harley raised her brows. She'd assumed the piece had taken him months to compose, as it had sounded so technically challenging and seamlessly performed. *And it probably would take most people that long,* she thought, if they could even create something of that caliber.

But, of course, this was not the case with Beau Arson. It came naturally to him, almost like a rote endeavor, just as the average person brushed their teeth, combed their hair, or tied their shoes each day. Beau Arson picked up a guitar, and he created, each day of his life. Harley wondered if the pain and sadness Beau carried inside him, had carried inside him since he was a child, fueled his creativity, acting as a muse, lifting his art to heights not otherwise reached.

He rose from his chair, and as he rose, his body extending to its full height, Harley seemed to lessen in his presence, cowering, if not physically, then at least internally. He stood over her, guiding his muscled arms through the sleeves of his shirt, and though she was not as susceptible to temptations of the flesh as others were, she could see, at least theoretically, the attraction women felt for Beau Arson, the "spell" as Jed put it, he cast upon them. It wasn't just that his body was physically beautiful and powerful, but that there was something of the animal about him, a virility that spoke to primitive, forbidden desires.

"You bake?" he asked, buttoning up his shirt to the chest.

"Huh?" Harley said, pulled from her reverie.

He gestured to the apron Tina had loaned her that morning.

"Oh," she said, feeling her cheeks color. "Yes. That. Well, you see, Matilda...my pig...she ate a hole in my dress at the festival this morning, and you could see my granny panties...I mean my underwear through the hole, so I borrowed this apron from a friend of mine who's a baker."

He released a gravelly chuckle. "Harley Henrickson, you never cease to surprise me. So," he said, clearly amused, "did you get any takers?"

"Pardon?" Then she realized he was referring to the apron's logo: *Bakers Knead Hot Buns.* "Well," she said, in serious consideration, "there was a drunk guy on Main Street this morning. He said I could knead his hot buns anytime."

"There you go," she said smiling.

"I don't know," Harley said, "it didn't look like he had many teeth. He probably can't eat much *but* buns."

A roar of laughter rolled from Beau Arson, one that surprised Harley, not only because it came from him, but because she hadn't been trying to be funny. Realizing the ridiculousness of it all, she began laughing too.

When the amusement had settled, and the two had returned to a comfortable silence, Harley approached the purpose of her visit. "Beau," she said, "there really is something I need to speak with you about."

Registering the seriousness of her request, he drew a chair from a nearby table and gestured toward it. "Please," he said with kindness, "have a seat. And would you like something to drink? I can make a pretty decent cocktail, but probably nothing compared to yours."

"I'll just have a scotch. Neat." She didn't usually drink during the day, but she needed something to help her get through the impending conversation.

Beau filled two glasses with shots of scotch and returned, handing one to Harley. "So what is it you'd like to talk to me about?" he said, returning to his seat.

Harley took a sip of scotch and savored the smokiness as it burned down her throat. She drew in a breath and in a soft voice, said, "Beau, I know about Patrick. I know what he did to you...to your mother."

Beau swirled his scotch, watching it collect on the sides of the glass. "You do?"

"Yes. I know that he killed your mother."

Sadness fell over his face, and his expression regained that haunted look. "How did you find out?"

"It's a long story. Let's just say I pieced it together over time."

"All those years," he said, shaking his head. "All those years I secretly always wondered why he'd taken an interest in me, why he was always helping me out. Nobody else sure as heck ever did. It was so strange. He just seemed to appear out of nowhere one day when I was kid, started showing up at the Boys and Girls Club after school, volunteering in the afternoons, tutoring me, mentoring me.

"I had no idea at the time that he'd already set up a trust fund for me, that if anything were to ever happen to him, I'd be taken care of, at least financially anyway. I asked him one time why he did all of it, why he helped me out. He said he'd lost a son once, and he wanted to help out another boy who would've been about his son's age. He even said he wanted to adopt me, at one point, but being a single guy who never planned to get remarried, it wasn't appropriate. So...he became like a benefactor to me instead."

"And you never knew the truth until he was diagnosed with cancer," Harley said.

"No. He said he was dying and that he wanted to confess the truth to me before he died. That he hoped I could forgive him, that maybe his kindness to me over the years would somehow make amends for what he'd done." His voice trailed off, and he added, "It didn't." He took a sip of scotch, and after rolling it around his mouth in thought, and swallowing, he said, "I'm not even mad anymore, I'm...just..."

"Sad?" Harley said.

"Yeah."

At that moment, the back door swung open and Marcus appeared, a bandage taped across the bridge of his nose. He looked as if he were about to ask Beau a question, then stopped when he spotted Harley.

"Oh, it's you," he said, glaring at her. "What are you doing here?"

"Leave us, Marcus," Beau said quietly.

Marcus turned to Beau and began apologizing. "I'm sorry, Beau. I mean, I don't know how she got in here. We thought the doors were all locked, I swear. She must've broken in somewhere." He returned his attention to Harley and made a face. "And gosh, Deliverance, you look even more hideous than usual."

Like a grizzly bear, Beau rose from his seat, his anger hurling like a fist across the room at Marcus. "I said leave us!"

Marcus stood stunned, his eyes moving from Beau to Harley, then back to Beau again. His look of surprise cowered to hurt, and he retreated through the open door, closing it quietly behind him.

"I apologize," Beau said, returning to his seat and working to calm his anger. "I care for Marcus. I do. We have a long history, but he tries my patience sometimes." He turned to Harley, and with an expression of compassion in his eyes, he said, "and he can be cruel...cruel to those who deserve it the least."

He returned to his glass of scotch. "Now, where was I?" He gathered his thoughts and continued. "Yes, so when I was growing up, Patrick was the only person except...." He stopped himself midsentence and decided to take another course. "He was the only guy who ever gave a crap about me. And the fact that he lied to me about something so important, so crucial to my very existence is just unforgivable."

He rested the glass on the table beside him and ran his fingers through the dark waves that fell across his forehead. "I knew nothing about my mother until he told me about her the other day. He said that when it happened, he'd just moved to Notchey Creek after losing his wife and baby, that he was deeply depressed, and that he'd been drinking at one of the bars in town that night.

"As he was driving home, he rounded a curve on Maple Bluff. He'd cut the curve too close, he said, and before he had time to throw on the brakes, he hit a car that was parked on the edge of the cliff. His head must've hit the steering wheel with the impact, he said, and he blacked out of consciousness for a bit. When he came to, the car he'd hit was on fire, and the front end was dangling off the edge of the bluff. He ran over and saw that there was a woman inside, a woman he said was my mother. She was already dead from the crash, but that I was in the back, crying in my car seat. The child locks were activated on the back door, so he broke the rear window with a rock and pulled me from the car before it careened down the bluff and exploded.

"Then, he took me to a Catholic monastery that was close by, Our Lady of the Mountains, and left me on the doorstep. The nuns there were French Carmelites. They named me Beau because they said I was the most beautiful baby they'd ever seen." He gave half a laugh. "Hard to believe now, isn't it?" He shook his head and resumed his story. "And then they gave me the last name Arson because of the soot I had all over my body. They said it was a miracle that a baby so covered in ash and soot didn't have any burns anywhere on him. They said I'd 'risen from the ashes unscathed.'"

He unfolded his leather jacket from the back of his chair and drew his arms through the sleeves, buttoning it at the chest.

"I've been thinking a lot about my mother the last few days," he said. "Wondering if she'd lived, what my life would've been like. If it would've all been different. Having a family. And now I'll never know, will I? All because of Patrick Middleton."

"And he thought he'd found your father too, hadn't he?" Harley said. "As another form of atonement for what he'd done?"

"Yes." He removed its guitar from its stand and placed it inside a black carrying case, which he then buckled to a close. "After Patrick told me the truth about my mother, he said he'd been looking for my father and had found him recently. He said my father was a vet who'd fallen on some hard times since he'd returned from overseas. That he had PTSD and it had led to some substance abuse problems and bouts of homelessness here and there. His name was Martin Evans and Patrick had arranged for the two of us to meet."

"Did you consider it?"

"No." He lifted the guitar case by its handle, and held it down by his side. "To tell you the truth, I'd rather just put all of this behind me. Sometimes I think I was better off just not knowing anything about my past. And this Martin Evans person could be anybody really. Who knows if he's even my real father? Maybe Patrick got it all wrong. Maybe this man would be somebody who'd just try to cash in on my fame?"

Harley did not mention she'd found Martin Evans, or at least the man she presumed to be Martin Evans, in the ditch in Briarwood Park, and no one had seen him since. Even though Beau seemed resigned to move on with his life, she thought this might only add to his hurt and confusion.

"The police know you were acquainted with Patrick," she said.

"Yes, your sheriff made that perfectly clear when he came by to see me earlier. He's convinced I drugged Patrick, that I killed him. And I did give him that bottle of whiskey they found at his house, that's true, but it was sealed when I gave it to him, unopened, just your label…."

He looked over at Harley with a playful grin on his face. "Wait," he said, "maybe you…"

Harley returned his smile. Despite her suspicions of Beau Arson, she found herself liking him.

He shook his head and took a sip of scotch. "I don't know, but it seems like your sheriff is out to get me."

Harley recalled her meeting with Jed at the shop that morning, about his suspicions about Beau, and his jealousy surrounding Cheri. "Well, I think part of the problem is his girlfriend, Cheri," she said. "Jed thinks she's attracted to you, that maybe something might've happened between the two of you."

Beau considered this, but Cheri's name seemed to hold no meaning for him. "I don't know her."

"She's a model. Tall. Icy blonde hair. Very thin. Wears black stiletto boots."

"That sounds like half of L.A."

"Well, you might not remember her, but she certainly remembers you, and she's not helping you make friends with Jed. Cheri is Jed's weakness, you see, and she keeps him hanging by a string most of the time."

"I'm sorry for him," he said, "but women like that are a dime a dozen. She might've come onto me, yes…a lot of them do, but I don't remember her, and there was nothing on my part. I'm not saying that I'm an angel or that I'm an innocent. There's plenty of things I've done that I'm not proud of, especially in my past, but I don't indulge in women who are in relationships of any kind. It's too messy and not worth my time. I like things easy. Unattached."

He looked squarely at Harley, the seriousness returning to his face. "And I didn't kill Patrick Middleton. I know that's really what you want to know. I was angry with him, yes, and it's true that I never wanted to see him again, but I didn't hate him, even then, even after everything he'd done to me. I loved him. And I still love him, as much as I don't want to. What he did to me…it didn't make me to want to kill him. It broke my heart."

He zipped up his leather jacket and picked up his guitar case again. "Mind giving me a lift, kiddo?"

"Where are we going?" she asked.

"To the festival. I promised them I'd play. And I'm not one to break promises."

"GREAT TRUCK," Beau Arson said, his elbow hanging out the open window as they made their way down the winding road from Muscadine Farms. "My first truck was like this. Except mine was a '62. One of the families I lived with when I was a teenager…the dad was a mechanic. He taught me how to fix it up. We put in a whole new engine, new tires, everything. That guy was my favorite of all of them, of the ones that fostered me. We still keep in touch occasionally, cards every once in a while. I wished I could've stayed there at their house. But his wife had a baby about a year after that, and they couldn't take the responsibility of another kid, so I went back into the system. But I'll never forget that summer we fixed up that truck. Man oh man, how I wish I'd kept it all these years."

"It was a similar situation with this truck and me," Harley said, keeping her eyes focused on the road. "My grandfather bought it for me when I was only thirteen. Granddaddy said he thought it'd take us at least three years to refurbish it into anything drivable, and by that time I'd have my license. And he was right. It did take us about that much time. I think we finished it just a month shy of my sixteenth birthday, and I've had it ever since. I don't know if I'll ever be able to retire it. I'll just have to keep adding new engines."

"You do that, Harley," Beau said. "Don't ever let it go."

They arrived in downtown Notchey Creek, where the morning crowds filled the sidewalks and streets with a sea of buzzing bodies. Harley stopped her truck in front of the sawhorses which had cordoned off the festival area from the remainder of downtown. Before she could put the truck into park, Alveda Hamilton was tapping on the driver's side window.

"What do you think you're doing?" she said.

"I just need to—"

"You just need to," she said in a mimicking tone, rolling her eyes. "You just need to move this truck out of the festival grounds right now before you get a citation. You can't park it here."

Beau leaned across the seat where Alveda could see him. "Harley parks where she wants, or there won't be any performance this afternoon."

"Why, Mr. Arson!" Alveda said, adopting a sycophantic tone. "Why, I had no idea it was you. What a pleasure. My apologies. I am so—"

"This truck still isn't moving, lady," Beau said, glancing at his watch.

"Why, yes, of course," she said, motioning to the festival workers. "Right this way."

Two teenage boys, dressed in Pioneer Days sweatshirts, removed two sawhorses from the perimeter, opening a path wide enough for Harley's truck. As they passed through, the two boys stared and pointed at Beau, who sat unaware in the passenger seat with his tattooed forearm still hanging out the window.

"That's him," one boy said to the other. "Oh, my gosh, I can't believe that's really him."

"Dude," the other boy said, "he's even bigger in person."

"You can just pull over there," Beau said, ignoring the boys as he pointed to the white gazebo in the middle of the town square.

When they arrived at the gazebo, Harley put the truck into park and turned to Beau. "Are you performing solo?"

"Nah," he said. "I've called in some reinforcements." He popped open the passenger side door, and with his right hand gripped to the truck's roof, he hoisted his long, muscular body from the seat. He grabbed his guitar case from the truck bed, and after closing the door, he lowered his head inside the open window and looked at Harley. "You're a good kid. You know that, Harley Henrickson?"

Then he disappeared from the open window and walked inside the VIP tent stationed alongside the festival stage.

CHAPTER 29

"Howdy, Harley," Uncle Tater called over a crowd of festival goers who'd gathered around him on the sidewalk on Main Street. As promised, he'd stationed his moonshine still in front of Smoky Mountain Spirits and was in the process of conducting a distillation demonstration. "Wilmer's inside the store yonder," he said. "Already got things set up."

He turned back to the small crowd and resumed his demonstration. "Now this here's called a thump keg," he said, the audience watching him with rapt attention. "Some folks calls it a doubler because, you see, what it lets you do is distill your output a second time. That way you don't have to run your distillate through the still twice. Amazing contraption, I reckon. Changed the course of moonshine making."

His voice trailed off as Harley entered the store, shutting the door behind her.

Aunt Wilma stood behind the check-out counter, ringing up purchases. She wore a purple velvet dress with gold fringe, the front slit exposing a pair of sausage casing legs in fishnet stockings. A wide-brimmed feathered hat covered her Oompa Loompa wig, and a choker peeked from the roll underneath her chin.

Beside her, with rote movement, an always silent Uncle Buck placed bottles of liquor in paper sleeves and handed them to departing customers. Uncle Buck didn't need to dress up for the festival, Harley thought. For as long as she could remember, he'd resembled the farmer in the painting, *American Gothic,* with the same dour expression, the same overalls, white shirt, and dark jacket. She'd only heard him speak twice in her life and that was to his turkeys.

"Mornin,' Harley," Aunt Wilma said, grinning. She handed a receipt to a departing customer and said, "Now you enjoy the festival, you hear, and come back and see us soon."

Wilma left Uncle Buck behind the counter and walked over to her great-niece. "Oh, Harley, don't you look right cute! Opha Mae done good makin' them outfits, didn't she? Matilda get hers?"

"Oh, yes."

"Guess what I am," she said, fanning her dress and flicking the feather on her hat.

Harley pondered the best and most delicate response to the question. "A lady of the night?"

"I ain't no prostitute, Harley," she said, defensively. She puffed out her chest. "I'm a madame."

As if that lended more dignity to her costume.

"Anyhow," she said, "it's been right busy here, I reckon. We're gonna make a nice profit off this festival." She looked past Harley to the back storage area. "Oh, and Tina's back yonder. Gettin' some more stuff for her recipes."

Harley left Wilma, passing through a sea of customers to the back room. Tina stood on a step ladder, removing a bottle of whiskey from the shelf. And if Aunt Wilma was a madame, then Tina was one of her employees. Their costumes were nearly identical except Tina's dress was red and she wore a black feather boa around her neck. Two stiletto booties peeked from the black fringe of her dress.

"Need some help, Tina?" Harley asked, entering the back room.

"Nah, I got it."

She removed a bottle from the shelf and groaned as she climbed down the ladder, her stiletto booties tapping against the rungs.

"Whiskey balls, whiskey balls," she said. "I swear that's all anybody wants today. I just can't seem to keep the darn things stocked."

"Then you shouldn't make them so delicious," Harley said, smiling.

Tina turned around and looked at her, then started laughing. "Lordy, that dress and apron look funnier every time I see them."

Tina saw the look on Harley's face, then swallowed her laughter. "Did Jed find you?"

"No. He was looking for me?"

"Oh, yeah. Everywhere. He came by my shop twice and then this place twice. Didn't say what he wanted, but I figured it had something to do with Patrick's death."

Perhaps they've found more evidence, Harley thought.

"Anyway, I gotta get back to the store," Tina said. "I tell you, I'm makin' a killin' from this thing, but boy am I slammed."

"Good luck," Harley said, watching her friend as she slipped out the back door.

Harley retrieved a series of bottles from the shelf and placed them on the prep counter, along with her cocktail shaker and spoon. For Pioneer Days, she'd planned a special recipe in advance, one consisting of Tennessee whiskey, apple brandy, apple cider, and a splash of vanilla liquor. She hoped to blend the spirit of the festival's historical significance with its fall setting.

She poured the "Pioneer Punch" into a large silver punch bowl and carried it into the main room where she placed it on the bar. She retrieved cups from the storage area, but before she could arrange them in any configuration, Wilma called to her from the checkout counter. "Hey, Harley, we got any more of that apple brandy, or are we clean out?"

"I think I have some more in my truck. I can get it."

"Would you, honey?"

Harley passed through the store and to the back room, then to the parking lot. As she reached into the truck bed to retrieve a case of apple brandy, a police cruiser pulled up beside her and Jed Turner rolled down the driver's side window.

"Get in," he said.

CHAPTER 30

*H*arley looked at Jed over her shoulder, still holding the case of apple brandy in her arms. "But Jed, we're right in the middle of the festival. Aunt Wilma and Uncle Buck need my help."

He reached over and pushed the passenger side door open. "I said get in."

Reluctantly, Harley walked over to the cruiser and lowered herself into the passenger seat, closing the door behind her.

Jed put the car into gear, and the two rode in silence, taking the long alleyway connecting downtown to Briarwood Avenue.

"Are you going to tell me what this is about?" she asked.

He remained silent, keeping his eyes fixed on the road. Something troubling had happened, Harley surmised, and while Jed hadn't wanted to bring her along, something had made it imperative.

As they progressed down Briarwood Avenue, the downtown buildings morphed into the tall pines of Briarwood Park. The park was closed because of the festival, and when they reached the entrance, two policemen appeared at the locked gates and opened them for Jed.

Jed parked in the public lot, empty except for two police cars and

Eric Winston's navy BMW. It was then Harley knew the cause of Jed's strange behavior.

He rose from the cruiser and instructed her to follow him on foot along one of the many dirt trails. As they walked, Harley could hear the festival noise in the distance, the sound of a mandolin above the low roar of street vendors and pedestrian foot traffic on Main Street. About a quarter-mile down the trail, Jed stopped at the periphery and said, "Just this way. Not much further."

They were off the path then, hiking through beds of pine needles and thick growth forest. Not many visitors ventured off the park's well-marked trails, and Harley wondered how Jed had found his way back.

As they drew nearer, she could hear voices ahead and a faint line of yellow crime scene tape stretched across the trees. Beyond the crime scene tape stood two police officers, a photographer, and Eric Winston, who was crouched by what was presumably a body.

At the sound of their approach, Eric rose to his feet. "Jed," he said somberly. "Harley."

The three of them stood over the body, looking down.

"Is this the man you saw outside the park the other day?" Jed asked.

"Yes."

There was no doubt about that. The same scarred face. The same tattered clothes. The same haunted eyes, staring up to the heavens as Patrick Middleton's had. But unlike Patrick, this man had a wound on the right side of his head, a gash caked and congealed with blood, never to heal.

Jed cleared his throat. "He was found by a hiker early this morning. We're trying to keep things hush-hush until the festival's over."

Eric looked at them with concern and shook his head. "Whoever killed this man desperately wanted him dead. So much so as to kill him twice."

"Now slow down, Eric," Jed said. "What do yo mean by 'killed him twice'?"

Eric lowered his gaze to the man's body. "Well, first, I think the murderer drugged him, probably using the same drugs he or she used on Patrick Middleton. That would explain the aberrant behavior you described the other day, Harley. And then when the drugs didn't kill him, I suspect the killer took a branch, presumably from the woods here and finished the deed."

Jed shook his head. "But why kill him? From what they said at the shelter, he was harmless."

Because he knew or found out something he shouldn't have, Harley thought.

"And there is something else odd about this," Eric said. "Whoever hit this man, hit him with a great deal of strength and anger. But why use drugs to kill a man so passively the first time and then a branch or club to beat him to death the second time?"

"Are you suggesting we have two killers on our hands?" Jed asked.

"Possibly." Eric looked to Harley. "Do you notice anything different about him? Anything unusual?"

"Yes," she said. "His dog tags. They're missing."

Eric lowered himself to the man's body, and guided his gloved finger along the man's neck. "There are some slight abrasions along here. Looks like whoever killed him, ripped the tags from his neck as well." He looked up at Jed and Harley. "Hoping to conceal any identifying information, I imagine."

"They shouldn't have troubled," Harley said. "I know who he was."

"What?" Jed barked.

"His name was Martin Evans," she said. "He was an Army veteran, and at one time, Susan Thompson's boyfriend...and Beau Arson's father."

Jed's mouth dropped open. "Beau Arson's father?"

Harley nodded.

"And who is Susan Thompson again?" Jed asked.

"She was the nineteen-year-old girl who was killed by Patrick Middleton in a drunk driving accident over thirty years ago. Prior to that, she was Martin Evans's girlfriend when was deployed to Afghanistan and went missing in action. Susan was pregnant during Martin's deployment and later gave birth to a baby boy, Beau Arson. When Beau was only a few months old, he and his mother's car was struck by an inebriated Patrick Middleton on Maple Bluff on Halloween night. Patrick was able to remove the baby from the back seat before the car careened down the bluff and burst into flames. That's why the baby's body was never found. At the time, everyone just assumed it had been carried off by wild animals. Then Patrick took Beau to Our Lady of the Mountains, where he was taken in by the clergy and placed in the foster care system."

Harley had never seen Jed Turner speechless, but this time he was.

The always calm and collected Eric Winston, however, merely looked at Harley inquisitively. "Are you sure this man was Martin Evans?" he asked.

"Not absolutely," she said, "but I have strong evidence that I believe proves it. You see, when Patrick found out he had cancer and only months to live, he decided to tell Beau Arson the truth. He'd carried the guilt over Susan's death for years, her ghost haunting him day after day, night after night. He wanted to atone for his sins, and when he found out Martin Evans was still alive, he thought he could reunite Beau with his father. So he invited Martin here and planned to meet him at Bud's Pool Hall. But Martin got the day wrong and ended up going to Bud's the night before. Then, not finding Patrick there, he went to his house instead, where he disappeared until Tina and I found him outside the park the next morning."

"And now both men are dead," Jed said.

Harley began pacing back and forth in the woods, her mind searching for answers, "Martin Evans," she said, thinking aloud. "What made his presence here so threatening? What did he find out? What did he know?"

Suddenly, a flash of intuition dawned on Harley, and she took flight to leave them.

"Harley!" Jed yelled at her receding back as she ran back through the woods. "What are you doing? Where are you going?"

"I'm sorry, Jed," she called over her shoulder. "I have to go. There's someone I need to speak to."

CHAPTER 31

*C*ynthia Thompson's robin's egg blue bungalow was just one of many identical homes along the tree-lined street known as Cypress Avenue. Each house boasted a perfectly manicured front lawn and a paved walkway that ran from the sidewalk to the front porch, each porch graced with a set of rocking chairs and a porch swing. Harley's grandfather said the houses were built after World War II for returning soldiers and their young wives, a structural reminder of the Baby Boom.

She parked her truck on the street and started up the paved walkway to the home. The curtains were closed and the house silent, but several pots of chrysanthemums lining the porch steps suggested someone lived there and that person was an active gardener. She approached the front door and rang the bell.

No answer.

She tried a second time.

Again no answer.

Harley felt her hopefulness depleting. Maybe Cynthia wasn't home. Or perhaps she was taking a nap. Or maybe she was home but did not answer the door for strangers.

"Mrs. Thompson," Harley said, knocking on the screen door. "Mrs.

Thompson, my name is Harley Henrickson. I live just a few streets down from you on Poplar. I was wondering if you might have a moment to speak with me."

Silence.

Harley turned with resignation to leave. She would have to find another way to glean the information she needed. But how?

Then she heard the front door unlock and the sound of the door being opened. She turned with anticipation to find a senior woman peeking from the crack in the open door, eyeing her suspiciously. The woman wore a lavender velour tracksuit and white tennis shoes, a decorative chain dangling from her wire-rimmed glasses. Before her arrival, Harley assumed she must've been engaged in doing cross-words, needlework, or reading.

"Mrs. Thompson," she said. "Hello."

"What did you say your name was?" the woman asked, still peering through the crack in the door.

"Harley," she said with a smile. "My name is Harley Henrickson."

The woman's squinting eyes widened. "Jackson Henrickson's grandbaby?"

"Yes."

"I always did like Jackson," she said, softening. "He was a very decent man."

Before Harley could respond, Cynthia added, "And you promise me you're not trying to sell me something? That you're not trying to con me out of some of my money?"

"No, ma'am," she said. "Of course not."

"You've been at the festival, I see," she said, looking at Harley's costume.

"Yes. I own Smoky Mountain Spirits on Main Street. And all of the vendors, as you know, are required to dress up."

"And you left the festival to come here and speak to me?"

"Yes. You see it's quite important. I need to talk to you about your daughter, Susan…and Patrick Middleton."

Surprise flashed across Cynthia Thompson's face, and she grabbed the doorknob, propping her weight against it. "Patrick Middleton?"

The mentioning of Patrick's name seemed to lend more credibility to Harley's visit, and Cynthia opened the door wider. "Patrick called me last week," she said, "not long before he died." She motioned for Harley to come inside. "I couldn't make sense of it."

The small house was warm and cozy, dimly lit by a crackling fire in the hearth and two lamps, a floor lamp in the corner of the room, and a table lamp beside Cynthia's wingback chair. A book of crosswords lay open on the side table, a pencil resting in the spine.

"I apologize for my rudeness," she said. "You just can't be too careful when you get to my age and you live alone. It seems like someone is always calling me on the phone, trying to sell me something or telling me I've won a prize, if only I'll send them my Social Security number and my bank account information. I may be eighty-two, but I'm not gullible. I know about elder fraud. Even if that does make me rude."

"No, Mrs. Thompson," Harley said. "You're right to act the way you do. It's good to be vigilant."

"Take a seat, won't you?" she said, motioning to the couch opposite her wingback chair. "Would you like something to drink?"

"No, ma'am. That's very kind of you, but it's not necessary."

"So," Cynthia said, lowering herself into her chair, "what is it you needed to tell me about Susan? You do know that this Halloween marked the thirty-second anniversary of her death."

"I did," Harley answered.

"And I'd wondered why Patrick Middleton of all people would've been calling me out of the blue on that very same day. And now you arrive here, too, wanting to speak with me about Susan."

Harley placed her hands in her lap and tried to think of the best way to proceed. Deciding the direct approach was best, she told Mrs. Thompson everything she knew, from Patrick Middleton having accidentally killed Susan in the car wreck, to Martin Evans's presence in town, and his subsequent death.

When she had finished, a stillness fell over the room like a blanket, and the two women sat in silence, listening to the fire crackle in the hearth and to the grandfather clock tick in the corner of the room.

Harley did not know how much time passed as they sat there, and she did not dare speak first. After all, it had been thirty-two years since Susan's death, thirty-two years of wondering who had killed her, and Mrs. Thompson needed time to digest and recover.

At last Cynthia spoke. "Never in all these years," she said, "did I think it could be Patrick Middleton. Never. All those times I saw him in town, passed him on the street, and he would always smile and speak to me so pleasantly...all the while he knew he'd killed my Susan. How could he live with himself?"

"I don't think he did," Harley said. "Not happily anyway. It haunted him for the rest of his life."

"And he'd found Martin too?" she asked. "Brought him here? For the same reason? To confess?"

"Yes, and to reunite him with his son."

She deflected her gaze to the floor, sadness softening her voice. "I never knew the baby. Susan and I had a falling out, you see, not long after she became pregnant. I didn't approve of her being an unmarried woman with a child, and I told her so. Martin was a nice enough boy, but the two weren't married, you see, and there he was being deployed to Afghanistan. I voiced my disapproval to Susan, and she moved out of the house not long after that." Her voice began to crack. "I never saw her again."

"Where did she go when she moved out?" Harley asked.

"She moved in with the Johnsons. Arthur and Pearl. They live in that big Tudor over in Briarwood. Pearl was volunteering at the high school when Susan met her. The two became very close, and they began spending more and more time with each other. I suppose the Johnsons were never able to have any children of their own, and Pearl, I think, considers herself some sort of mother to the community. Always helping out children and their families."

Harley agreed that this was indeed true, and mentioned that Pearl had babysat her as a child too.

"Do you have any photos?" Harley asked, looking about the room.

"Of Susan?"

"Yes, of Susan, but I was really hoping to see a photo of Martin."

"I'm sure I probably have some somewhere," she said, lifting herself from the wingback chair. She walked across the living room to a large oak bureau and slid open the center cabinet. Inside were several old photo albums, stacked in two rows. She ran her finger along the spines, searching for the right year. Finding it, she removed the album, placed it on top of the bureau, and began thumbing through the pages. Photos flashed from the pages as Cynthia skimmed through them. At last, she stopped paging and tapped her index finger against one of the pictures.

"Here he is," she said, beckoning Harley to join her.

Harley walked over to the bureau and peered over Cynthia's shoulder to the photo album. "There he is in his uniform," she said, pointing to the young man in the photograph. "Not long after he met Susan. Before he fought overseas."

And there he was at last. The young Martin Evans, young and unscarred and hopeful, before combat and post-traumatic stress and substance abuse had mangled his features into something unrecognizable, something that had protected a long-held secret.

Harley placed her hand over her mouth and gasped.

"Are you all right?" Cynthia asked, staring at her with concern. "You look like you've just seen a ghost."

Harley's breath remained caught in her throat, and she found it hard to speak. "I'm sorry, Mrs. Thompson," she said, struggling to pull her truck keys from her pocket. "I have to go now." She made her way to the front door. "I'm really sorry about what happened to Susan. I've never had a child. I don't know what it is like to carry someone in my body for nine months, to love them unconditionally, only to lose them."

"Wait, Harley, please," Cynthia said, following behind her. "I think there's something else you need to know." She placed her hand on Harley's shoulder and the young woman turned around, their eyes meeting. "I loved Susan...so very dearly...and I did consider her my daughter, but I'm not the one who carried her inside of me. I'm not the one who gave birth to her. You see, Susan was adopted."

CHAPTER 32

The largest crowd the Pioneer Days festival had ever seen flooded the stage area where Beau Arson was performing. Several local musicians had joined Beau on stage, and to get things started, he'd asked them to play a few measures of a song, any song. The group of smiling male and female musicians chose Earl Scruggs's "Foggy Mountain Breakdown," and after listening to a few measures, Beau repeated them note-for-note with ease. The exercise continued until they were playing the entire song together.

Just when the audience became accustomed to the music, Beau signaled for the sound techs to turn on his amplifier, and he added his electrical guitar interpretation to the traditional bluegrass favorite. The effect was mind-blowing. The crowd went wild. Men, women, and children cheered from the festival grounds, lifting their arms, their beverages, their small children in salute.

"Where's Pearl?" Harley asked, rushing inside the VIP tent behind the stage. Hazel Moses stood behind the table, guarding the filled glasses and trays of food.

"She went to run an errand a few minutes ago," Hazel said, looking at Harley with concern. "Is something wrong?"

"Did she say where she was going?"

"I believe she said she was going to get more dishes in the storage area…above the pharmacy."

Before Hazel could stop her, Harley dropped her arm to the table, and in one sweep, knocked the row of filled glasses to the ground, shattering and spilling their contents across the pavement.

"What are you doing, Harley?" Hazel shouted.

"Did Beau have anything to drink yet?"

"No," she said, a confused look on her face. "I don't believe so. They've not taken their break yet."

"Don't let him," Harley said. "Whatever you do, don't let him."

"Harley? Harley, what are you talking about?"

Harley ran from the VIP tent, hoping she could still find Pearl above the pharmacy.

Most people were too engrossed in Beau's performance to notice a young woman in period clothing raging like a mad woman among them, and she passed through the sea of bodies mostly undetected.

Harley stood before the pharmacy on Main Street and gazed up at the second floor windows. The lights were on, and she assumed Pearl must still be inside. If memory served, the pharmacy had a back entrance with a staircase leading to the upper floors. She made her way down the narrow alleyway that ran alongside the building and pushed open the back door.

Taking a deep breath, she drew her cell phone from her pocket and called Jed. When he did not answer, she left a hurried message, telling him to meet her at the pharmacy immediately. Before she returned the phone to her pocket, she activated the voice recording application, ensuring the microphone was in an ideal position to record.

She started up the stairs.

CHAPTER 33

The pharmacy's upper room was empty. A row of large double-paned windows overlooked Main Street and the festival stage beyond. Beau's concert was still in full-swing, the crowd cheering as he and the local musicians played "Man of Constant Sorrow," a bluegrass song made famous by the movie, *O Brother, Where Art Thou?*.

Harley searched between the long rows of makeshift shelves, stacked with plates, cups, and cutlery, then among the piles of fall harvest decorations grouped in the room's corners. Perhaps Pearl had already left and was on her way back to the VIP tent. Then she heard a noise coming from the stairwell, the sound of feet tapping up the steps, and Pearl Johnson appeared, wearing a Pioneer Days volunteer sweatshirt and wool slacks, her gray-blonde hair styled immaculately in a chin-length cut.

"Harley?" she said with a pleasantly surprised look on her face. "I wasn't expecting to find you here."

When Harley did not answer, Pearl's pleasantness turned to concern. "Harley, what is it? Is something wrong?"

"You switched the babies," she said.

A shock of surprise struck Pearl's face, the color draining from her cheeks. "I'm sorry," she said. "I'm afraid I don't know what you're talking about."

"Beau Arson and Michael Sutcliffe. You switched them when they were just months old, didn't you, after you murdered Beau's real father, James Sutcliffe. You're the one who pushed James off the cliff that night at the Sutcliffe party. He didn't fall like everyone believed. You killed him. You did it so that Arthur would inherit James's shares in the Sutcliffe real estate company."

Over the years Pearl Johnson had mastered the subtle art of deceit, of concealment. While most people would've cowered or grown defensive in the wake of such accusations, she stood resolute and composed as always, a master manipulator who was always cool under pressure.

"James Sutcliffe wanted to die," she said. "He was only a shell after his wife passed away, so depressed he could barely function. He could no longer run the company the way it needed to be run, the way Arthur could run it. I did he and Sutcliffe Real Estate a favor."

"And then you took his son," Harley said, "his real son, Beau Arson, and you switched him with your illegitimate grandson when the babies were only months old. I saw Martin's photo, I saw what he looked like before he went to war and became unrecognizable. He and Michael are almost identical. Michael is really Martin's son, isn't he? And his mother is Susan Thompson, the illegitimate daughter you gave up for adoption."

"My, my," she said, her voice still calm, "you have been busy, haven't you? And still just as bright and perceptive, I see, as you were as a child." She drew a box cutter from her pocket and ran her finger along the sharp edge, "That is unfortunate."

She crept back ever so slightly and shut the room's door so that no one would hear them, no one would witness what she inevitably had to do. But first, it seemed she would explain herself.

"Yes, Susan was my daughter," she said, and for the first time, sadness wilted her calm and collected demeanor. "My only daughter. I never had another child after her, and I knew I would never have another. You see, Arthur never wanted any children. He was adamant about it, said it was the only contingency he had when we got married. And so I agreed, though I realize now, after all these years I've hated him for it. At the time I told myself I didn't mind because I had my Susan. Even though she'd been adopted by someone else, I could still be close to her here in Notchey Creek, I could still look over her like a mother. After all, that is why I moved here in the first place."

"And Susan's real father?" Harley asked.

"Susan's real father," she said, looking wistfully past Harley to the row of windows overlooking Main Street, "was the only man I ever truly loved."

Her eyes met Harley's. "Oh, don't look so surprised," she said. "You think I don't know about Arthur's late-night dates, his preference for cheap women? Of course, I know it. I've always known it. The difference is I don't care. You have to love someone to be made jealous by them, and I don't love Arthur, never have."

"But you've always acted so convincingly," Harley said.

"Oh, yes, I'm quite the little actress," she said, a smile forming on her face, then disappearing. "Always have been, even when I was a child. That's what you do when you grow up one of seven in a two-room housing project, fighting for every little scrap you have. You become crafty, artful, doing anything within your filthy little means to rise above the squalor. And I did. Oh, how I did."

A look of triumph lit up her face then darkened. "My father was a drunk, you see, always between jobs, could never keep one for very long because he couldn't stay sober for any period of time. And when he did have a job, he squandered all of his wages at the neighborhood bar, leaving nothing for us. My mother...she started bringing men home when my father wasn't there...for money...just to buy food for us. The men..." She swallowed hard and exhaled. "When they would leave my mother, some of them would try to come into my room and."

Her face tightened with disgust then relaxed. "Anyway, I left after that. I ran away from home when I was sixteen, and I got a job at one of the department stores in Knoxville, convincing women that if they would just buy that new pair of gloves, that new dress, that new pair of shoes they would feel beautiful. And it worked. By year's end, I was number one in sales in my department. I also knew that if I was going to rise above my station at work or anywhere else, I was going to have to look the part, so I started stealing little things from the store, just here and there, nothing that would be noticed. First a pair of earrings, then a pair of stockings, and then graduating to clothes. By the time I was eighteen, I had a complete wardrobe I could wear to my evening typing classes and then to my job interviews in the afternoons.

"Sometime thereafter, a law office hired me as a secretary, and that was where I met Susan's father, one of the partners in the firm. He was handsome and charming and dignified, tall and regal in his suits and ties. He was quite a bit older than me, at least fifteen years, I think, and married with children of his own, but it didn't matter. I was so taken with him from the very first time I ever saw him, ever talked to him, that I knew my fate had already been sealed.

"I didn't want to fall in love with him, of course. I didn't want to fall in love with anyone. But then again, you can't choose who you love, can you? It happens even when you want to be completely self-reliant, like I did, not letting anything interfere with the goals you've set for yourself. But Susan's father was a weakness I could not resist, and to this day, he's been the only weakness I've ever had besides Susan.

"It all started very innocently. Our affair. He'd begun staying at the office late some nights, working on cases, and it was just the two of us there, all alone, in the dim office, just the streetlights and table lamps keeping us company.

"When I'd first started working there, you see, I pledged that I would always be the last to leave the office and the first to arrive in the morning. That was the key to success, I told myself. And so you see, I wasn't going to leave there until after he did. So there I would sit at my desk, typing away, the light filtering in from his corner office as he poured over his cases.

"I would catch him looking at me from time to time, and when our eyes would meet, he would blush with embarrassment, and return to his work. But over time, the looks grew longer between us, lingering, until there was no embarrassment behind them at all, no blushing, just an understanding.

"One night he asked me to come into his office, said he needed to ask me something. I knew the real reason behind his request, of course, and I knew what was going to happen between us when I crossed that threshold that night, that my life was about to change, that my world would be forever altered.

"And when I did go in there, and he rose from his desk, and he stood over me, so handsome and dignified and strong, his eyes caressing my hair, my face, my figure, I knew fate had dealt a heavy hand. And then he closed the door behind us and shut off the lights, darkness covering our desire, our sin, a sin that has followed me like a shadow for over fifty years."

She closed her eyes and paused in a moment of silence, then opened her eyes once more. "The affair carried on for a few months after that, in the same way it had that first night. I thought he must love me by that point, the way he would send me flowers, jewelry, dresses, tell me how beautiful I was, how desirable I was. And his interest did not wane, did not abate until I asked him what his intentions were for our future. He was married, I knew, and with two children, but I assumed that the love he felt for me, the passion that had caused him to betray his family in the first place, would drive him to leave them, to start a new life with me.

"But this wasn't the case. I began seeing less and less of him. He would avoid me, leaving early in the evenings, inventing fabricated meetings that took him outside the office. Before long, I wasn't seeing him hardly at all. I thought perhaps he needed time to think, to mull over what his next step would be for us. After all, it was a major life decision, leaving your family for a woman who was so many years your junior, and who came from nothing.

"But this wasn't the case, of course, either. I knew the affair was over between us, that he had wiped his hands clean of me completely, when one of his colleagues, a fellow partner, came into my office one evening after everyone else had left. He set a pair of diamond earrings on my desk, told me that they could be mine if only I would meet him at a hotel after work the next day. He said he'd heard I liked nice things, that I liked to have a little fun too for the right price, and that he would give me those earrings, and other things, lots of other things, if I did what he wanted.

"I handed in my resignation the next day. But by this time, I'd found out I was pregnant with Susan. I confronted her father about it, told him about the child, that I expected to keep her, expected him to help me raise her. He said the baby probably wasn't even his, that I should get an abortion, that a child didn't deserve to be brought up by a soiled woman who turned tricks for anybody with a wallet."

Pearl paused, her mind suspended by the memory as if it were happening all over again in that very moment, as if Susan's father was standing right before her eyes. "It's amazing, really," she said, " how love can turn so quickly to hate. How you can live your entire life for someone in one moment, then want the world rid of them the next. Susan's father was the first person I ever loved. He was also the first person I ever killed. It was so difficult for me that first time, so conflicting were the emotions I felt over him. It gets so much easier, you see, over time, the more you do it, the more experience you have of separating your emotions from the act of killing. But his death…his death was the hardest."

She looked at Harley. "So hard for me," she said, "but so easy in the execution."

She deflected her gaze back to the windows overlooking Main Street. "My father was a drunk, you see, but he was a good mechanic when he was sober. He taught me a few things about cars, enough to know my way around an engine without any problems, and while Susan's father was working late one night at the office, probably seducing the poor girl who'd replaced me, I cut the brakes to his Mercedes while it was parked in the office lot.

"A few hours later, as he was driving home to his precious family, he tried to brake for a deer in the road, and his car swerved, striking a tree head-on. It killed him instantly." She paused and her eyes met Harley's. "Can you believe that even after everything he'd done to me, even after all of the hurt and pain he'd caused me, I mourned him? That I missed him? That I still miss him to this very day?"

She drew in a deep breath and released it slowly. "The human heart is a mysterious thing. Anyway," she said, continuing, "I gave birth to Susan some months after that, and as much as I hated to, I gave her up for adoption. You see, it wasn't as accepted back then as it is today. People frowned upon unwed mothers, placing a disgrace on them, a shame that followed you for the rest of your life, killing any chances you might have at marriage with a respectable man.

"Giving up Susan was the only voluble option I had at that point. Some time thereafter, I discovered Susan had been adopted by a child-less couple here in Notchey Creek, the Thompsons. When the opportunity arose, I moved here and took a job at the public library as an aide. I met Arthur, we were married soon after, and I still had the opportunity to be near Susan. I volunteered at the school, always ensuring that I would get to interact with her class, spend time with her in a safe environment. We became very close over the years, and she adored me, just as I adored her. It was almost like she somehow knew I was her real mother, and that made the bond between us that much stronger.

"Then, when she became pregnant with Martin's child, and she moved out of her mother's house, she came to live with us. Arthur didn't care, of course, as long as it didn't interfere with his extramarital liaisons, and he never expected, not once that Susan was my daughter.

"And then everything started coming together in a way that seemed like it was ordained from above, that what was about to happen had been fated in the stars. You see, Susan was terribly unhappy, clinically depressed. There she was with a newborn child, and no husband, the child's father missing-in-action and presumably dead overseas. She was still so young, still wanted to go to college, to start her life over. If she could just find a safe home for the baby, a family that would take him so that she could start anew.

"Then, there was James Sutcliffe. He'd just lost his wife, was alone and depressed and useless to care for his newborn son, or for his family's company. James had already told Arthur and me that if anything were to happen to him, he would leave Michael in our care, as his legal guardians, with a generous trust fund and all of the comforts a child could desire. And at that age, all babies tend to look alike, and Michael and Beau had the same blond hair and blue eyes."

Noticing the expression of surprise on Harley's face, she said, "Oh, yes, Beau Arson is really a blond, didn't you know? A full golden Sutcliffe crown. Always has had it, from the time he was a baby to when he was a teenager and until now. I assume he must dye it dark as part of his public persona. The golden hair wouldn't have worked with that Gothic image his band had, I imagine.

"And so after James died, I switched the two babies. By that time I'd told Susan the truth, that I was her real mother, and that we could give her the freedom she wanted and the baby the best home possible under my and Arthur's care. As Michael Sutcliffe, her child would have the life others only dreamed about. She agreed and said she would put James's real son, the person we now know as Beau Arson, up for adoption, claiming he was hers.

"But I explained to her that this couldn't be the way of things, as Beau Arson was living proof of what we'd done, and the only way to keep our secret safe, was to get rid of him. Permanently. It was the only option. After some reluctance and much persuasion from me, she agreed, and we constructed a plan. On Halloween night, she would take Beau to the edge of Maple Bluff and drop him into the ravine. No one would ever find his body there. Then she would leave town, start a new life, no one would be the wiser.

"But Patrick Middleton threw a wrench in our plan. I wasn't expecting him to hit Susan's car that night as it was parked on Maple Bluff, to kill her, and to save Beau's life in the process.

"No," she said, shaking her head. "And I was so crushed by Susan's death afterward, and realizing that the baby was still alive somewhere out there, knowing that he was the one link to all of this, was still discoverable…it kept me in a perpetual state of anxiousness. But time passed, and no questions were ever raised…no one ever suspected what we'd done or even linked Beau Arson with Susan's car accident."

"Except Patrick Middleton," Harley said.

"Yes, but I didn't know that at the time. I didn't find that out until very recently." She paused. "There was one other time, too, years after the car accident, when I worried someone might catch onto our secret, might guess."

Harley waited for Pearl to continue.

"It was around the same time I realized who Beau Arson really was, what had happened to him after Patrick had saved him from Susan's burning car that night. He was a teenager by then, I imagine. As a favor to Patrick, the Winstons had agreed to keep him for the summer at their house."

Pearl met eyes with Harley. "You may not remember it now, but you knew Beau Arson all those years ago, the two of you became unlikely friends the summer I babysat you. Oh yes, that was him. The blond boy next door. You thought he was Eric Winston, didn't you, and I wasn't going to tell you the truth. None the wiser, I told myself."

She seemed to take delight in Harley's shocked expression, to relish in the fact she'd one-upped her. "And I remember he gave you that book by Charles Dickens. What was it called?"

"*Great Expectations*," Harley muttered, still stunned by the revelation.

"Yes, that was the one. And he saved you from those bullies. Put the fear of God in them, I remember, and filled your head with all of those grand predictions for your future. Such nonsense.

"Anyway," she said, "he was in between foster homes at the moment, and the Winstons' son, Eric, was away in Europe for the summer. They'd heard the boy was musically gifted, and being sad that Eric was away, they thought it would be nice to help out an aspiring prodigy, one so highly esteemed by Patrick Middleton.

"But what worried me at the time, after I'd seen him all grown up, was that he looked so much like his father. I knew who he was immediately. So tall and handsome like James, the features, the likeness was unmistakable. It probably still is underneath all of that hair and scruff. But the summer passed, and Beau Arson moved on and no one made any connections. Everything was quiet until Martin Evans seemingly rose from the dead and came back into our lives.

"I was home the night he came looking for Patrick. They were supposed to meet at Bud's, but Martin had gotten the day wrong and had come looking for Patrick at his house instead. I was seated on the porch, I remember, finishing a novel for book club when I saw him knocking on Patrick's front door.

"I never would've known it was him. Goodness, he was so unrecognizable with all of the scars, nothing like he was when I knew him as a young man. I called across the yard and asked if I could be of any help to him, and that's when he recognized me. You see, he remembered me from when Susan had been living with us.

"Oh, the timing couldn't have been more horrible. Just as Michael had returned to Notchey Creek, had established himself at Briarcliffe, that Martin Evans had to appear. I wanted to kill him right then and there.

"But that's not how one gets things done, is it? So I feigned to Martin that I was so very happy to see him again and wouldn't he please come inside for a cup of hot tea, to catch up on old times. I'd already decided at that point what I was going do, what I had to do... and with Arthur out with one of his floozies that night, there was little to deter me.

"Martin accepted my invitation for tea and joined me in the living room, and over a few cups of Darjeeling, he told me everything. How Patrick Middleton had confessed to him that he'd killed Susan in that car accident all those years ago, that his son was still alive somewhere, that he hoped to reunite the two.

"But then Martin noticed Michael's photograph on the mantle, recognized the strong likeness between them, and asked if Michael was the long-lost son Patrick hoped to reunite him with. I told him, 'absolutely not,' that the young man's name was Michael Sutcliffe, and he was James Sutcliffe's only son. But he didn't believe me, pointing out that Michael had the same heart-shaped birthmark on his neck that his son had had.

"By that time the drugs had taken effect, thankfully, and I decided to just confess and admit the truth, that yes, he was right, that Michael was his son, and wasn't it good that I'd saved the child from being raised by a useless, derelict father like himself.

"Martin was downright stumbling, asking what had happened to the real Michael Sutcliffe, what we'd done with him, saying that the boy had been 'innocent.' He said he was going to go to the police, tell them the truth, that the world needed to know what I'd done. When he left, his speech was slurring, no longer making any sense. So I just let him go. I knew it wouldn't take very long for the drugs to kill him, and it didn't. I predicted the police would find him in a day or two and rule his death an overdose.

"Then I just had Patrick to deal with. I knew I would have to kill him too, of course, and do it quickly. I wasn't sure how much he knew already, and how much he was bound to find out. He was too much of a liability. And with all of the controversy swarming around the new history museum, there would be a multitude of suspects who would've had motive to kill him. I would use that angle.

"So that night, at the historical society meeting, I was the one who threw that rock through Patrick's living room window, with the note, STOP NOW OR FACE THE CONSEQUENCES."

"When you excused yourself to go to the restroom," Harley said.

"Yes. It was quite easy really. I'd typed up the note beforehand, placed the rock in my pocket, and once Tina was distracted in the kitchen, I sneaked out the back door, crept around front, and the broke the window. Everyone would think one of the museum protestors had done it.

"Then I asked Patrick if I could please stop by his house after the meeting for a chat. There was something important I needed to speak with him about, and it couldn't wait. Of course, being that it was me, he accepted. I knew Arthur had a date with one of his women that night, so there would be no interference on his part.

"When I arrived at Patrick's house later that evening, he invited me into his den, and offered me a seat in the leather chair across from his. There was a bottle of your whiskey on the side table by his chair and two glasses. He poured himself a glass then offered one to me, which I then accepted.

"We began talking, and I told him the purpose of my visit was to tell him that I supported his plans for the living history museum in Briarwood Park, and that I was glad he'd thwarted Arthur's plans of developing the land into a shopping center. Arthur needed to slow down, I told him. He was getting older, and the shopping complex would require too much of his time and energy and wasn't good for the town's posterity. This was all nonsense, of course. The history museum was a piece of idiocy, I thought, and I wanted Arthur to have his shopping center if it would keep him out of my hair and put more money into our retirement fund. But Patrick wasn't to know this, and he would never know it after I drugged him.

"Then I asked Patrick if I could please borrow a copy of his meeting agenda. I said I'd misplaced mine, and I wanted to make sure that my meeting minutes lined up with the agenda. When he went to his office to get it, I reached over and poured Ambien in his glass, and topped it off with more whiskey. He never suspected a thing.

"I placed the whiskey glass he'd given to me in my purse, and, wished Patrick a good evening, promising I would smooth things over with Arthur for him. Then I went home to my still-empty house, destroyed the whiskey glass, and watched Patrick's house from my bedroom window.

"All was quiet over there until about midnight when his bedroom lights came on, then the lights to his outdoor kitchen. He should've been dead by then, I thought, and I was worried I hadn't put enough of the sleeping pills in his drink, or he hadn't consumed enough.

"I dressed in black from head-to-toe and crept into his backyard. He was holding one of those outdoor lanterns, and he was walking along the creek bank, searching for something or someone in the water. Then he started calling for her. He started calling for Susan! He was begging her to forgive him, saying her death had haunted him all those years, would haunt him until the day he died. I truly think he believed that silly Samhain legend Iris had shared at the meeting earlier that night, and with the drugs making him see and hear things, he thought he'd somehow been reunited with Susan.

"I crept up behind him as he stood there, searching for Susan's ghost in the water, and I placed my hand on his shoulder. I wanted to be the last person he saw before he died, for him to realize the hurt and pain he had caused me over the years. He turned around, and when he saw me, he gasped, and I pushed him into the creek. He fell on his back and was thrashing in the water, so I held him down until he lay still, staring up at the night sky in horror.

"I returned to my house, removed and washed the damp clothes, and waited for Arthur to come home a little while after. I was done with both of them. Patrick and Martin. Our secret was safe."

"But Martin didn't die," Harley said, "not as you planned it anyway. He made it to Briarwood Park, and Tina and I found him the next morning. He was disoriented, yes, but he was still very much alive until someone bludgeoned him to death."

"What?"

"Yes, someone killed Martin Evans in the woods."

"But no," she said, her voice growing desperate, "no one knew about Martin besides me, no one knew but Patrick."

"You're wrong about that," a male voice said.

Pearl turned in horror to see Michael Sutcliffe emerging from the storage aisles. He was pale and distraught, dark circles around his eyes as if he'd been awake for days.

"Michael," Pearl said with a gasp. "Michael, what are you doing here? How long have you been here?"

"Long enough to hear the truth," he said. "Long enough to know my entire life has been a fraud. I'm the one who killed the tramp in the woods," he said. "I'm the one who killed my real father."

Pearl stood frozen in disbelief, staring at Michael.

"Oh, yes," he said, glaring back at her with hatred. "I came upon him in Briarwood Park one night, after I'd followed Savannah to Patrick Middleton's house. He was stumbling and drunk and mumbling crazy things, saying I wasn't entitled to the Sutcliffe inheritance, that I wasn't James Sutcliffe's real son. That I was *his* son. He pulled a photograph from his pocket and pointed to a man in military uniform. He said the man was him when he was younger, and didn't I see the likeness between us." He shrieked. "Good god, he looked just like me!"

His face scowled with disgust as he aimed the gun at Pearl. "And then he told me that you'd confessed it to him, that you'd told him the truth about who I really was. He said he was going to the police and tell them, then to the trustees. I knew Savannah was only marrying me for the money, that she'd only stay with me for the money. And my life's nothing without her and the Sutcliffe name. I…I…didn't know what to do. And then, suddenly, I had the chance to kill him."

He cocked the gun and swallowed hard. "Savannah has left me," he said. "She said the two of you had a discussion, that you agreed it was best to end the engagement."

"And it is best," Pearl said. "Savannah doesn't care for you. You deserve better than her."

Michael narrowed his reddened eyes at Pearl. "There were only two things that I loved in this world. The Sutcliffe name and Savannah. And now they're both gone because of you."

"But Michael," Pearl said, "no one knows about your real identity but Harley, and we can get rid of her. You can still have your money, your name."

His face tightened in anger as he placed his finger on the gun's trigger. "I don't care about the money if I don't have Savannah."

"If you really want her back," Pearl said, "we'll get her back, I promise. I'll figure out a way. Then once we've gotten rid of Harley here, everything will settle back to the way it was before."

"Oh, the police aren't stupid. Even if we do kill Harley, they'll still find out who I really am. That I'm not really Michael Sutcliffe." He narrowed his eyes at Pearl, squeezing the gun. "You're the one who's caused all of this. You're the one who deserves to die."

The gun fired, and Harley leaped, knocking Pearl to the floor beneath her. But she'd hit her head on the side of a table, and the room was spinning.

The last thing Harley saw was Jed Turner breaking down the door and tackling Michael Sutcliffe to the floor. Her final thoughts, as the room dimmed and the sound of Beau Arson's music lilted into silence, was that Pearl Johnson was alive, that she would have to account for what she'd done, that the truth would finally be known.

CHAPTER 34

*H*arley woke to the sound of Eric Winston's calm, soothing voice as he stood over her. She lay in a hospital bed, and through partly opened eyes, she could see him searching her face with a mix of hope and concern. In the hallway she could hear nurses and doctors and orderlies making their rounds, and the sound of TV game shows blaring from neighboring rooms.

"Harley?" Eric said, drawing his face closer to hers. "Harley, are you awake?"

He wore blue hospital scrubs and a white lab coat, a surgeon's cap still perched on his head. He'd been working in the morgue and had taken a break to visit her.

"Eric?" she said, the words coming forth in a weak croak. "Eric, what's happened?"

"You've suffered a concussion," he said, placing his hand on top of hers. "You've been in and out of consciousness for the last three days."

She drew her hand to her still-throbbing forehead and flinched with pain.

"Now, now," Eric said, guiding her hand back down to the bed. "You still need to take it easy. You won't be out of the woods for a few days yet. And it's best that way. Believe me, you don't want to leave the hospital right now. It's an absolute press frenzy. Everywhere. Reporters from all over the world are here, trying to get more of the story. The whole thing is so sensational, so incredible on its own, and then the fact that it involves Beau Arson at its center...well, I don't believe they'll be leaving here anytime soon."

"What about Pearl?" Harley asked. "What happened to her? To Michael?"

"Pearl fared much better than you did, I'm afraid. When you tackled her to the ground, you saved her from Michael's bullet. It would've killed her. She's in police custody, as is Michael. When the EMS arrived on the scene, they found your cell phone still recording inside your pocket. They were able to attain Pearl's and Michael's confessions. They'll be going away for a very long time." He looked at Harley in earnestness. "Is that why you saved her?"

"Yes," she said, her voice still hoarse. "I wanted her to be held accountable for everything she's done, to all of the people she's hurt. Dying would've been the easy way out for her. Before she atones for her sins in the next life, she needs to atone for them in this one."

"And she will," Eric said, patting the top of her hand. "There is no question about that."

A thought entered Harley's mind, and she squeezed Eric's hand for emphasis. "I want Jed to get all of the credit for solving the murders," she said. "I don't want to be mentioned in the press, I don't want any publicity. Please let Jed know this is what I wish, and ask if he would please comply."

"But Harley, it was you who solved the case. You deserve the credit."

"No," she said, squeezing his hand again. "Eric, please."

"If you wish." His expression conveyed that while he disagreed with her request, he understood it, understood that Harley Henrickson thrived in the shadows, leading a life of quiet humility. Being in the public eye would only dampen her little light.

"And Beau? How is Beau?" she asked.

"Ah, yes, Beau," Eric said. "The person everyone is talking about. He's still here, and with a wall of security around him. The reporters have been absolutely relentless trying to get a photo of him or a piece of information. And you were right, Harley, about Beau. He is Michael Sutcliffe. The real one. They collected DNA from James and Marian Sutcliffe's old hairbrushes and matched it to Beau's. He is their son and heir, all right, the rightful owner of Briarcliffe."

Oh, thank goodness, Harley thought.

"It's quite a strange coincidence really," Eric said, "but did you know that Beau stayed at our house one summer, years ago when I went abroad to Europe?"

Harley gazed past Eric to the large window overlooking Notchey Creek, where the morning sun filtered through the open blinds, casting golden ribbons across the bed. "Yes," she said. "Yes, I remember him quite well now."

Eric shook his head. "Back then, none of us, especially my parents, would've ever guessed who he really was. He was...well, not what you would expect."

"Yes," Harley said in a whisper. "Yes, he never is, is he?"

The light from the window danced across the walls in speckles of gold, as the trees outside shook the last of their leaves, the brittle browns and reds and oranges sweeping toward the heavens. Harley watched the leaves as they swept back and forth before the window, making their way this way and that, down to the earth where they would at last die.

"I'm finding that so many of my beliefs," she said, "about people, about situations...about memories...aren't at all what I thought."

"Well, I'll tell you what," Eric said, changing the subject to something more pleasant. "So many people have been by to see you, have left things for you."

He gestured to a table stationed in front of the room's large windows, a variety of gifts displayed along it. Nestled among several bouquets of flowers were several presents: a tin of cupcakes from Tina, a longneck beer from Uncle Tater, a cheeseburger from Floyd, a box of expired HoHos from Aunt Wilma, and a stuffed chicken wreaking of cigarette smoke from Opha Mae Shaw. There was something else there too, rectangular and flat, wrapped in simple parchment.

"What is that one there?" she asked, pointing.

Eric directed his eyes to the wrapped present, his face adopting a curious expression. He walked over to the table and searched the package. "Hmm," he said, "I don't know. And there's no tag." He turned and smiled at Harley. "Would you like to open it?"

"No," she said. "That's okay. I can just open it when I get home."

Eric came back to the hospital bed and took a seat on the edge. "And you'll also be pleased to know that your Matilda won the Prize Pig contest at the festival."

"Really?" Harley said, her face lighting up. "Well, Aunt Wilma will certainly be pleased." *And Matilda will get the little house we promised her,* she thought.

Eric rose from the bed and patted Harley's ankle which was tucked beneath the blanket. "Gets some rest, and I'll be back by to check on you later.

When he turned to leave, she stopped him. "Eric," she said.

"Yes?"

"Thank you."

A WEEK PASSED and Harley Henrickson was at last home again. Her yellow cottage, surrounded by beds of fallen leaves and acorns was a bevy of activity for the birds and squirrels, scurrying among the maples, foraging nuts and berries and seeds, as they prepared for the winter ahead.

Harley sat on her front porch swing, a cup of hot cider in her hands, swinging back and forth, enjoying the brisk fall morning. Two women passed along the sidewalk in tracksuits and sneakers, pumping their arms and legs as they laughed and chattered, sharing experiences from a friendship that had lasted decades. As she watched the women's joyful expressions, she wondered if that would be she and Tina when they reached middle age, looking back on a life of triumphs and pain, trials and laughter.

Inside the house, Aunt Wilma was cooking a pot of beans on the stove, singing along to the radio as she added a ham bone to the steaming cast iron pot, the Southern Gospel Choir lilting throughout the house along with the aroma of country ham. Wilma was a bit tone deaf, and Harley wondered if the foul notes would rouse the neighborhood dogs to howling.

"Then sings my soul, my Savior God to thee
How great thou art, how great thou art!"

Tina, who was also in the kitchen, baking a batch of cornbread, dropped the cast iron skillet on the stove and clamped her hands over her ears. "Aunt Wilma! Now, look, I know as a good Southern Baptist, you're called to make a joyful noise, and that the good Lord loves all kinds of singin' if it's done in praise, but I swear that racket is makin' my cornbread fall!"

In the backyard, Matilda's little house was under construction, a project Uncle Tater and Floyd had volunteered to take on. Harley could hear the two old men arguing behind the house, the choice of window treatments being a matter of much contention.

"Now, if you're a pig, Floyd," Uncle Tater said between sips of beer, "and you're wantin' to look out the winder, which of them two you think you're gonna want? Curtains or mini-blinds? Curtains, of course! That way you can take your nose and push 'em aside while look out yonder at the scenery. You can't do that with no mini-blinds."

"Well, maybe Matilda wants somethin' more modern for her house," Floyd said. "And mini-blinds is easier to clean."

"She's a pig, Floyd. I doubt she's gonna be the one cleanin' them."

A Dodge Ram truck descended Poplar Street, and Harley could see it was Sheriff Jed Turner, off-duty in his street clothes and a University of Tennessee Volunteers baseball hat. After parking in the driveway, he stepped outside the truck and zipped up his Indianapolis Colts jacket before making his way up the sidewalk. When he reached the front porch, he stopped at the bottom of the steps and looked at Harley, expressionless.

Harley pondered the purpose of Jed's visit, and feared the prospect of bad news, that perhaps she was in trouble yet again for something.

But to Harley's surprise, Jed's large baby blue eyes creased in the corners and he smiled, the first time he'd smiled at her since they'd taken that summer art class together when they were children.

"Henrickson," he said, his boots clomping up the steps. He made his way in her direction, the porch boards creaking under his weight. She gestured to one of the two rocking chairs across from the swing, but he lowered himself beside her in the swing instead. The metal suspension chains buckled and locked, unaccustomed to so much weight, and Jed extended his legs out in front of him, resting his feet at an angle on the porch.

"Are you doing all right?" he asked.

"Yes," she said. "To tell you the truth, I think this is the most rest I've had in years."

"Good."

He lifted his legs and pushed them underneath him, launching the swing in motion. As the swing creaked back and forth, shifting the two of them to and fro, she waited for Jed to address the point of his visit.

"I wanted to thank you," he said, at last, staring down at his feet as they moved along with the swing. "You didn't have to give me the credit for solving this case, but you did. And it's given me the respectability I've been needing, made me something more than just a retired NFL player playing sheriff."

He stopped the swing and looked at Harley intently. "Why did you do it?"

Without speaking, Harley rose from the swing and left Jed to go inside the house, the screen door shutting behind her. She ambled up the steps, the aroma of Wilma's cooking and the sound of gospel music following her up to the second floor, then to the attic. There, among the dust of pink insulation and holiday decorations, she located the old canvas, wrapped in a cotton cloth.

She returned to the porch and to Jed, unveiling their long-lost artwork, a field of wildflowers and a summer sky, left unfinished by a father's anger and a little boy's shame.

"This is why," Harley said, placing the canvas in his hands. "At least this is part of the reason."

In his muscled arms, Jed held the canvas of their childhood, a canvas of shared joy and collaboration, a piece of artistry and friendship cut short by things beyond their control.

"My flowers," he said, running his large hand across the surface. "And your sky." He fought back emotion as he smiled at the canvas in reverie. "I still remember you saying that the sky is never really one color. That it's nuanced. Lots of shades and colors, like people." He looked up from the artwork and locked eyes with Harley. "You were right."

"I'd like you to finish it, Jed," she said. "That's all I ask."

He nodded and hugged the canvas to his chest, gazing up at Harley. "I will."

He rested the canvas in the swing beside him and reached into his jacket pocket, removing an envelope. "I have something for you too," he said, handing the envelope to Harley. "It's just a little something from some of the members of the community."

Harley opened the thick envelope and thumbed through a series of twenty-dollar bills.

"We know you've had to be out of work since everything happened," Jed said. "And we wanted to help you out a little financially."

"Thank you," Harley said. "Really. But this wasn't necessary."

Before Jed could reply, a second car pulled into the driveway. This time it was Eric Winston's navy BMW. He rose from the car, and he smiled when he saw Harley and Jed on the porch.

"Good Morning," he called across the yard. He reached into the back of his car and lifted a covered casserole dish from the seat.

"What is that?" Harley asked, her face lighting up.

"Oh, just a lasagna I made."

Jed snickered. "Yeah, and what's in it?"

Eric made his way up the path, listing the various ingredients. "Bolognese sauce, slow-cooked for ten hours, porcini mushrooms, sautéed with truffle oil, egg pasta made in my pasta machine, and homemade béchamel."

Jed snickered again and poked Harley. "Yeah, so among his many other talents the man is a gourmet chef."

"Where would you like it?" Eric asked, smiling at Harley as he stood on the porch.

"You can just take it in the kitchen." She held open the screen door for him. "And give it to Aunt Wilma or Tina." She smiled as she watched him progress past the living room to the kitchen, charming the two women with a cheerful greeting.

"Now, I don't want you to get your hopes up about Eric," Jed said, behind her from the swing.

Harley looked over her shoulder as she stood in the open doorway. "What?"

"About Eric. I've seen the way you look at him, how your face lights up every time you see him. I know you're getting sweet on him."

"Jed, I'm not—"

He held up his hand to stop her. "It's okay, Harley. It's okay. And I'm not saying this to be mean or to hurt your feelings. Goodness knows, I'm not after everything you've done for me, for this town. But I want you to know that Eric has a girlfriend. She's still in Connecticut, but she'll be moving here soon. And Harley, she's incredible. Gorgeous, accomplished, smart, educated. She makes Savannah Swanson look homely."

"But not Cheri?" Harley asked.

"Well, I can't be objective about that." He repositioned himself in the swing and changed his tone to one of empathy. "Look, I just don't want to see you get hurt. Eric's a nice guy, and he wouldn't do it on purpose, but he's charming, Harley, really charming, and his attentions could be taken the wrong way."

Harley's heart sank, and she worked to conceal her disappointment. "I understand," she said quietly, bringing the screen door to a close.

Jed was right. After all, she'd already told herself to be realistic regarding her feelings for Eric, that he was out of her league, that he could never feel romantically about someone like her.

"Thanks for telling me, Jed," she said.

Within the half-hour, the seven of them, not counting Matilda, sat down at Harley's dining room table for a noon meal, a smorgasbord of bolognese lasagna, Pabst Blue Ribbon, Hardees cheeseburgers, pinto beans, cornbread, and a vintage Merlot, courtesy of Eric Winston.

Opha Mae Shaw arrived in time for dessert, offering a case of pina colada wine coolers and a pack of Virginia Slims, which she added to Wilma's collection of expired Little Debbies and Twinkies. The Litte Debbies and Twinkies remained untouched until Matilda, some hours later, raided the kitchen and carried them back to her little house.

When everyone had left, and Harley and Wilma had finished wiping down the kitchen, Wilma said it was time for her great-niece to write thank-you notes for the presents she'd received in the hospital.

"I'm not sure anyone's really expecting that after what happened," Harley said, drying a dish and placing it in the cupboard. "I mean, I did almost die."

Wilma cocked her index finger in the air. "This is the South. You *always* send a thank-you note. *Always.* Even if you're dead, you still find a way to send one."

"How would you do that?"

Wilma rolled her eyes. "Why, through a psychic medium, of course." Wilma plopped a box of cards and envelopes on the table in front of Harley. "And I even got you your own stationery," she said. "Monogrammed."

"Monogrammed?" Harley said, looking at the bolded hot pink letters on the white stationery cards.

"Of course, it's monogrammed. You don't use nothin' but mono-grammed." Wilma leered at Harley, narrowing her eyes. "Are you sure you're really a Southerner? Are you sure I helped raise you?"

And so they commenced, Wilma going through the table full of gifts in the living room and Harley scribbling messages of apprecia-tion on her stationery. They'd worked their way through most of the gifts when Wilma paused, looking down at the table, a perplexed expression on her face. "Now, where'd this one come from?" she asked. "Don't believe I saw it there before."

Wilma lifted the gift from the table, and Harley surveyed the rectangular, flat package, wrapped in plain brown parchment and tied with kitchen twine. "Oh, yes," she said, "I remember it being at the hospital. It must've gotten buried beneath the others."

Wilma handed the present to Harley. "Well, why don't you open it already?"

Harley returned to her seat and rested the package in her lap, carefully removing the paper from what was clearly a book. A flash of green emerged from the parchment, then a little boy raising his arms to a tree.

Harley placed her hand over her mouth. *The Giving Tree.* She opened the inside cover and ran her finger down the page, searching for the inscription she hoped would be there.

To my darling baby girl,
    My sweet angel love,
    Our giving tree.
Love you always,
Mama

But how? The book had been destroyed by Kevin Grazely and Spider Buttle, she was sure, destroyed all those years ago when they'd invaded the Johnsons' backyard and stolen it from her, tearing out the pages, throwing it in the mud puddle.

But there it was. Restored. She fanned through the pages, studying with amazement what an excellent job the restorers had done. It must've cost a fortune.

A note fell from the spine and landed in Harley's lap.

Come to Briarcliffe, it read.

CHAPTER 35

*A*ll was quiet in the early morning hours on Main Street as Harley parked her truck in the lot behind Smoky Mountain Spirits. The shop had remained closed during her sabbatical, and with the pomp and circumstance of Pioneer Days at an end, Main Street was observing a day of rest, the stores, the bars, the restaurants recovering from the celebration, the hay bails and pumpkins and chrysanthemums sagging outside their doors.

Harley entered the back room and traveled into the shop area and to the row of hardback novels stationed above the bar. She retrieved the copy of *Great Expectations,* and as she placed it in her bag, she saw a car pull up outside the shop.

Hazel Moses rose from her green Volvo, the car's luggage rack covered with suitcases and trunks. She approached the glass windows, and placing her hand over her brow, peered inside. Upon seeing Harley, she waved and smiled enthusiastically, beckoning the young woman to let her in.

"Hazel?" Harley said, unlocking the front door and opening it. She gazed over Hazel's shoulder to the packed Volvo. "And your car. Are you moving?"

"I am," she said, still ecstatic. "That's why I stopped by. I was hoping to say goodbye to you before I left."

"But where are you going?" Harley asked, matching Hazel's enthusiasm.

"Well, first let me explain." She walked past Harley through the open doorway and entered the shop, taking a seat in one of the chairs beside the potbellied stove.

When Harley had taken a seat across from her, she said, "He left them to me. *All* of them. His first editions. Patrick did. *Every single* one." Jittery with excitement, she crossed then uncrossed her legs. "And a small inheritance too! Can you believe it?"

"I do believe it. That's wonderful."

"You were right, Harley. I wanted to come by and tell you that you were right. About Patrick. He *did* love me. He really did. Not in the way I wanted initially, of course, no, not in a romantic way, but in a way that now I think was even better, more special."

"You were a true friend to him, Hazel."

"Yes," she said, exhaling with relief. "And now I can finally leave Notchey Creek like I always wanted, do whatever I want, be whoever I want."

"And what will you do?" Harley asked. "What are your plans? Where are you going?"

"New York. At least at first. And then, well, I don't know…wherever the notion takes me."

She reached into her bag and removed a book which she then handed to Harley. "Patrick wanted you to have this," she said. "He left me a note, asking me to give it to you. He said it had shared meaning for the two of you, from when you were a child."

Harley gazed down at the first edition printing of Alfred, Lord Tennyson's poems. She opened the book and paged through, stopping when she'd found "The Lady of Shalott."

"Yes," she said, smiling at Hazel over the book's cover. "Yes, it does have special meaning."

Afterward, when Harley had said farewell to Hazel and wished her

228 | LIZ ANDREWS

well, she closed the shop and began her pilgrimage to her next stop, the county homeless shelter.

"I'd like to make a donation," she said, placing the envelope of money Jed had given her on the front counter. "Anonymously, please."

The female volunteer working behind the desk, looked at Harley, then at the envelope, a quizzical expression on her face. Then she proceeded to open the envelope and count the succession of twenty-dollars bills. "But there's hundreds of dollars here," she said. "Are you sure you want to give away all of it?"

"Yes," Harley said without hesitation. "I'm absolutely certain, and I want it made in honor of the memory of Army Private Martin Evans. He was a veteran, and though he didn't die in battle overseas, he fought his own personal battles when he came home, terrible ones, like so many of our brave men and women in uniform." She paused and looked at the volunteer intently. "Martin fought a lot of demons, but he was a good man, and he chose to do the right thing before he died, the best thing he could've done."

"I will see that it is put to good use," the volunteer said, closing the envelope and smiling at Harley. "And thank you."

"No," Harley said. "Thank you. What you do here is so important."

Harley returned to her truck, thinking of Martin Evans as she drove along Briarwood Avenue, passing the ditch where she and Tina had found him on that fateful morning, when he'd tried to tell her about Beau Arson, about the boy who'd been 'innocent.'

She slowed the truck when she spotted Savannah Swanson ahead, wearing a pair of old jeans, a sweatshirt, and a hard hat, her long blonde hair tied in a ponytail, her face free of makeup. She stood at the edge of Briarwood Park, watching as two men surveyed the land.

Harley stopped her truck and rolled down the window. "Savannah?"

"Harley!" she said running over. "It's so good to see you. I'd heard you were on the mend. Did you get my gift?"

"I did," she said, remembering the beautiful set of notebooks and pens. "Thank you."

"The museum is going forward," she said, gesturing to the green space behind her. "Beau Arson bought the land, and he's decided to move forward with the construction, as specified by Patrick's plans. It's going to be called 'The Patrick Middleton Museum of Appalachian History,' and I'm going to be the curator."

"I'm so happy for you, Savannah."

She yanked the hard hat down on her forehead and grinned. "And guess what else? Beau Arson is giving his entire inheritance to the National Park. Can you believe it?"

"Yes. Yes, I can believe it."

Harley deflected her gaze to a line of trees at the edge of the park. "Savannah, would you mind doing a favor for me? Those trees," she said, pointing. "Will you see that they remain there, untouched?"

Savananah gave Harley a quizzical look. "Well, sure, but may I ask why?"

"Because they were planted by the town's World World II veterans, and it would mean a lot to…many of us if they remained there as a memorial."

"Sure," she said. "I think that can be arranged."

"Thank you."

Savannah lowered her head into the open window, her excitement settling into seriousness. "Hey, I was wondering if I could maybe stop by your shop sometime. Maybe we could have lunch? I'd like to get your thoughts on the history museum and maybe catch up on the last nineteen years."

"That would be great," Harley said, "and I can't wait to see what you do with the museum." She rolled up the window, and after waving goodbye to Savannah, she progressed along Briarwood Avenue, making a right-hand turn into the exclusive neighborhood.

Cars with out-of-state license plates lined both sides of the street, and numerous people, all unknown to Harley, milled about on the sidewalk holding microphones and cameras, eager to get a shot of Beau Arson.

Three police cruisers cordoned off the remainder of the drive, blocking the portion leading up the hill to Briarcliffe. Harley stopped her truck in front of one of the cruisers and rolled down the window.

One of Jed's deputies approached the Chevy and lowered himself into Harley's view. She wasn't sure of the young man's name, as he was new to the force, but she hoped he might recognize her.

"I'd like to go to Briarcliffe, please," she said. "I've received an invitation from Mr. Arson."

"You don't have to ask permission, Harley," the young officer said with warmth. "You're free to go wherever you like. Jed's orders. And besides, Mr. Arson already told us to be expecting you."

He motioned for the officers to move their police cars temporarily, allowing Harley's truck to pass through them. In her rearview mirror, she could see them watching her truck as it ascended the street toward Briarcliffe, as if they couldn't believe that she was the young woman who'd solved the biggest murder case in Notchey Creek's history.

But Harley wasn't in the clear yet, for as her truck approached the tall iron gates of Briarcliffe, Boonie Davenport appeared behind the bars, his muscled arms crossed at his chest. He gave her a smug look, and she drew in a deep breath, preparing herself for an experience similar to the one she'd had with him at Muscadine Farms. Instead, the gates opened and Boonie stepped aside, and as her truck passed by him, he raised his hand to his brow in a salute.

Miracles never cease.

The truck progressed through the tall pines lining the drive, and then to the clearing, where in centuries past, a family of timber barons had leveled hundreds of trees, the same barons who'd leveled millions more in what was to become the Great Smoky Mountains National Park, the profits used to erect the immense limestone mansion of Briarcliffe, overlooking the small town of Notchey Creek.

Harley parked her truck near the servants' entrance, and as she opened the door, Stevie ran from the terrace, waving to her.

"Harley," he said, breathless and smiling, his cheeks rosy from the cold. "It's so good to see you."

"Hi, Stevie," she said, returning his smile.

Still catching his breath, he extended his right hand and shook hers. "Are you okay? I'd heard you were in the hospital."

"All better."

He dropped his gaze to the paved driveway and shook his head. "I can't tell you how much this means to us, to Beau. I think maybe he's finally found his other bookend, so to speak. Finding out about his real family, his home is... priceless."

"I'm so glad."

"Well," he said, "I'm sure you've probably come to see him, not me, so I'll let you be about your visit." He motioned to a wrought iron gate behind them, one leading into the backyard. "He's out back, down by the creek. You're free to go through there if you like. He's been expecting you."

Harley bid Stevie farewell and made her way through the iron gate and to the vast expanse of green, littered with fallen leaves, the lawn rolling and gliding to the creek and the row of piney woods beyond.

Harley stopped beneath an oak tree and rested her back to the trunk. In the distance she could see a solemn, lonely figure lounging beside the creek beneath a weeping willow, the autumn sun casting threads of sunlight through the trees, his golden hair falling in careless waves over his forehead. He peered down at the shimmering water as if casting a spell over the currents, a spell that traveled across the expanse of grass and beneath the tree where Harley stood.

Suddenly she was a little girl again, surrounded by a sea of lilies beneath the oak tree in the Johnsons' backyard. She lowered her eyes to her lap, where in her tiny arms, browned and scraped from endless days climbing trees and skipping rocks, she held *The Giving Tree*, the last present she'd received from her mother, a book she'd promised her mother she would read before summer's end. She pushed her finger along the open page, studying the text.

Once there was a tree and she loved a little boy. And every day the boy would come and he would gather her leaves and make them into crowns and play king of the forest. He would climb up her trunk and swing from her branches and eat apples. And they would play hide-and-go

*seek. And when he was tired he would sleep in her shade. And the boy
loved the tree.*

The wind whipped through the oak tree's branches, its limbs
waving toward the heavens, leaves rustling in crescendo. The sweet
redolence of coming rain filled the air, blending with the aroma of
freshly laundered linens as they flapped on Pearl Johnson's clothesline
and of fresh-cut grass forming ridges behind Angus Pruitt's lawn
mower as it droned across the yard next door. There, situated beside
the Johnsons' Tudor-style home was Patrick Middleton's three-story
brick mansion, the home's shutters gleaming from a fresh coat of
black paint, the foundation framed by flocks of white hydrangea
bushes. A screen door creaked open and sandaled feet clomped across
wooden boards, their impact silenced by pads of grass.

Patrick Middleton appeared beneath Harley's oak tree, dressed in
low-slung khakis and a white linen shirt, his round spectacles pushing
back strands of dark hair from his lined forehead, his smile lighting
up his handsome face. He greeted her as he always did. "Ah, tis the
fairy, the Lady of Shalott, floating in a sea of lilies, I see."

Harley hugged the book to her chest and smiled up at him. "I'm
reading a book. It's called *The Giving Tree.*"

"Exploring a magical world in it, are you?"

"Not really," Harley said with a shrug. "It's just about a tree in a
boy's backyard. It's nothing special really."

"Well, I don't know about that," Patrick said. "In *The Wizard of Oz,*
didn't Dorothy say that if I ever go looking for my heart's desire again,
I won't look any further than in my own backyard. And if your heart's
desire isn't there, you never really had it to begin with."

"Kind of like treasure?"

"Yes, kind of like treasure, treasure in your imagination."

Harley's eyes danced around the Johnsons' backyard, expecting
black pirate chests to burst forth in shoots on the lawn, their gold
coins clinking to the grass in puddles.

"Well, I didn't want to disturb you, my lady," Patrick said. "It's just that I saw you out here and thought you might like a glass of lemonade or some cookies."

Normally, Harley would've jumped at the chance for a glass of Patrick's freshly squeezed lemonade or a plate of his butter cookies, but her stomach was sour, had been sour for weeks. "No, thank you, Dr. Middleton," she said.

Patrick smiled, watching the little girl as she lounged in the grass. "Well, all right. Keep exploring then."

"Dr. Middleton," Harley said, pointing to the blond boy in the Winstons' yard next door. "That boy over there. Why is he always so sad?"

Patrick watched the boy as he slept beneath the willow tree, a hardback copy of *Great Expectations* spread across his chest. Tucked inside the book's spine was a bookmark made by a little girl's hand, one with a red heart and an inscription that read, *You are Loved.*

Sadness fell over Patrick Middleton's face as he continued to watch the boy, his voice adopting a melancholy tone. "Because he's all alone in the world, Harley. He's always been all alone."

"But I don't understand," Harley said. "It looks like he has everything over there. Everything in the whole world."

"I'm afraid not," he said. "It's only for the summer."

Patrick returned his attention to Harley and forced a smile. "Well, I must be about my work, my lady."

"Bye, Dr. Middleton."

"Goodbye, my sweet girl."

Minutes passed and Harley could hear the incessant raps of a keyboard emanating from Patrick's office window. She returned her focus to the boy in the Winstons' backyard. He had risen from his bed of grass and was standing on the creek bank, gazing down at the water in thought. He lifted his arms over his head, and ruffling his wavy blond locks, removed his white t-shirt and tossed it to the ground by his feet.

Rays of sun cut through the trees, casting ribbons of sunlight across the boy's back. There in varying shades of indigo, a pair of angel's wings traveled from the blades of his shoulders to the small of his back.

"Like the archangel," Harley whispered, smiling at the boy, watching as the wings of indigo moved in motion with his back. "Yes, like Michael."

Harley was transported back to Briarcliffe, to the immense, rolling grounds where on a summer day thirty-two years ago, the towns-people of Notchey Creek had gathered on quilts and blankets for the Sutcliffes' annual picnic, waiting for their host, James Sutcliffe, to give a few words of welcome. And there he was, handsome and tailored and tall, holding his baby son in his arms, standing before the micro-phone on the stage where hired musicians were set to perform.

He'd welcomed them all, thanking the town for all they'd done for Sutcliffe Timber and Real Estate, for his family, and for Briarcliffe, over the years. Then he held up the baby in his arms, beautiful and golden like his father, and the crowd cheered, and James Sutcliffe, sadness filling his eyes, said that he wanted them all to meet his son, the love of his life, Michael.

But everything had changed after that day, after James Sutcliffe had been killed, after his life had been robbed from him long before its due time, his son, too, sentenced to death, only to be saved by a man who thought he'd been the infant's undoing.

Harley directed her eyes to that baby, to the boy of her childhood, who was all grown up, tall and powerful and golden, like his father had been, his eyes saddened by tears, as he lay once again by the creek, gazing down in quiet concentration as he once had, searching for something just beyond his grasp.

Eighteen years had passed between them, eighteen years in which Beau Arson had risen from being an abandoned baby to a penniless orphan, passed from one derelict set of parents to the next, supposed guardians who'd cast aside the boy they'd been paid to love, only for that unwanted boy to be lifted up, through his incredible, God-given talent, to the greatest of heights, achieving money, power, fame, but nothing to fill the hole in his heart.

Nothing until now.

For Michael Sutcliffe was home, home at last.

Harley approached and rested her hand on his shoulder, just as he had done to her all those years ago when she was a little girl, after her mother had died and she'd sat helplessly in the mud with the last remnants of *The Giving Tree* falling apart in her soiled hands, lost, she thought, forever. And just as he had gazed down at her with so much compassion in his eyes, so much care, she too gazed down at him.

"'We need never be ashamed of our tears,'" she said, "'for they are rain upon the blinding dust of earth, overlying our hard hearts.'"

Beau Arson turned and looked at Harley Henrickson, and with his dark blue eyes reddened, he smiled and said with his deep voice, "Hey, kiddo."

"Hi," Harley whispered back.

"You remembered."

"I did."

She knelt and took a seat beside him on the creek bank. "I wanted to—"

But before she could finish he'd pulled her tightly to his chest, embracing her with muscular arms. "Thank you," he said, whispering the words into her hair as it fell across his folded arms, his chest, his breath warm and comforting on her cheeks. "Thank you for all that you've done."

Then he released her gently and the two sat in comfortable silence, listening to the creek as it babbled happily before them.

"Beau," Harley said at last. "I wanted to thank you too...for the book. *The Giving Tree*. I can't tell you what it means to me to have it back." She peered at him, emphasis growing in her voice. "But it's not just the book. Your words of encouragement that day...after Kevin and Spider did what they did...you were the first person who taught me to believe in myself."

She removed *Great Expectations* from her bag and handed it to him. "I think I have something of yours to return too."

Beau smiled and placed the book in his lap, then leaned his back against the weeping willow, gazing past the creek to the forest. "I still remember it...just like it was yesterday. I still remember that sad, lonely little kid, the little girl who would sit underneath that oak tree, day after day, all summer long, reading her books, crying for her mother. That same little kid who took the time to leave gifts for me under that willow tree.

"I remembered asking Patrick about you, and he said that you were an orphan like me, that your mother had just died, that she'd been killed by a roadside bomb in Afghanistan where she was stationed with the Army." He pondered this for a moment and shook his head as if scolding himself. "I felt so sorry for myself back then. So defeated all of the time. I thought I'd been given the absolute worst lot in life, going from one foster home to another, from one set of crap hole parents to the next.

"But then there you were, this little kid who'd just lost everything, so tiny and vulnerable and sad, taking time from your grieving to think and care for somebody as undeserving and selfish as me. I never forgot it. I never forgot you. It was a changing point for me, you see. Never again, I told myself, would I wallow in my misfortunes. Never again would I feel like I'd been given a bum rap. If I wanted to change my life, I told myself, I was going to be the one to do it, to lift myself out of the hell hole I'd been born into."

"And you did."

"In some ways," he said, "and in others ways I've failed horribly." But he did not expand on this further. "When I came by your shop the other day, it was you I came to see. I wanted to know what had happened to you, what had become of your life. The last I'd heard from Patrick, you'd been awarded a scholarship to Harvard, and you were headed to Boston. I was so proud of you."

Harley frowned. "I'm afraid my life hasn't turned out the way I expected it to, Beau. My granddaddy became ill right before I gradu- ated from high school, and I stayed here to take care of him. I never left. I never went to Harvard."

"I hate to hear that," he said, and she could tell he truly meant it. "But you're still young. You can still go wherever you like. Become the writer you wanted to be."

"You remember that?" she said with half a smile.

"Yes. And I don't see why you can't still do it. A person can write from anywhere, can't they?"

"Yes," she said solemnly. "Yes, I suppose so."

He fixed his gaze on the canopy of pines above them. "I've decided to stay here. In Notchey Creek. This is my home now, this is where I was always supposed to be, where my father would've wanted me to be." He paused. "It'll be a big change for me, I know, but I can't go back…not now…not to the way things were…not the way my life was before." He looked behind them to Briarcliffe, to the home of his ancestors. "And I don't want to go back."

And none of them would, Harley realized. Not Beau. Not she. Not Notchey Creek. They were all forever changed.

"It's kind of like that quote from *Great Expectations*, isn't it?" she said.

She deflected her gaze to the blue-gray peaks of the Smokies as they swept toward the rising sun. The mist had gathered in the foothills and was working its way upward through the trees, to the between place, where the mountains meet the sky.

"'We changed again, and yet again, and it was now too late and too far to go back, and I went on. And the mists had all solemnly risen now, and the world lay spread before me.'"

ABOUT THE AUTHOR

Liz Andrews is an emerging author of mystery fiction. Born in East Tennessee, she currently resides in Western Pennsylvania with her husband and goldador, Scout. This is her first book.